Pulse of Evil

"Bless me Father, for I have sinned."

The dark confines of the confessional room felt like a coffin.

"And how long has it been since your last confession?" the priest asked, his features and voice obscured behind a mesh screen.

"Years? I don't know. Since high school," I said.

Silence.

My hands wrestled with each other in my lap. I shivered, suddenly cold. Squeezing my eyes shut did nothing to ease the pain that throbbed inside my skull.

"What are your confessions?" he asked. The monotone voice masked boredom or interest.

Such a simple question. If I wanted forgiveness, redemption, salvation all I had to do was list the things I'd done wrong since my last confession.

More silence.

This time, it was up to me to break it.

I brushed one hand though my hair, and pushed my bangs to the side so I could see. Seemed pointless. There was no light, just the smell of wood polish and the sound of the priest breathing evenly on the opposite side of the wall that separated us.

"This isn't easy," I said. My bottom lip rolled into my mouth. I bit down.

"Admitting sins committed rarely is."

It felt like my heart had left my chest and was now fighting for space alongside my brain—beating, beating, beating. I dropped my elbows to my knees as I bent forward, my hands clasped together, extended out in front of me. "Father," I said, or thought, I can't be sure.

The silence that surrounded me, seemed to pulse—throb—in my ears, in counterpoint with the beating of my heart. The tempo wracking its way through the inside of my head was draining and intensified.

"Father, I witnessed a murder. Two. And I did nothing to help," I said. I wasn't ready for tears. It seemed I had no choice. As they fell, I allowed them, refusing to wipe them away. "I didn't try to stop it. I didn't call the police. I didn't do a thing!"

Did I hear the priest suck in air? This had to be so different from what he was used to hearing people confess. Bad words. Bad thoughts. Not informing a clerk you'd received back too much change at the check out.

"How far away from the murders were you?"

In the middle of them. "Close. Too close."

"Does anyone else know that you witnessed these murders?"

"The killers know I was there."

Wings

PULSE OF EVIL

Phillip Tomasso

A Wings ePress, Inc.

Horror Novel

Wings ePress, Inc.

Edited by: Jeanne R. Smith
Copy Edited by: Joan Powell
Senior Editor:Jeanne R. Smith
Executive Editor: Marilyn Kapp
Cover Artist: Richard Stroud

All rights reserved

Wings ePress Books
http://www.wings-press.com

ISBN 978-1-61309-919-3

Published In the United States Of America

Wings ePress Inc.
3000 N. Rock Road
Newton, KS 67114

Dedication

This one is for my Kids. Phillip, Grant, Raeleigh—you are my inspiration to keep at it.

And a special thanks to Jeanne R. Smith – a wonderful editor who took my good story and made it better!

Prologue

"Bless me Father, for I have sinned."

The dark confines of the confessional room felt like a coffin.

"And how long has it been since your last confession?" the priest asked, his features and voice obscured behind a mesh screen.

"Years? I don't know. Since high school," I said.

Silence.

My hands wrestled with each other in my lap. I shivered, suddenly cold. Squeezing my eyes shut did nothing to ease the pain that throbbed inside my skull.

"What are your confessions?" he asked. The monotone voice masked boredom or interest.

Such a simple question. If I wanted forgiveness, redemption, salvation all I had to do was list the things I'd done wrong since my last confession.

More silence.

This time, it was up to me to break it.

I brushed one hand though my hair, and pushed my bangs to the side so I could see. Seemed pointless. There was no light, just the smell of wood polish and the sound of the priest breathing evenly on the opposite side of the wall that separated us.

"This isn't easy," I said. My bottom lip rolled into my mouth. I bit down.

"Admitting sins committed rarely is."

It felt like my heart had left my chest and was now fighting for space alongside my brain—beating, beating, beating. I dropped my elbows to my knees as I bent forward, my hands clasped together, extended out in front of me. "Father," I said, or thought, I can't be sure.

The silence that surrounded me, seemed to pulse—throb—in my ears, in counterpoint with the beating of my heart. The tempo wracking its way through the inside of my head was draining and intensified.

"Father, I witnessed a murder. Two. And I did nothing to help," I said. I wasn't ready for tears. It seemed I had no choice. As they fell, I allowed them, refusing to wipe them away. "I didn't try to stop it. I didn't call the police. I didn't do a thing!"

Did I hear the priest suck in air? This had to be so different from what he was used to hearing people confess. Bad words. Bad thoughts. Not informing a clerk you'd received back too much change at the check out.

"How far away from the murders were you?"

In the middle of them. "Close. Too close."

"Does anyone else know that you witnessed these murders?"

"The killers know I was there."

"When did the murders happen?"

Last year. Last month. Last week. "Last night."

The women tried to run. The others were too fast. It had been a game. Cat's playing with mice before eating them.

"And you haven't gone to the police." It wasn't a question. "Did you ... help kill the two people?"

Gasping, I sat up straight. My mouth went dry. "No! No, but they wanted me to."

Their eyes had demanded I help, while their hands kept the women from escaping.

I opened my eyes wide, hoping to drown out the vivid memory. Despite the darkness, shadows seemed to swirl around above me.

The priest remained silent for a long time. I couldn't tell if he was thinking of what to say next, or waiting to see what I would say. I heard him breathing, thought I could hear his heart beating. I could smell him.

I turned and let my fingers grate the mesh between us. "Can God forgive me for doing nothing?" I said.

"God forgives all sins, if you ask for His forgiveness," the priest said. "You are asking for forgiveness right now. And there is still time."

"Time?" I said.

"Time to do the right thing."

"And what's the right thing?" I knew the answer.

"Confessing your sins to God redeems you spiritually. You have a moral obligation, as well. And the police should be notified."

The pain in my head was either caused by hunger I felt growing in the pit of my gut, or the need to block out memories, which came in flashes. A fast-paced slide show.

Skin torn. Blood splattered.

Blurred images of movement. Fleeing. Attacking.

I heard screams—screams that resounded over and over in my mind long after the actual screams abruptly stopped.

"I can't go to the police," I said. "I shouldn't even be here, telling you."

"What you've told me is confidential—kept between God and the two of us."

I knew this. It's why I came. I needed to talk to someone. Aside from a priest, there was no one I trusted. "But will it matter?"

"Will what matter?"

"If I ask for forgiveness when I know my soul is damned?" One side of my face pressed against cool pine, trapping tears between skin and wood.

"Witnessing a murder will not damn your soul, I can assure you," the priest said. "And going to the police with what you saw will also help eliminate some of the guilt you carry around inside you."

Guilt. I wanted to laugh. If it were only guilt that coursed through my insides, keeping-on might not be so difficult.

"They'd never believe me, Father."

"Whether they choose to believe you or not, is their choice. You must first give them the chance to believe you."

"You wouldn't believe me, either," I said. A whisper.

The one young woman's skin—flawless—shredded as if paper, and at that moment her eyes shot open so wide I thought her eyeballs might pop out of the sockets.

"What else would you like to tell me?" he said.

"The ones who did the killing, the murderers, they weren't human," I said. I heard my voice speak. I imagined the priest—once intently listening to my every word, ready to deliver a penance and bless me, and send me on my way—rolling his eyes.

"Murder is inhumane," he said.

I laughed. Couldn't stop it from escaping my lips.

Pieces of what remained were tossed onto a fire, the remnants turned to ash and smoke.

"I'm sorry I laughed," I said.

"I can go to the police station with you, if you'd like."

"You would do that?" I asked.

"I would."

"I *will* think about going to the police, Father."

"You should do more than think about it, son," he said. "You should pray about it."

I nodded in the darkness; eyes shut tight against insistent memories, and said, "Maybe I will."

One

St. Catherine's Hospital, Rochester, NY

"Joseph?" she said.

"Joey," I said. Although I sat facing her general direction, I couldn't focus my attention. With crossed arms and legs, I kept looking over her shoulder to the barred window. How strong could bars on a window actually be? I knew they were there to keep people like me locked inside. Right now, it didn't matter. Those bars served a double purpose as far as I was concerned. Those bars would keep *them* out.

At least I hoped they would.

I smiled, almost laughed.

"Is something funny, Joey?" she asked.

I rolled my eyes. I didn't need to be psychoanalyzed. I didn't buy into psychiatry as a legitimate science. If I'd lost my mind, then I was crazy and deserved to be stored away in the bowels of some nut house. If I wasn't a toy-short-of-a-Happy-Meal, then everything that has happened was real. If everything that has happened was real, then I preferred to be trapped behind barred windows and forced to have daily talks with Dr. Sanchez.

"I just thought of something a little funny," I said. I brought my thumb up to my mouth. I chewed at the tab of raised skin alongside the nail. My teeth ground the flesh like a saw. I felt the small severed square of skin on my tongue for a moment before spitting it onto the floor.

It was not even four. So many sinister clouds filled the sky, it resembled night. Outside was so dark I could barely see white snow settled on bare tree branches.

I scratched at my chin, the stubble scratched back, brushed hair out of my eyes as I leaned back in the chair.

"And what was funny, Joey?"

She wasn't going to give up. It didn't matter that I didn't want to talk. She couldn't understand why I was here. Insane or not, I just needed to be somewhere safe. Prison would be safe, but I didn't want to break laws just to gain protection. And, I don't know, the secured floors of a hospital seemed more impenetrable than even a maximum-security penitentiary. But what did I know? I'd never been locked away a day in my life, not in a prison. Not in a hospital. Until now, that is. But I came here. I committed myself. So this is a totally different story, a totally different situation, no doubt.

"Joey?"

I closed my eyes and sighed. "You know that old joke, the one about, 'Why is there a fence around the cemetery'?"

When I opened my eyes, she was still nodding. "I know it," she said. "But I don't remember the punch line. Can you tell me the punch line?"

Man, was she full of it. It was a kid's joke. She knew the punch line. Everyone knew the punch line. "Because people are dying to get in," I said. Only now it wasn't funny. "I was just staring at the bars on the window."

"And that reminded you of the joke about the fence around a cemetery?"

I leaned forward, rested my elbows on my knees and dropped my head into my hands. "The way I see it, the same joke applies to this place."

"People are dying to get into the hospital?"

I shrugged. "I'm not really talking about the whole hospital. I'm talking about here, the psycho-ward."

"That's interesting. I'm not sure I understand," she said. "Can you explain it a little more?"

"I know. It doesn't make any sense," I said. "Not to you. But to me, the joke would be, why are there bars on the psycho ward of St. Catherine's?" I paused for effect. I had the doctor's attention. She waited for the punch line. "Because the dead are trying to get in."

I snorted out a short grunt that could have been mistaken for a laugh. I sat back in the chair and went back to chewing the loose skin on my other thumb, my eyes trained on the window, on the bars, straining to see into the thick of night. Was anything out there, on the other side, straining to see in—to see me?

"Can you tell me about what you saw, Joey?" She must not have cared for the joke. Keep things moving. That must be what they teach in psycho school. Keep things moving.

Dr. Sanchez sat behind her paper-cluttered desk in a burgundy leather chair, maybe five feet from me. No doubt the desk served as an obstacle, should I go crazy and attack her. I'd bet anything a panic button was at her fingertips and that the room was monitored. Someone was probably watching the session, maybe even recording it.

I wasn't planning on attacking her. Not even sure why I was thinking about an attack. But if I *did* attack Dr. Sanchez, orderlies would burst through the door and restrain me. No doubt about it. I was being watched. I felt it the way you felt the prick of a needle in your arm before the needle ever touches skin.

That was fine. I hoped the whole place was under surveillance. If any of *them* ever got in here, if any of *them* came for me . . .

I shook my head and closed my eyes.

If any of them got in here, if any of them came for me, it would be over. The orderlies might be big and strong, but what could they really do to protect me?

They couldn't do a thing, that's what they could do.

Not. A. Thing.

"Joey?"

This doctor had a bad habit of pulling me out of my thoughts. I rolled my eyes, pursed my lips and exhaled through my nostrils. "What happened," I asked. "You want to know why I'm here?"

"Would you like to talk about that?" She sat like a perfect lady with legs crossed at the ankles, hands folded in her lap. The session was definitely being recorded, or she'd be taking notes, right?

Thinking about what I'd witnessed had me craving coffee. Extra sugar. I did not want to sleep. I hated the dreams that plagued my nights. Sweat pooled behind my knees, and beads formed on my forehead.

My forearm wiped away the perspiration. I went back to nibbling at the skin around my thumb. I tore at it. "It must be in my file, what I told the police," I said.

I'd been here less than forty-eight hours. The first twenty-nine I spent alone in a room, medicated. Today was my first session with Dr. Sanchez, my first session, and she wanted to jump right in and talk about what I'd witnessed? Absent seemed to be the art of finesse and subtlety.

She cocked her head slightly to one side. Though her eyes were obscured behind thick lenses encased by gold frames, the weight of her stare could not be ignored. She'd been intently studying my *everything* since we started the session.

"I have information from the police. But what I'd like most is for you to tell me what happened," she said. "Police reports read flat, one dimensional. I'd much rather you tell me about what took place."

"You know, believe it or not, I want to talk about that night," I said, and leaned forward again. "I think I need to talk about it."

"That's good, Joey. Then why don't we talk about what you remember?" she asked.

"I can't start there. You can't start a story in the middle, you know what I mean? We have to start at the beginning. We can't start with that night," I said.

She nodded, but looked a little uneasy, startled even. "You're bleeding," she said. Her eyes locked on my hand.

Most of the skin by my fingernail was gone. I stuck my thumb into my mouth to stop the blood; its warmth filled my mouth. I could smell it, like copper and acid, and felt hungry, as if someone had placed a burger and fries in front of me.

"Joey, maybe we should continue this talk later," she said. She stood up. I stayed sitting. "I think you should have that looked at."

I pulled my thumb out of my mouth. I felt blood drip onto my lips, and chin. "It's nothing," I said.

"Let's have someone look at your thumb," she said.

I rolled my eyes, and got to my feet. "I want to talk," I said, or shouted. I'm not sure.

Her brow furrowed some, her smile frowned, her mocha skin paled. I saw her eyes flash to her desk, perhaps thankful it sat like a wedge between us. "Mr. Tresca—"

"What happened to Joey?"

The office door banged open. Two male orderlies in stereotypical hospital whites entered the room and took hold of my arms.

Dr. Sanchez held up a hand. "Mr. Tresca—Joey—we had a very good first session."

The guys held my arms so tightly circulation was cut off. My fingers tingled. I wasn't resisting at all. Their aggression was uncalled for, out of line.

"We can't possibly talk about everything in one evening," she explained. The polite tone of her voice rippled with—what was it? *Fear?* "We'll pick up where we left off tomorrow, Joey."

"I'm done talking to you," I said.

The orderlies pulled me away from the doctor and toward the office door.

"We'll talk more tomorrow," she promised.

"I'll listen, Doc. But I'm done talking," I said over my shoulder. The orderly on my right had fingernails like a woman. They cut into my flesh. "Get your hand off me!"

I tried to shrug my way out of his grasp. My jerking caused him to crank closed the vise that much more. His grip made me wonder if his hand was part Rottweiler.

Two

After bandaging my thumb, the orderly escort led me back to my room. The first thing I noticed upon entering was that the second empty bed, was no longer empty.

"I've got a new roommate?" I asked.

"Take some time to cool down, Joey," one of the orderlies said. Far as I was concerned, they shared a brain.

They released me simultaneously. I wanted to rub my sore arms, but did not want to give them the satisfaction. I walked into the room, eyeing the bag of clothes and supplies on the bed across from mine.

I sat on my mattress and studied the belongings of my new roommate. Besides some pajamas, jeans, underwear, socks and toothpaste was a big black, leather-bound Bible.

Pushing back to lean against the wall, I brought my knees up to my chest and wrapped my arms around them.

"Great," I said out loud about nothing in particular. Maybe I'd said it because I didn't want a roommate, but I sure didn't want some holier-than-thou fool living with me. With my luck, the nut probably thought he was Moses, or Peter, or Jesus Himself. "Great," I said again.

With my door open, the sounds from the psycho floor filtered into my room. A woman screamed relentlessly, as if being beaten. I heard someone moaning and high-pitched wails like they had a painful bellyache. Announcements blared over the PA system calling doctors here and there. To top it off, all I could smell was urine, despite an obvious attempt to mask the pungent stench with an overdose of ammonia.

I didn't want to be in here. I had nowhere else to go. Nowhere was safe. Was anywhere really safe? I might not even be safe here. I probably wasn't. In my heart, I knew I wasn't losing my mind. Everything had seemed so real. Even the dreams.

But it wasn't all a dream.

Couldn't have been.

From where I sat, looking out the barred bedroom window, I saw streetlights already on in an attempt to battle the premature darkness. With the manufactured lighting I saw a flock of crows, or pigeons, or some kind of big dark bird perched on a rooftop.

I thought of lyrics by the Red Hot Chili Peppers that talked about *birds* and *lonely views.*

I felt alone. Empty, and alone. Also frightened. I didn't trust the birds, whether we shared an empty view together or not. Still, I was in here. Bars allowed me a sense of security, real or false, that let me feel somewhat secure. For now, it would do. For now, it had to do.

We didn't have to wear white gowns like you see the crazies wear in movies. We wore our own clothing. Minus shoelaces or belts, or anything we could use as a weapon to hurt ourselves. I had on jeans, the same pair for a second day in a row, a gray sweatshirt and slippers. I leaned forward and dug into my little four-drawer dresser for a sweater. I felt cold. When barefoot, my feet froze on the linoleum. The last two days I wore socks and hospital-issued slippers.

What I really wanted was a drink and a cigarette. Apparently there was no smoking in the hospital except for designated spots outside, far from the campus parameter. I was told during my admission that if I was good—get that, like I'm some child—I could earn the right to be escorted out for a cigarette. I told them I'd been meaning to quit anyway. My answer seemed to make them happy. I didn't have plans to quit, didn't want to quit. I just didn't want to be outside. *They* were outside. If I went out there to smoke a cigarette, they'd find me. They were looking for me. I hated feeling paranoid, but I didn't think they'd ever stop looking.

I was trouble to them. I'd brought trouble to their door.

Outside I'd felt vulnerable and exposed, which was why I was now locked away in here.

I might have self-admitted, but if I told them everything, or anything, the doctors would have me committed for sure. Only Father Daly knows the truth.

I wasn't sure that was a bad thing. If I were right about them, then being released would prove deadly. And if I was wrong about them, well, then, I guess in here is where I belonged.

I slid off the bed and walked up over to the window. I pulled the sweater tight and crossed my arms. Leaning against the wall, I stared out at the city.

The birds on that rooftop seemed to stare right back. Were they really looking at me?

I believe they were.

I closed my eyes. In my brain, I knew the birds were not looking at me. It was my imagination. But I had doubted my sensibility a lot the last several months. Things I would have called impossible suddenly seemed plausible. *Seeing is believing*, has recently become my life's motto. And the things I've seen made it hard to doubt much of anything.

The birds moved about on the rooftop, huddling closer together, perhaps shielding each other from the bluster of a cold early winter wind. All at once they turned beaks upward and stared directly at me. All of them. At the exact same time. I stepped away from the window. I shook my head, my only defense at battling the impossible. I needed that cigarette. The birds were outside. I wasn't planning on going outside any time soon, maybe not ever again. I laughed out loud.

"What's so funny?"

Startled, I turned around. The man filling the doorway was my extreme opposite. He stood at least six five, weighing roughly two eighty, where I was only five eight, and about a hundred pounds less. His head was shaved bald; my hair reached my shoulders and was mostly one length. I brushed strands from my eyes to make sure the giant wasn't some kind of illusion.

"What's so funny?" he asked a second time.

I rolled a finger in a circular motion and pointed it at my temple. "I'm crazy, man. I laugh for no reason at all."

The hulk smiled and nodded as if he understood what I was talking about. I walked toward him, wanting to exit the room. His presence made me feel suddenly claustrophobic. "Excuse me," I said. My tone of voice was far from polite.

He didn't budge. Instead he held out his hand. "I'm Wayne. I think we're roomies."

I closed my eyes and shook my head. "Roomies? What is this, a sorority?"

I pushed by him. Once in the hallway I felt like I could breathe again. I hated the rooms. I hated the hallways. Everything was white: the floors, the empty boring walls, the orderly uniforms, the nurse uniforms. It was maddening.

After taking two steps down the hallway, no destination in mind, I stopped and turned around. I expected to see my roomy still in the doorway staring at me. He was gone. Had he been there in the first place?

I could go back to the room and peek in, but didn't want to. It didn't matter. If he was merely a figment of my imagination, then when I did decide to return to my room, or our room, he'd either be there, or he wouldn't. So what difference did it make?

Instead, I decided to head down to the lounge and mingle with the rest of the *loonies*. The lounge sat directly across from the nurses' station, and consisted of two doors, one at either end of a wall made of what looked like thick glass, making us like zoo animals for the staff's entertainment, no doubt.

Inside were several round tables and chairs. In front of the corner wall-mounted television set were a few sofas and recliners. At the opposite end was a countertop housing a sink; there was a fridge and cupboards. I had no idea what was stored in the fridge or cupboards, and didn't much care.

I stood in the doorway. Four people occupied the lounge. I found the woman responsible for the moaning I'd heard. She sat in a wheelchair in front of another barred window. Long, greasy gray hair covered her shoulders and draped down her back. She wrung her hands in her lap and slowly rocked back and forth as she moaned. The moan started out low and guttural, before getting louder and higher pitched. Then she would abruptly stop, before starting out low and guttural again.

Two men watched television from one of the sofas. I didn't think the volume was on at all. At least I couldn't hear any sound coming from the set. Not that it mattered. Moaner was making enough noise to prevent me from hearing myself think, but the men on the sofa didn't seem aware of this annoying distraction.

One man walked in circles around one of the tables. His right arm was bent up toward his chest, his wrist limp, and his fingers were rolled into a fist. "Push over," he said to no one. "Push over. Come on, push over."

Whoever it was he saw, or was talking to, they weren't moving over. This seemed to agitate him. He walked faster around the table, banging into chairs as he continued to beg the unseen to *push over*.

The two on the sofa giggled, and turned from the muted television to watch the show unfolding behind them.

"Push over!" His hip hit a chair, which slid in front of him. He stumbled over the chair, got around it and continued to circle the table. Drool pooled in his mouth, dripped over the side of his lower lip.

Excited now, the two on the sofa bobbed up and down, laughing at the man on display.

The moaning woman wailed. Apparently, she was competing for noise level and attention.

I turned and walked out of the lounge.

If I wasn't crazy when I checked myself into this place, rest assured I'd go crazy before I left.

If I ever left.

Three

When I returned to my room, Wayne was already in bed, under the covers and reading his Bible. I closed my eyes and walked past him and sat on my mattress. I didn't want a roommate. I wanted to be alone. I kept thinking there had to be something I could do that would get me thrown into solitary confinement, or whatever they called it in the hospital. I needed time away from everyone.

For five minutes I sat quietly on my bed. I thought that at any second Wayne would start talking, asking me questions. Surprisingly, he seemed intently focused on his reading, almost as if he did not notice me enter the room.

Thankful, I laid down. I wasn't tired. My days and nights were off kilter. I rested more during the day, and tended to be up most of the night. It didn't matter. I was on a medical leave from work, so there wasn't a reason, really, to get to bed at a reasonable hour. Besides, I didn't want to sleep. Lately my dreams consisted of nightmares.

"Good book?" I heard myself ask. I was propped on an elbow, facing Wayne.

He looked over at me for a moment before laying a ribbon bookmark between the pages. "Was that a joke?" he asked, getting up on an elbow too.

I smiled and shrugged, lying down, lacing my hands behind my head. "I guess," I said.

He laughed, which lasted too long. When it didn't stop after a good minute, I felt a bit uncomfortable.

"That was pretty funny," he said.

"Yeah," I mumbled. "I'm like a comedian."

"Good book. Good Book. I get it."

I closed my eyes, rather than roll them. "Yep."

Wayne sat up. He wore no shirt and briefs. I saw more than I expected, more than I wanted. I closed my eyes again. Didn't help.

"You read the Bible?"

"Nope," I said.

"But you used to," he said. It wasn't posed as a question.

I pulled myself up into a sitting position. "Nah. I never read the Bible," I said.

He nodded at me. It resembled the kind of nod a parent gives to pacify a child. "Okay."

He lay back down, and started reading again. Why was he in here, I wondered? He didn't look crazy, didn't act it. Did I?

I dropped my head down onto my pillow and turned to face the wall, eyes closed. Blackness made up the backs of my eyelids. Tiny white dots floated across the dark inside my sockets. Were they cells I saw? Illuminated Dust?

I opened my eyes. It was a good thing I didn't want to sleep. I was absolutely wide-awake.

Awake, and hungry. My stomach ached. I didn't touch dinner. It was served at three and had been some kind of chicken with mashed potatoes. The chicken looked all right, better than expected, but I couldn't eat it. I was just in the mood for something else. Not sure what. But I knew it wasn't chicken-whatever and mashed potatoes. Right now, though, I wish I'd eaten at least some of it. Morning was a long way off, which meant, so was breakfast.

"I read the Bible all the way through each year, from Genesis to Revelations," Wayne said.

I looked over at him. He looked like he hadn't moved. He was still on his back, his face buried in his Bible.

"Excuse me?" I said, wondering if I might have been hearing things. It did not look like he had spoken.

"Some people read just the New Testament. Some alternate, reading one book in the Old, one book in the New. I like to read it straight through, starting with the book of Genesis and finishing up with the last chapter in Revelations. It makes for a more complete story," he said, never looking away from the pages.

I closed my eyes. I suddenly wished to be tired. I welcomed sleep, nightmares and all. Getting into a discussion on how one reads the Bible was not what I was in the mood for. "Whatever works for you," I said.

"How about you?" he asked.

I opened my eyes, turned my head and saw Wayne sitting up again. This time his finger sat between the pages of the Bible to mark his place. "How about me what?"

"Do you read the Bible straight through or bounce around?"

"I think I just told you, I don't read the Bible," I said, using a clearly agitated tone of voice.

"When you did, I mean."

"And what makes you think I ever did?" I asked.

"Everyone reads the Bible at some point in their life."

"Yeah? Well, not everyone."

He pursed his lips tightly together, and then relaxed his jaw. "I'm pretty sure most people pick up the Bible and read from it at least once in their life. Every year it ranks as the best selling book." He looked up at the ceiling for a moment. "I don't mean everyone reads the entire Bible. Most people don't, not even Christians. But I believe that everyone at least reads from the Bible at least once in their lifetime. So, going on that theory, I'm curious as to how you read the Bible, when you read the Bible."

"And what do you base this theory of information of yours on?" I asked. My stomach growled. I placed a hand on my belly to silence it. I didn't care what was served for breakfast. I planned on being a good little patient and eating every last crumb.

"Have you ever read from the Bible?" he asked.

He was right. I had. "I suppose."

I waited for an I-told-you-so that never came.

"New Testament?"

I just nodded.

"Book of John?"

I nodded again.

"That's the book of love," he said. "One of my favorites. So why did you stop reading it?"

"Look, I'm not like you. I'm not a holy roller," I said, gritting my teeth as I spoke. "You aren't going to hook me on your religion."

"I don't have a religion. I have a relationship."

"Whatever. Same difference."

"It's not, actually." He flashed me a smug smile. "Why'd you stop reading?"

I used to read the Bible. Every day. Somehow, this whack-job knew this about me. "I stopped because I no longer wanted to read it. That simple."

"Doesn't sound simple," Wayne said.

"You're not going to pull me into this conversation. I'm not interested in discussing God…"

"So you believe in Him?"

"Of course I do," I said. I shook my head. Wayne was pulling me into this conversation. I needed to turn the tables. "Why are you in here?"

Wayne's confident expression faltered. He no longer strived to make eye contact. Instead, he looked down at the floor as if studying his toes. "Why are you in here?"

"I asked first," I said. Some satisfaction filled me. Wayne liked to ask the questions. Not answer them. Maybe if I asked him enough questions, he'd stop asking me so many.

"Fair enough. You did ask first."

I sat up. Although still fully clothed, I felt cold. It seemed like I was cold all the time, as if my body were a corpse rather than a living, warm-blooded being. I took a blanket and wrapped it around my shoulders.

Watching Wayne, I could tell by the crumpled expression on his face that he was struggling with opening up. His brow furrowed and his nose wrinkled. I didn't push. If he wanted to keep talking, he'd have to share; otherwise, I was going to lie back down and pretend to sleep. Actual sleep might be the only thing to get my mind off my empty belly.

"You won't laugh?" he said.

"Don't know, you haven't told me," I said.

This did not comfort him. In fact, Wayne seemed to flinch at my words.

"Fine. I won't laugh," I promised. It was an empty promise. If he told me something funny, I'd laugh. I laughed at funny things. Doesn't everyone?

"God talks to me," Wayne said.

And I almost did, I almost laughed, but didn't.

Four

As soon as I closed my eyes, I opened them. I don't think I'd fallen asleep, but when I'd closed my eyes it felt as if my mouth had suddenly filled with something like gravel. I slowly bit down, and swooshed my tongue around. How had anything gotten into my mouth?

With the shades drawn closed, the room was dark. I threw the covers off and stumbled to the bathroom, my mouth filled with saliva and . . . rocks? I switched on the light and leaned over the sink to stare at my reflection in the mirror. It might be almost winter, but I don't recall ever looking so pale. My skin looked pasty-white. My eyes were extremely red; dark bags encircled them. My hair needed serious attention, messy and matted from lying down. I wasn't sure if a brush could help at this point, nor did I see why it mattered.

Opening my mouth, I half expected to spit out a large amount of colorful aquarium pebbles. What I saw inside caused me to gag.

Blood. It wasn't saliva inside my mouth. It was blood. There was so much of it I couldn't figure out what else was in there.

I spit out as much as I could, then ran the water to wash it down the drain, and rinse everything else off to see what it was I'd been crunching on.

My gums hurt.

I massaged my jaw as I stared into the sink. Whatever it was that had filled my mouth was now covering the drain. The sink slowly filled with blood-red water. I reached down and washed the stuff around with my hand. The water level receded, leaving behind a small mound of crushed and crumbled pieces of teeth.

I looked up and into the mirror. When I opened my mouth, I wasn't ready for the horror awaiting me. My teeth were chunked away, dangling by threads of gummy flesh.

Cupping my hand over my mouth seemed like the only thing I could do to preserve what remained in place. I closed my eyes, wanted to cry. It looked horrible. I looked horrible, like some crazed mountain man trying for the lead in *Deliverance the Sequel*.

Putting my face as close to the mirror as possible, I moved my hand away and smiled. More fallen teeth sat on my tongue. I spit them into the growing pile in the sink, along with more blood.

The hot water was still running. Steam rose from the faucet and fogged the mirror. I wiped away a section on the glass, and could do nothing but stare at my jagged grin.

My tongue was not happy to leave well enough alone. It poked and prodded at the few remaining teeth still in place. And when it did so, those few remaining teeth wiggled. They too were loose.

I touched my bottom row of… what? Mangled bone?

It was as if I'd depressed a release button and like a dental partial, my entire bottom row of teeth came out, all attached to a section of gums. I tried to stick the partial back into my mouth, holding it in place, but the pressure applied caused the teeth to erode and slip to the dam that was my inside lower lip.

I spit more into the sink and stared at the gathering pool of blood water, and knew that the depths were not made up of beachy-sand, but rotting teeth. How could this happen? What could I do about it?

Fake teeth? Would I have to go to a dentist for a complete set of dentures? Teeth didn't just fall out like this.

I dropped to my knees. My stomach felt as if it were filled with acid. It churned and groaned. Breathing became difficult. I knew this feeling all too well from spending too many nights out drinking. I was about to vomit, was ready to vomit, needed to get it out of me, but my body hadn't reached the eruption phase just yet.

My stomach heaved once, twice, and then a flood of bile and blood raced its way up my esophagus and gushed out of my mouth like water from a fire hose. I didn't want to fight it, but it felt like I was about to die if I let it continue. And just when I was sure I was about to pass out from lack of oxygen, it stopped.

I gasped, and attempted to catch my breath. My eyes watered. A strand of bloody drool dangled off my lips. I reached for a strip of toilet paper, dried my eyes and wiped my mouth. The toilet bowl was filled with blood. I hadn't eaten in a while, thank God. But seeing all that blood scared me. It had to be way too much for me to lose. Had to be.

Someone knocked on the door.

"You going to breakfast?" It was Wayne.

I flushed the toilet. "I need a minute," I said, mumbling. My words sounded slurred. How could I could I go to breakfast? I didn't have teeth. I needed to be taken down into emergency, is what I needed.

Teeth just didn't fall out like that.

I used the toilet for support as I pushed myself up. I lowered the lid and sat down. A cold sweat encased my body.

Another knock.

"Just give me a minute," I yelled.

"You're going to miss breakfast."

"I don't care about breakfast!"

There was a moment of silence before a third knock. "Want me to wait for you?"

"Leave me alone!" I shouted.

I reached over and shut off the water. I needed to stand up. I needed to get help. I leaned on the counter, over the sink. The mirror was totally fogged. I wiped away the steam, my lips tucked safely into my mouth, hiding the monstrosity inside. When I gathered enough courage, I parted my lips and again tried to smile. And then fell back to my knees and threw up again. I could not believe what I saw this time. My teeth. All of them. In place. Pearly white, and in place.

When I snuck a peak into the sink from where I kneeled by the toilet, I saw that the water was gone. No blood stains. And no teeth piled up over the drain.

I stood up. My stomach felt queasy. I had to hold it with my hand to comfort it. I looked in the mirror again, and stared for a good three minutes admiring my teeth.

It had to have been a dream... all of it. But I was here. In the bathroom. I was awake. Wide awake. I puked... twice. How could I puke twice if I'd been sleeping?

Was I losing my mind completely? Did I actually belong here in this ward?

~ * ~

I couldn't help but feel like I was back in elementary school, preschool even. We gathered for meals in the lounge. The lounge was in full pandemonium. People shouted, both patients and staff. As I waited in line with my food tray, I watched debris sail across the air from one table to another and from one person to another, or at another, whatever.

One guy laughed so hard he started coughing, and was practically choking on his food, but that didn't stop him from laughing and pounding his fist on the table as if he were throwing back beers and exchanging dirty jokes with his buds down at some bar. The problem was he was the only one at his table.

The woman sitting across from the slow-shuffling line I was in, stared at me while she ate. And before I knew what was happening, before I could turn away, she stopped chewing, opened her mouth and stuck out her tongue. Half-munched scrambled eggs and what appeared to be sausage and toast oozed out of her mouth and off the sides of her tongue.

I'd been hungry. Whatever appetite I hoped to satisfy this morning was gone. I left my tray and cut to the head of the line where the juice was and grabbed a couple of cranberry cartons and went to find an empty table.

Unfortunately, I made eye contact with my roomy. Wayne smiled and waved me over. How could he want me to sit at his table when only a few minutes ago I'd yelled at him? Looking around the lounge, I realized I was not going to find a place where I could sit and be by myself. I looked at the juice in my hands. I could just take it back to the room. I wasn't eating. I didn't need to stay in the lounge.

"Joey!" Wayne called. "Over here, sit over here."

Relenting, I made my way toward his table. Two other people sat with him. One man, one woman. I wasn't interested in meeting people here. They were crazy, and I already had enough drama in my life, not to mention my own bouts with reality that increasingly demanded more of my attention.

The guy sitting with Wayne wore his long, stringy, greasy hair in front of his face. His grungy beard contained bits of breakfast that must have fallen from his mouth while chewing, hopefully it was food from today, and not last week. Though he was sitting down, I could tell he was frail, all skin and bones. Couldn't weigh more than one-ten.

I sat between him and Wayne. The guy ignored me as Wayne shook my hand.

"I was worried about you," Wayne said. "Thought you were going to miss out on breakfast." He looked at my two cartoons of juice. "Did you miss breakfast?"

"Not hungry," I said.

The woman sitting across from me stared. She didn't seem to blink. She just locked eyes with mine, but otherwise wore an expressionless expression. I lowered my head some, but did not break eye contact. Finally, I passed my hand up and down in front of her face. She did not appear to notice my hand.

"Want some of my eggs?" Wayne offered.

I thought of the chunks of chewed food in the other woman's mouth. "Nah, I'm good," I said. I pointed at my juice. "This is plenty."

"What were you doing for so long in the bathroom?" Wayne asked.

The man beside me giggled. He was looking into his coffee cup. Our eyes met. I nodded at the guy and turned my attention back to my roomy. "I didn't feel well," I said.

"It sounded like you were getting sick in there," he said.

"Yeah, well, I kind of was," I admitted.

"You tell the staff?" he asked.

"No need," I said. "I'm fine."

The guy next to me reached for one of my juice cartons. I had two. There was no reason he couldn't have one of them. Instead, I grabbed it out of his hand.

"Mine!" The guy screamed. Before I knew what was happening, he used his plastic knife and stabbed it into my forearm. I released my grip on the juice and pulled my hand away. The cheap plastic should have snapped in two, but there it was sticking out of my arm.

"Oh my. Oh my. Ah, my goodness," Wayne gasped, reaching for my arm.

I pulled away from him, and hugged my arm close to my chest. "Just great."

It hurt, but not terribly; giving blood at the Red Cross hurt worse. As I pulled the knife out of my arm, orderlies ran at our table; one grabbed the crazy, longhaired freak, the other grabbed me.

"Why you grabbing me? All I did was get stabbed," I said.

The longhaired freak thrashed about. Another orderly joined the fight to restrain the maniac. The one holding me by the shoulders knelt beside me.

"You all right?" he asked. "Here, let me see the arm."

I showed it to him, while watching the orderlies wrestle the longhaired freak to the floor. The excitement riled the rest of the residents. Whoops and hollers filled the tiny lounge. Staff rushed in and started clearing people out.

The orderly took a napkin off the table and wiped away the blood from my wound. My own blood did not affect me in the least. Blood from someone else was another story entirely.

"Hmm. Not sure where that blood came from. But this looks all right," the orderly holding my arm said. "I thought he'd broken skin."

I pulled my arm back. "What are you talking about? The damned thing was sticking out of my arm."

When I looked at my forearm, there was nothing. No hole where the knife had been. Not even a scrape. "Wayne, you saw it, the knife was sticking out of my arm."

"It was," Wayne vouched.

The orderly smiled, a *hey-I'll-humor-you* kind of smile. "Well, it looks fine to me," he said. "Does it hurt?" he asked me.

I thought about it for a moment, ran my hand over the place where I'd been stabbed. "No, I guess not."

"Okay. That's good," he said. He stood up, focusing his attention on getting the longhaired freak out of the lounge and to, hopefully, somewhere where he couldn't violently lash out at people—like to some basement lock-up cell, or something.

"Wayne, you saw it, right? The knife, it was buried into my arm?" I asked. I held my arm out so that Wayne could look over the area.

The woman across from me had not moved, flinched, and as far as I could tell, had not blinked. She still stared directly at me.

"Maybe I didn't see it," Wayne said.

"What are you talking about?" I asked. "The thing was sticking out of my arm."

"I thought that's what I'd seen," he said, and shrugged.

"Well what's God tell ya? Did he see anything?" It was a low blow. Couldn't be helped, though.

Wayne pursed his lips together, stood up and walked out of the lounge without looking back.

I turned my attention to the woman. "You saw it," I said. "The knife was sticking out of my arm."

Nothing.

I stared at her for a good ten seconds, then stuck my tongue out and wiggled it at her. Nothing. Not a smile, smirk, or a blink.

"What the hell am I doing," I asked myself. "Why am I here?"

Five

Dr. Sanchez actually was an attractive woman with dark skin and large brown eyes. She couldn't be more than five-two. The degrees and certifications framed and hanging on her walls didn't impress me so much. They were just bond paper with fancy writing and gold seals. Anyone could earn a degree. So maybe it was the business suits she wore, or the way she kept her hair tightly pulled back and tied off in a dangling pony tail that lent credit to her craft. The glasses—dark, round frames—were a nice, professional touch, too.

"How are you Joey?" she asked. "I heard about what happened at breakfast this morning."

"Apparently it was nothing," I said.

"Apparently?"

I nodded. "Yep."

"Did you get hurt?"

"Apparently not," I said.

"Apparently?"

"That's right."

"Can I see your arm?" she asked.

I showed her.

"You look all right."

"I feel all right."

"Would you like to talk about the fight?"

"There was no fight," I said. "The guy went crazy, or crazier, and stabbed me with his plastic ware."

"I see. And what did you do?"

"I held my arm and let the orderlies restore peace, love and harmony to the lounge," I said with no attempt to hide the sarcasm.

"So you don't want to talk about it?"

"We just did."

She waited a moment before she asked, "So, other than that, how are you today, Joey?"

I remembered my promise. I wasn't talking. I was done talking.

Like our first encounter, the good doctor sat behind her desk. Something happened yesterday. Something scared her. I found it hard to believe a bleeding thumb would have upset her much. I know I was a little agitated, but she'd started it, asking questions and then abruptly ending our session.

I did not have a psychology degree, but I'd bet my life that doing what she'd done to me was not the best way to establish any kind of meaningful doctor-patient relationship.

"Dandy, doc." I would make small talk. That couldn't hurt. I was not going to share, or open up, or divulge anything more substantial. "My new roommate thinks God talks to him." I shrugged and crossed my arms, and arched my eyebrows, as if to say, *what do you think about that?*

"Your new roommate? And what's his name?" Her pen poised over a pad of paper.

"Isn't that in my file?"

"I'm asking you," she said.

"It's Wayne," I said. "God's messenger."

She smiled, nodded and made a note in my file. I rolled my eyes. "And how do you like rooming with Wayne?"

"No complaints, so far."

"That's good," she said.

"Would you like to talk more about Wayne?"

"Is he important to my… healing?"

"Not necessarily," she said. She waited. When I said nothing, she added, "You look tired. Long day?"

Considering I slept maybe a wink last night, I'd say long day and longer night indeed. "I'm fine."

"Everything all right?"

I thought about my teeth falling out of my mouth. Spitting them into the sink. Rinsing off all the blood. I just shrugged. "As good as can be expected, I suppose. Considering…"

"Considering?"

I waved my arms about, indicating the surroundings. "Where I am. Where I live."

"I see. This is your third day at St. Catherine's," she said, hands folded on the thick file sitting on her desk.

"And I would highly recommend this place to all my friends," I said. "Drinks, meals, lodging—it's all inclusive, you know?"

"You're upset with me," she said, stating the obvious.

"That's right, I am," I said. "We were talking yesterday. You asked me about what was going on. All I was trying to do was tell you that we needed to go back farther and talk about before everything went crazy in my life. And then you cut me off," I said. I was mad at myself. I shouldn't have said even this much. I wanted to be true and not say a word about anything. Somehow she got me talking.

"I'm sorry about that," she said.

"So why'd you cut me off?" I asked.

"You were bleeding," she said, but she wasn't looking at me. She was looking down at her hands. Was she concentrating on the file under her palms? "And I could see you were suddenly upset. So at that point I thought it best to end our session together."

"It was just my thumb. And I wasn't upset."

"You seemed it."

"I'll tell you this, I'm far more upset right now than you think I might have been last night," I said.

"Something was different yesterday. I'm trying to be open and honest with you, Joey. I think that's important so we can restore the bond we were forming."

Bond? Right. But she didn't sound like a doctor right now. She sounded like a normal human being. Her doctor defenses seemed to be down. She appeared a little weak, vulnerable.

I crossed my legs, and leaned back in my chair. She was trying to connect with me. It was her game. Had to be. And let me tell you, she wasn't doing too badly.

But not *that* good, either.

I was on to her.

"Different how?" I asked.

She shifted in her chair. "I would like to talk about what happened before your life got all crazy."

"I'm sure you would," I said. I couldn't figure out how old this lady was. With all the degrees and stuff on the wall, I'd have sworn early fifties. Right at this second, she didn't look it. She looked like she might be closer to my age, somewhere in her mid-thirties. Her skin looked so soft and smooth. I couldn't see a visible wrinkle, not by the corners of her eyes or lips or anywhere. And she smelled good. It was more than her perfume. It was *her* that I smelled. The scent was sweet, alluring. I bit down on my lower lip. I could not remember a time when I was ever so aware of someone else's scent.

"You don't want to talk about what happened?" she asked.

I wanted to talk about what happened this morning, in the bathroom. I had to have been dreaming. It had seemed so real. But if I was dreaming, it was a dream of a different kind all together. "Not sure we'd have enough time," I said. "I'd hate to get started only to have you cut me off in few minutes saying we're out of time."

"I apologized for that," she said.

"No. You never apologize."

"I was trying to explain what happened."

"But you didn't apologize."

"No. I didn't apologize. Joey, I'm sorry I cut you off yesterday. I mean that. Sincerely," she said.

I closed my eyes. She was messing with me. And it wasn't hard to do, because I actually wanted to talk. I needed to get everything off my chest. I wanted someone to listen to me. Dr. Sanchez wanted to listen to me, whether she was being paid by the hospital for her time, or not, I could tell she really wanted to hear what I had to say.

Or was I just fooling myself?

Didn't matter.

"Let me ask you this, Joey. You mentioned having nightmares."

"I have them."

"Did they start before or after the car accident?" She grasped the file on her desk, and then let go of it. She knew plenty about me.

"After the accident," I said, collapsing internally. I didn't want to fight Dr. Sanchez, not physically, not mentally, and not emotionally. She was here to help. I had to remember that. I was here because I wanted help, because I needed help. What good was it to play some stubborn, psychotic idiot?

I leaned forward in my chair, elbows on my knees, hands clasped together in front of me.

"Do you want to talk about the accident?" Dr. Sanchez stood up, the file in her hand, and walked around to sit in the chair across from me, showing trust.

I still wanted to know what caused that lack of trust in the first place. It wasn't because I was getting agitated. It wasn't a bleeding thumb. Something happened to our trust first. Then she'd quit the session. Then I'd become agitated. It wasn't the other way around. That much I knew for sure.

"Joey?"

"The accident," I said. I lowered my head.

I knew a lady who was in a bad bike wreck. It should have killed her. When she wiped out, she broke bones, had internal bleeding, and had sliced her liver in half. If you asked her about the accident, she could tell you everything that happened before the crash, and about her ride in the ambulance to the hospital. But she couldn't remember the accident itself.

Aside from the injuries, I considered her lucky.

Me? I remembered the night, everything about it, including the accident—every sight, smell, sound, taste and sensation. I'd give anything to wipe it out of my brain forever.

"Joey? Do you want to talk about the accident?" She asked.

"I don't know," I said. "I'm not sure."

The answer was honest. I'd almost died that night.

"When was it?" she asked.

"Just a few weeks ago. October thirty-first," I said. "Halloween."

When I finally opened my eyes, I didn't see the carpet in Dr. Sanchez's office. Instead I saw the night of the accident, as if transported back in time.

We were in my car. The roads were wet from endless hours of a cold rain. It had been an awful night for trick-or-treaters, no doubt. It wasn't raining then, though, not as we made our way back from a party to my apartment.

"I was drinking, but wasn't drunk," I told her, same as I told anyone who'd listen.

"The police tested your blood-alcohol levels," she assured me. "And you're right. You weren't drunk. In fact, they found no trace of alcohol in your blood at all."

That's what I'd been told at the hospital that night, too. It couldn't be right, though. Beer. Whisky. I'd pushed my tolerance to the limits that night. It should have taken days for me to sober up. It was like back in college, drinking more than I should with little regard for anything else. I had no business behind the wheel of a car.

At the time, I had no idea how the tests could have come back showing I was sober. It wasn't even remotely possible. And yet, it is what happened. I passed the sobriety test. No one arrested me. No DWI was tacked onto my license. And luckily, no one died, not really.

"Were you alone in the car?" she asked.

She knew all the answers already. It was all in the file in her lap. She was just trying to draw it out of me. She wanted me to talk.

Had I been alone?

God, no, I wasn't alone. I wiped tears from my eyes. "She trusted me," I said. "I wasn't just responsible for myself. I was responsible for her, too."

"Who?" Dr. Sanchez asked.

"Carissa. My girlfriend," I said.

"And what happened to her?" she probed.

She went through the windshield. "She was okay," I said.

"No broken bones, no cuts, no bruises," Dr. Sanchez said.

"That's right," I said.

We'd come up on a curve in the road. I was going far too fast. When I slammed on the brakes, the car skidded out of control. The sound of tires screaming on slick pavement overpowered the blaring of the car stereo. Inside the car I could smell the strawberry air freshener, Jack Daniels and cigarette smoke. The truck coming around the bend in the opposite lane swerved to keep from hitting us. All I could see was its headlights, they shone like an atomic explosion against my front windshield. My hands gripped the steering wheel so tightly that my fingernails dug into the palms of my hands. The sound of one loud, lone horn blast filled my ears as we careened off the side of the road, and rolled and rolled.

We weren't wearing seatbelts. My thighs slammed into the lower half of the steering wheel with so much force the wheel snapped off the column. My head banged against the interior roof so hard that when I bit my tongue, I was sure I'd severed off a good chunk of flesh and muscle.

It didn't matter though. All I saw was Carissa . . .

"Joey?" She held out a couple of plucked tissues from the box of Kleenex in her hands. "Joey? Your friend, Carissa, she was all right. You were all right. No one was injured, isn't that right?"

I nodded. Even with my eyes closed, the heels of my hands pressed against them, I still saw the scene play out in my mind's eye. Carissa shouldn't have been all right. She smashed through the front windshield, her body twisted and cracked. She was bent and twisted and broken. She should have died. She should be dead.

We should both be dead.

But we weren't. After she got up, she came to me—I was trapped inside the car. It felt as if both my legs were broken, and I couldn't breathe. I thought a rib might have punctured a lung. I thought my spine might be broken because I couldn't move at all— she hugged me, and then...and then...

We walked away from the wreck in one piece. We walked on legs that shouldn't have worked at all.

"Are any pictures in there, in that file?" I asked. "Are pictures of my car in there?"

She held the file up to her chest as I reached for the folder. "I can't share the contents of this with you," she said. "I'm sorry, Joey."

"It's my file, right? Pictures of my car, right? I was at the damned scene of the accident," I hollered. "I was driving that car."

She stood up. She looked at me the same way she had the day before. Her eyes were open wide, full of fear.

I clapped a hand onto my head. "No. Not again. Not this again." It was *me* this time. This time I was angry first, or agitated, or whatever she wanted to call it.

"Joey, I think we need to end this. We can talk more about this tomorrow."

"Don't do this to me, doctor. Please. I want to get this out." I wanted to stop crying. Couldn't. "Please, Dr. Sanchez, I need to get this out of me."

Slowly, she lowered herself back into the chair.

"You've looked through the file?" I asked.

"I have."

"And you saw the pictures from the accident?"

"I did," she said.

I opened my eyes and stared at her for a moment, ignoring the tears that rolled down my cheeks. "So tell me, how could I live through that? The car was crushed. I should be dead, shouldn't I? We both should have died, right?"

"That question, Joey, is beside the point. For whatever reason, neither of you died. Some might say an angel was watching over you that night. I mean, it was truly a miracle that you survived," she said, and I'm sure she thought she was being helpful.

She wasn't.

This all had to be a dream. I almost laughed. A dream? I was losing my mind. Nothing about this resembled a dream. A nightmare, yes, but a dream, I don't think so. Dreams made you feel warm and fuzzy. When in them you floated everywhere, your feet never quite touched the ground. When you woke up from a dream, you tried to remember every last detail. I even remember times when I tried to go back to sleep, and hoped I could plug myself back into the same dream.

What I was in now existed at the extreme opposite end of a dream. And *nightmare* didn't work as a descriptive word, either. Not really.

Living nightmare.

That was better, living nightmare, because I was not asleep. I would not wake up. If I closed and opened my eyes, nothing would have changed. I'd still be here. *They'd* still be out there.

I don't think a miracle happened that night. I don't believe a guardian angel was anywhere near the crash site. I'm not so sure I survived the wreck, not at all.

Six

Webster, New York

The Tantalo Mansion sat on the edge of the bluff overlooking Lake Ontario. At times, on extremely clear days, it seemed like you could see the outlining shores of Toronto, but couldn't. The idea of seeing land was merely an illusion playing off the water shimmying along the distant horizon. It didn't matter. The view remained spectacular.

Victor decided it was far too cold to sit outside. And although he never felt warm, he did not wish to immerse himself in the elements. His blood was far too thin to extract any enjoyment from wintery months. Always cold and bundled under layers of clothing, he couldn't help but feel like an animal forced to hibernate.

He made himself comfortable in the leather chair in the study by the window. He kept the lights off. The darkness *did* comfort and relax him. He set his ice-filled tumbler on the stand next to the chair and stared out at the white caps and rolling waves.

Moving south made the most sense. Florida, Georgia, even South Carolina. Unfortunately, it didn't work that way. Not anymore. Western New York was his territory. Each family was responsible for a territory. For whatever reason, Victor and his family had been unlucky enough to wind up here.

Once known for sporting four splendid seasons, Rochester had somehow fallen victim to climate change. There were a few weeks of spring, barely three months of summer, a few weeks of fall, and then six months of winter. Not fair, but if Victor knew one thing for certain it was that life was rarely fair. And death even less so.

The moon was out, and shone brightly, but was not reflected on the rough water. The gray clouds all around the suspended orb overpowered the moon's glow.

"I knew I'd find you in here," Katrina said, like an elegant silhouette she entered the study. As she got closer, the moonlight that managed to pass through the study's windows lit her features. She looked wonderful for her age. People who met her would have sworn she was not a day over fifty. They'd be surprised to find out her actual age. As a lady, and as a rule, she never divulged that secret. Only he knew her true age. Raven black hair, copper complexion and vibrant blue eyes complemented her still stunning figure, complete with long shapely legs and flat belly.

He didn't mind that his own hair had gone mostly gray. He wore it slicked back. Katrina said the gray made him all the more distinguished. He was not one of those guys who fooled around with hair coloring. If Katrina liked his hair color natural, then that was how he'd wear it. He kept in shape, exercising in their basement gym daily. That was as much for her enjoyment as for his health. Everyone gets older; how one aged was up to the individual.

She carried a cup on a saucer and sat in the chair across from her husband. "You want to be alone?"

He smiled. "Of course not, dear. You know I enjoy your company. What's that you're drinking?" Of course he knew the answer.

"Espresso," she said, smiled. "I just enjoy the flavor."

Some things were hard to do without, he realized.

"Worried?" She said.

"I wouldn't say I was worried. There's just a lot going on, always so much going on. I guess I'm just getting tired."

"We've been at this a long time," she said, sympathetically. She lifted the tiny cup and sipped her espresso without slurping. "When the time is right, maybe you can retire."

Victor laughed. He lifted his bourbon, held it in between the fingertips of both hands and sloshed the thick fluid and ice cubes around some, mixing them, before taking a drink. "We won't get to retire, dear. We are the leading force. We are the explorers on this latest frontier. There is so much work to be done. There is so little time."

"Our people have been at this for centuries," Katrina reminded him.

"Yes. And we've never been this close. We are on the last leg of this journey, dear. The last leg. And though I'd love to think this could all be finished in our lifetime, I'm a realist. Possibly, just possibly, it will be the next generation who sees the day of victory. But, to be honest, it may be the generation after that, or even the one after that who lives to see the glory of a new age." Victor drained his drink, and frowned as he set the empty glass back down. He stared out the window.

"You're thinking about him?"

She knew her husband too well. "You are a beautiful woman. You know that," he told her.

"He'll turn up," she said. "Your boys won't stop until he's found."

"I know. I know it, dear. It's just rotten timing." He reached for his empty glass. "Now the police are involved, and the church. It's such a mess."

"Would you like me to refill that for you?"

"No dear," he said, pulling his hand away from the glass. "You already do enough for me."

She set down her espresso next to his glass and then stood up. He held out his arms. She came to him and sat on his lap. He held her tight to him. Smelled her hair. Smelled her. "I love you so much, you know that?"

"I know that. And I love you."

"After all this time, you might think we'd lose interest in each other, but my Katrina, with you I actually believe I fall more in love every day," he said. He was talking more to himself, actually, but had said the words out loud.

She gently lifted his chin, looked into his eyes and kissed him, just as the sound of a door slamming shut shattered the mood. "I believe our boys are home," she whispered. "We will continue this later?"

He smiled. "Yes, we will," he said.

"Mom? Dad?" It was Marcus. The oldest.

"In here, son," Victor called out. To Katrina he said, "Why do they do that, go yelling through the house? They're not children anymore. They know we're home."

She laughed. "Tell them that."

"They need to grow up," he said. "I'm not going to live forever."

"And they'll need to step in and take over, I know. They know. And when the time comes, your boys will make you proud," she said. She stood up. "Do you want to be alone with them?"

He shook his head. "I don't want you out of my sight," he said, lovingly. "Stay, sit."

The door to the study opened and the light was switched on. Victor shielded his eyes against the sudden contrast. "Do you have to go through the house turning on every single light?"

"Sorry, Dad," Marcus said, and switched off the light.

Antonio and Dean entered in birth order behind their oldest brother. There was no mistaking they were brothers. Each stood within half an inch of the other, all about six-one. Long, curly dark, almost black hair draped over broad shoulders. They were built like gymnasts, sporting that V torso. Solid muscle covered their bodies, and they wore their clothing a bit too tight to flaunt it. The most distinguishable feature was eye color.

Marcus, the oldest, had azure-blue eyes that resembled the sky on a clear, cloudless day. Antonio's eyes were steel blue-gray that looked like a charged magnetic storm cloud. Dean had andiridia eyes, and since he lacked irises, they looked black.

All three boys walked over and kissed their mother hello. Dean sat on the armrest and wrapped an arm around her. She snuggled into the embrace. Antonio leaned against the table by the window; his bulk blocked most of the moon's light, while Marcus squatted down in front of his father.

"Where's your sister?" Victor asked. He now wished he'd had a refill on his drink. He lifted the glass off the table next to Antonio and held the empty tumbler in his hand. It was cold from the ice cubes.

"She's here," Marcus said. "Home. In her room."

"Yes. I realize that. She's always in her room," Victor mumbled. "Any word? Anything new? Anything?"

As the oldest, Marcus did the talking. He was next in line to run the family business. "We hit a million dead ends," he said.

Victor grunted and lowered his head. He hated hyperboles.

"Until Dean came up with an idea," Marcus added.

"That's my boy," Katrina said, patting her son's chest.

Dean smiled and bobbed his head from side to side as if it was no big deal. Victor knew Dean was Katrina's favorite. The others knew it, too. Victor was surprised Marcus would hand out such a compliment, especially in front of his mother. That's what made Marcus so remarkable. He was a leader. A leader didn't hide the truth; didn't need to make himself look good.

"And this idea?"

"Well, first we went to all the clubs and stuff that Carissa told us about, to see if anyone had seen Joey in the last week or so. No one's seen him," Marcus explained.

Victor impatiently rolled his finger at his son, urging him to move the story along. He didn't need to hear about all their failures to appreciate the weight of what they considered a breakthrough. "And?"

"We already knew Joey had no family," Marcus continued, drawing it out slowly, letting the suspense build. "And Carissa said he was always something of a loner, so there really weren't any friends to track down."

"Marcus, you're killing me here, what'd you find?" Victor hated when he raised his voice and lost his composure. His boys, no matter how old they got, never changed. They knew how to gnaw at his nerve endings—whether on purpose or not.

"Sorry, Dad," he said, bowing slightly to show his submission and respect. "That's when Dean…"

"I said, 'what about Joey's job,'" Dean blurted.

Victor wasn't amused. This kind of thing wasn't done. Marcus talked for the boys. It wasn't Dean's place. If anything, Antonio had more of a right to talk than Dean. And, as it were, Antonio had no right at all.

Without looking at the youngest, Victor locked eyes with Marcus who wore an expression of embarrassment. "I'm sorry, Dad," Marcus said. He turned his attention on Dean.

Without a word, Dean stood up and lowered his head. "I'm sorry, Father."

Victor nodded his approval.

Dean wasn't done. "I'm sorry, Marcus."

Marcus ignored his brother and said, "Joey works in some law firm as a paralegal, right? So tomorrow we're going to hang out around that firm and see if we can't see him coming in to work, or find out if he ain't been at work, then maybe find out if they know where he's at."

Victor sat thoughtfully for a moment. He tapped his fingers on the tumbler. "It's a good plan. I like it. I do. Okay, you boys keep me in the loop."

Marcus' cell phone rang to the tune of some rock song that absolutely drove Victor crazy. Marcus reached his hand into his pocket and silenced the ringing. "Sorry, Dad."

Victor smiled. "Go on. You've put in a long day. Enjoy the night," he said, offering his blessing.

They all kissed him and their mother goodnight.

"Dean," Victor said, as Marcus and Antonio filed out of the study.

"Yes, Father?"

"Come here," he said. "What you did to your brother just now was disrespectful."

"I know, Father. I said I was sorry. And I am."

"When people speak out of turn, it shows weakness. You see what I'm saying? Our family needs to not just *look* strong and united. We need to *be* strong and united. We understand each other?"

"It won't happen again."

Victor nodded. "And Dean?"

"Yes, Father?"

He held up his tumbler. "Grab me a refill, will ya?"

Seven

Wayne kept knocking on that bathroom door as if there weren't any other johns on the floor. I stopped yelling at him to go away five minutes ago, but for some reason he couldn't understand I was ignoring him.

Bang! Bang! Bang!

"Joey? You all right?"

I leaned over the sink, half expecting my teeth to fall out while I stared at my arm. There should be, at the very least, a scrape. But there was nothing. There had been blood. I saw the blood. The orderly wiped it away. Where had the blood come from?

It came from me. It appeared after the plastic knife sawed into my arm! The stinking plastic blade broke skin. I saw the knife buried into my forearm. Wayne saw it. I know he did. And I'd bet anything the crazy woman across from us, the one who never blinked, saw it.

Bang! Bang! Bang!

"Wayne, please!" I shouted.

"You all right?"

"I'm fine, just constipated!" There. Let him think about that for a while.

I looked at my face in the mirror, brushed the hair out of my eyes. My skin looked so pale, so ghostly white. I needed sun. What sun? Rochester used all the sunshine up in the summer. The sun left this itty, bitty city dark and desolate for the winter months. I'd have to wait until April for sunlight, maybe May.

I ran the faucet, cupped my hands and splashed cold water onto my face. When I opened the door, Wayne was standing right there, smiling. I jumped.

"Didn't mean to scare you," he said.

I walked past him and fell onto my bed.

"Who's Kelly?" he asked.

My jaw tightened. "Who?"

"Kelly. You talked about her in your sleep last night."

"I didn't sleep last night," I said, remembering that when I closed my eyes, I opened them immediately, my mouth filled with teeth that had fallen away from my gums.

"Seemed like you were talking in your sleep," he said. "Maybe you were up."

Or maybe I had fallen asleep.

"So who is she?"

"Who?"

"Kelly," he said.

"No one."

He nodded, clearly pacifying. "So you hear God talk to you?" I said, changing the topic.

"That's right. I do."

"So how come you're in here?"

"This is where He wanted me," he said.

"God? He wanted you in a mental ward?"

"I believe so," he said. "Getting in was easy. I practically walked in, and wound up in your room."

What a poet. "So you self-committed?"

"Did you?"

"You here to save someone's soul, or something?"

"Not sure yet," he said, sincerely. He sat on his bed, picked up his Bible and squeezed it between his large hands.

"Kelly was my wife," I said. I had no idea why I'd said it. Wayne wasn't my therapist, or psychiatrist, or even sane. Talking to him would not help me one bit. Maybe, just maybe, that's why I told him.

"Ah," he said.

I closed my eyes. What a mistake. But what had I expected? Him saying *Ah* made perfect sense, a fitting response.

"We were married for just over five years," I said.

"Kids?"

"No, no." I hated thinking about Kelly. I had loved her so much. Kids would have made her loss all the more unimaginable, but perhaps kids could have been my saving grace.

"What happened?"

What happened? That was the question I asked myself a million times. "She was stubborn, I guess. She wasn't feeling well. I don't know if she knew, but I never understood just how sick she was. Until it was too late," I said. She was always tired. She never seemed happy. She had to have been in pain, but never complained about it. "Things got really bad the last year," I said.

"The last year?"

"She died. Cancer." I could see her in the hospital room. There was nothing more the doctors could do. They made her last few weeks tolerable, feeding her drugs intravenously. Morphine numbed her pain. They prescribed nothing to ease mine.

"I'm sorry."

"So was I," I said.

"You're not now?"

"She gave up on me," I said. "She could have gone for help when she first got sick, but she didn't. She hid it. She kept it a secret, even from me."

"She knew she had cancer?"

"She knew she was sick. And she never did anything about it. Nothing." I came home one night. She was in the bathroom, on all fours, puking blood into the toilet. I remember falling to my knees beside her, crying, trying to hold her hair back and out of the way. "Even when I wanted her to go to the hospital, she wouldn't. She refused."

"So you're mad at her?"

It was a good question. "Don't you get it? If she loved me, if she ever truly loved me, she wouldn't have turned her back on me. She wouldn't have quit. Because that's what she did. She quit. We dated for four years. We had nine years together. I'd have done anything for her, anything. And what did she do? She gave up. She didn't even try to fight her illness. She didn't even try to get well. She gave in to it, let it overpower her, and then she just died."

When she flat lined, doctors and nurses came into the room. I stood back, out of the way, expecting them to attempt reviving her. Instead, one doctor held her wrist, looked at his watch and pronounced her dead.

"How do you just give up like that? How do you not fight to keep alive," I asked. I didn't want Wayne to answer. He kept quiet, and I was thankful. "She left me, Wayne. I don't care how you look at it. I don't care what anyone says, she left me. She just gave up."

"How long ago did this all happen?"

"Last April," I said, eyes closed. "Just after Easter."

"Joey?" Wayne said, his tone of voice so soft I could barely hear him. "Joey?"

"What?" I said, my tone harsh. I'd shared so much with him, more than I'd shared with anyone before.

Opening up was never easy for me. Talking about something so personal, so intimate was not easy.

"So then, who's Carissa?"

~ * ~

Hamlin, New York

She stood by the open window in her bedroom. With her eyes closed, she concentrated on the sound of waves crashing onto the shore. The brisk breeze chilled her to the bone, but she refused to close the windows, or to even wrap herself with the comforter off her bed. She could smell winter coming and the smell reminded her of death. It was such a barren and desolate season.

Her long red hair blew with the wind, wrapping around her face and whisking over her ears to flap freely behind her head, only to wrap back around her face. She didn't brush away the hair; it worked as a tissue drying tears her eyes shed.

Everyone was mad at her, her brothers, her father, maybe not her mother, but she couldn't be sure. They'd talked, and her mother swore she understood, but did she really? Could she possibly?

He was out there. She could feel him. He hadn't fled the city. He was still in Rochester. She knew it. In her heart, she knew it. If he had taken off, she would have sensed it. And soon, her brothers would find him. That's what they did. They found people, and things. Whatever they looked for they found, always making Daddy so proud. While all she could do was disappoint everyone. Continually disappoint him.

Her father never wanted a daughter. He never said as much, but she knew this to be true. The way he looked at her, the way he talked to her, the way he treated her, spoke volumes. He wanted four boys.

She pursed her lips and held back sobs that threatened to escape.

They didn't understand her. Not even her mother.

She didn't ask to be part of this family.

If she could have chosen her parents, she'd have picked some normal family from Wisconsin or something. Or some family in Rochester, so she could still have met Joey.

But she believed in destiny, and if she'd of been born to some family in Wisconsin, she believed she and Joey would still have met, would still have fallen in love, regardless.

It was her family that ruined everything; her brothers that had scared him away.

And as much as she hated to admit it, Joey had a right to be scared, and every reason to run. She would have run and hid too, if she had been in his shoes. She felt like running and hiding, anyway. She'd do anything to get away from her family. Anything.

But two things stopped her from running: her brothers, because they would find her, and Joey. Sooner or later her brothers would find him. When they found him, he would need her support and love and power more than ever. She might be the only thing that could keep him alive. Without her, the family would execute him for sure.

She turned from the window, ran and fell onto her bed. There was no stopping the crying now.

Eight

Rome, Italy

The small forest was backlit by floodlights, forcing the shadows of the trees to extend toward unnatural heights. Dressed in black, like ninjas, three figures stood at the center of a small clearing, shoulders touching, backs facing in, allowing them to slowly walk in a circle and watch the dark crevasses for signs of movement.

The only sound was their breathing. Nothing stirred in the darkness surrounding them. Crossing one foot over the other, they continued to step around, taking in everything, intent on finding something. They were not alone. The tension felt like electricity as it raced up and down each of their nervous systems.

The silence sounded almost overwhelming.

The attack would come. Waiting for it was the hardest part. They were on defense. Splitting up and running blind into the thicket did not make sense. They'd be picked off one by one for certain.

Just when it seemed like insanity from anticipation would set in, something big and dark, almost featureless, fell from one of the trees.

The one facing it reacted, expecting an imminent attack—the arrow was in place. In one fluid motion, the sight was locked, the arrow released and the target hit. The mass fell backwards.

With that, four more things emerged. Two more fell out from treetops, ready to pounce, two stepped out of hiding from behind large trees. Though resembling humans, the things had no faces to speak of. No eyes, no noses, no mouths. It appeared as if they were wearing black stockings over unusually round heads.

Without words, the trio stepped into action.

The one armed with a bow, drew and fired another arrow, piercing a second thing in the head. Before it fell, face down onto the ground, a second arrow stuck the target in the heart.

One of the others moved out of the tight circle. The thing, about to pounce, seemed undeterred. The two collided. The person in black cupped the thing's head and snapped the spine when it twisted the neck almost a full one hundred and ninety five degrees.

The third person, dressed in black, was chased into the trees; he jumped and grabbed onto a branch. He pulled his knees up to his chest and the thing passed under him. The branch he'd hung suspended from broke. He fell, squatted on the ground and picked up a rock in his free hand. When the thing stopped and turned, he smashed the rock into its face three times in quick succession before he drove the sharp end of the broken branch into the thing's heart.

The fourth thing flew at the man with the rock. It raised its hands, ready to lunge forward, but then fell to the ground, an arrow stuck out of the center of its back.

With all the things down and out, the trio stepped back into formation, and made their way back to the clearing, ready for more unsuspected surprises.

~ * ~

Cardinal David Bonsignore stood with his hands folded behind his back in his Vatican office. He stared out the window into the midnight darkness. He had been looking at files from the Pope all day. His eyes hurt, his neck ached and he simply needed rest.

When he first became a priest, he never once expected to become a cardinal, and he surely never expected to be working out of the Vatican. He always felt his calling would lead him more toward missions work, spreading the Word to those who had never heard God's message of salvation, freedom, hope, love and redemption.

He felt more like some FBI agent than a man of God. Perhaps it was his military background that allowed the Pope to zero in on his personnel file. Whatever the reason, the Pope had assigned him this daunting task. He must have known the inner turmoil such a task would render on the soul of a Cardinal.

No one said following God's plan would be easy. In fact, the Bible promised just the opposite— that following could prove to be a constant test of one's faith. Throughout history followers have been tormented, tortured and killed for their set of beliefs. Bonsignore only hoped it never made it to such an extreme, but with what he read day in and day out in those files, he wasn't so certain.

He needed to release it to God.

The trouble was, as much faith as he had, as much as he believed, he was never one to leave work for others. He had a job to do. Ignoring it was not an option, and neither was going at it only halfheartedly.

A knock at the door pulled the cardinal from his thoughts, from his doubts. With a passing glance over the ever-accumulating files gathered by intelligence, Bonsignore gladly welcomed the interruption.

"Come in," he said.

Father Pete Cano entered Bonsignore's chambers. This priest used a bow and arrow with such skill and accuracy, Robin Hood would have been impressed. The two of them had utilized the archery field behind the rectory a few times. Each outing had left

Bonsignore feeling as if he should concentrate on honing some other talent, since Cano obviously owned it all. Built like a marine right down to the buzz haircut, broad shoulders, bulging biceps and thick muscular thighs, no one would ever suspect that Cano led worship most Sundays in the Vatican choir.

Next, Sister Brianna walked in. Sister Bri. With shoulder length light brown, almost blond hair, she couldn't be more than five-four, and couldn't weigh more than a hundred and five pounds, and didn't look like she could hurt a fly. Her small stature definitely misled most. On Saturday nights, Bri taught self-defense hand-to-hand combat for women over at the Vatican gym.

Last to enter was Father Brandon Padilla. Perhaps the most undisciplined of the group, of Bonsignore's team, but also one of the most fearless, and dedicated. At five-nine, one seventy-five, he was solid and a master at improvisation. His hair was so blond, and his eyes so blue and his skin so light that it was hard to believe fifty percent of his bloodline was Puerto Rican.

The Catholic Church is bigger than most governments combined, and as filled with as many secrets, too. Bonsignore knew plenty, but hardly all. He wondered if anyone but the Pope himself had a grasp on just how powerful and widespread the church actually was. However, he wished a few more had been assigned to his team. The four of them were about to wage a secret war. War was hell. No doubt about it. Four just didn't seem like a sizable army. Even Jesus had twelve.

"Your Eminence?" Pete said.

Bonsignore nodded. His team was anxious, maybe even a bit excited. "You've completed your last simulation this evening. The games are over. Training is complete. When we go into the field, there won't be mechanical mannequins on wire coming at you. It will be the real thing." He paused, swallowed and looked out the window. He knew the job they'd been assigned needed to get done.

In the last several years he'd come to think of Pete, Brandon and Bri as family, and not just as his *team*. They were about to put more than their lives in danger. They were about to put their very souls on the line. "Plane tickets are on my desk," he said. "Get packed. We leave in the morning."

Nine

Marcus drove his SUV with both hands on the wheel, eyes on the road. Antonio rode shotgun, tuned the radio to a station he liked and then played his thighs like bongos. Dean sat in back, leg crossed, elbow on the door's armrest, chewing on his thumbnail.

"You ever wonder what it would be like if we were like them?" Dean sat slouched in the seat as he nodded his head toward the people outside of their vehicle, his finger lightly tapping against the window.

"I've thought about it," Antonio admitted. "Then it depressed the hell out of me."

"I think about it, but no matter how hard I try, I just can't imagine it. I can't even begin to fathom being like them, living a pathetic existence like them. I can't imagine waking up every morning and going to bed each night without any purpose, without any meaning to such a dismal existence," Dean said. "And then I wonder, how do they do it? Where do they get that drive to continue, because look at them—they don't stop. Even though they have nothing to look forward to, they keep going and going, day after miserable day."

"They're like goldfish, Dean, that's all." Marcus signaled a turn at the next intersection.

"What's that supposed to mean?" Dean said. "You mocking me? Because I'm being serious here."

"So am I," Marcus said. "You can go to a pet store and buy a goldfish for a quarter. You stick him in a tiny bowl with a fake plant and some fluorescent stones, you pepper in some food once a day and they can live for years—day after day, swimming in circles, never going anywhere, never doing anything worthwhile. Then one day you find them, what? Floating at the top of the bowl. So what do we do? Flush 'em and drop a new quarter goldfish into the bowl to replace the one that died. And if you looked at the new one, you'd swear it was actually the old one. No one would ever know the difference. But even then, it would only be a glancing thought, because they're goldfish, who really cares?"

Dean smiled and nodded. "Yeah. That's exactly what it is. Goldfish. That's why I spend so much time watching them. They're in like an aquarium out there, living useless lives."

"Exactly," Marcus said. He pulled the SUV up to a curb. "We're here."

They climbed out of the car. Antonio dropped coins into a parking meter. Under similar long leather coats, they were dressed in expensive Italian dark suits; solid colored ties and monogrammed white shirts. With hair greased and slick backed, and clean shaven faces on display, there was no denying that the three of them resembled models right off the cover of GQ.

"Big building," Dean said, looking up toward the sky.

"Joey works near the top."

"You want me down here?" Antonio asked.

Marcus nodded. "Blend in, though."

"We *shoulda* got here earlier, catching people coming into work," Antonio said.

"It was a rough night," Dean said, snickering.

"If we need to, we come back tomorrow," Marcus said. "At five a.m. if we have to." He stared at Dean. "Got your phones?"

Dean and Antonio patted pockets and nodded.

"Dean, you come with me," Marcus said.

Downtown Rochester was busy, but not crowded. As winter months approached, both people and vehicle traffic seemed lighter than during the other three seasons. It was almost nine. The sun was barely visible, fighting to shine through thick gunmetal gray clouds. Still sensitive, Antonio slipped shades on to cover his eyes.

Inside the front foyer, Marcus and Dean consulted an information board by a bank of elevators. A security guard sat behind a desk in the far right corner, and other than nodding a quick hello to each of them, he focused his attention on the folded newspaper held in one hand and the sugar-powdered, jelly-filled doughnut in the other.

Dean used a finger to help him read through the columns and names on the board. "What's the firm, again? Like Dewey, Cheatum and Howe?" He laughed at his own joke.

"This is it. Mynheir and Mapes. Fifteenth floor," Marcus said, and depressed the up button to call an elevator. He straightened his knot at his collar while he waited for the next car. "You let me do the talking."

"Whatever."

"No, I'm serious," Marcus said, teeth clenched. "We're not going to mess this up."

"Did I say, 'whatever'? That means whatever. You do all the talking. I got it." Dean stuffed his hands into his coat pockets and slowly twirled around on the heel of one foot. His jacket parted like a cape in the wind.

Marcus grabbed his arm. "Will you act professional?"

Dean stood shoulder to shoulder with his brother. "Tell you what, don't ever grab my arm like that again."

Marcus turned to look at his kid brother. "You threatening me?" he whispered.

"See all these people around, they're the only reason you're still standing. If you want to take that as a threat, fine. It's a threat. You want to run to Father, and squeal like some fat pig? Best of luck to you," Dean said as an elevator opened, people got off and they stepped on. "I'm your brother," he said, despite people crowding in all around them. "Not your slave. Don't ever treat me like one again."

As the elevator doors closed, Marcus pressed the fifteen button, and stood with hands folded in front of him. He looked up and watched the numbers change as the elevator ascended. He ignored Dean's outburst. He'd address it later, no doubt. Now, it just wasn't the time.

After a few stops at other floors, people getting off, people getting on, they finally made it to their floor. Marcus let Dean step off first, no longer comfortable with his back vulnerable to the little monster.

"Mynheir and Mapes," Dean said, pointing at an office door on the left. The firm name was painted in black on frosted glass doors.

As Marcus reached to open the door, Dean made a show of using a key to lock closed lips, and then, like a demented mime, tossed the imaginary key over his shoulder, and dusted his hands together.

Rolling his eyes, Marcus pulled open the door and stood aside to let Dean walk in ahead of him. The first thing Marcus noticed was the gorgeous receptionist. She had to be barely twenty, with long, curly blond hair. Bright green eyes set under long, thick lashes. High cheekbones, a cute turned-up nose and full lips completed the facial ensemble. Her scent was strong, and he knew his nostrils flared, sucking as much in as possible. Marcus worried Dean would not be able to control himself. Right now, he struggled as well.

The nameplate at the edge of her desk simply read, Receptionist.

"Good morning," the receptionist said, smiling warmly. "Can I help you?"

"We're hoping you can. We've been waiting for a return call from a paralegal, Joey Rossi, or Joseph, rather?" Marcus said.

"I'm sorry, he's not back to work yet," the receptionist said. "Perhaps I can have you talk with one of our other paralegals, or set up an appointment to meet with one of our attorneys? What was your name, sir?"

"Do you know when Mr. Rossi will return?" Marcus asked.

She held a clipboard and pen out to Marcus. "I'm not really sure. He's been out a few days. If you want, you can have a seat and fill out this intake form?"

He waved off the form. He locked eyes with the receptionist. "Is Mr. Rossi on vacation?"

Her face wrinkled, lips puckered, brow furrowed, as if she didn't want to talk, but was somehow forced to answer against her will. "No."

"Where is he?" Marcus asked.

The receptionist winced, as if in pain, as if someone had grabbed her arm and twisted it behind her back. "He's sick. He's on some kind of medical leave. That's all I know. He's out sick."

Marcus stared for three more seconds before looking away. "That's all she knows," he said to Dean.

The receptionist gasped, planted a hand on her chest. "I'm going to have to ask you to leave," she said. She looked around her desk, appeared confused and disoriented. She jumped to her feet and turned, perhaps on her way to the restroom, but before she could take two steps she vomited on the carpet behind her chair.

"We'll show ourselves out," Marcus said.

Dean leaned over the receptionist counter to get a look at the woman down on all fours, heaving, as other office workers rushed to her side. Smiling, he turned and followed Marcus out into the hallway. "Tell me that wasn't fun?"

"Goldfish."

Dean laughed as they stepped into the elevator car and headed back down toward the front lobby.

Once in the SUV, Antonio asked. "Well?"

"We start checking hospitals."

"When?"

"Right now."

Antonio put a hand to his head. "He's in a hospital? Dad's gonna flip. He ain't gonna like this. Not one bit."

"We don't know for sure if he's in a hospital. We know he's out on a medical leave. That's what we know. We know he ain't home, and he has no family, so hospitals are the next best place to start checking," Marcus said.

~ * ~

"I think we should talk, today, about your dream," Dr. Sanchez said. She didn't look the same. It took a minute to recognize what was different. No glasses and her hair was not tied back in a pony. It went just past her shoulders, thicker than I'd have guessed.

"Date tonight?" I teased.

"Excuse me?" she said sharply, and then cocked her head to one side.

"I was, it was just, you look nice, so I was just asking if you had a date..."

"We are not here to discuss my personal life," she said, her tone of voice softening some, but not much.

"I'm sorry," I said, sighed heavily showing my self-disgust.

"Is that a problem?"

"Look, I wasn't trying to invade on your personal life. I was actually just trying to be friendly," I said. "I was just trying to give this, you and me, this doctor-patient, thing a chance."

Before I could look away, I saw her features soften. Thankfully, her head readjusted back to normal—she had started to remind me of Dustin Hoffman in *Rain Man,* standing the way she'd been standing.

When she sat down across from me, I looked up. She was smiling. "I'm sorry, Joey. It's been a long day. You don't want to hear about that, though," she said.

"I don't mind sharing some of my time with you," I said.

She laughed. "Let's talk about your dreams."

I looked at the clock on the wall behind me.

"No clocks today, Joey. Just you and me."

"No clocks?"

"Just you and me."

I clenched my jaw, felt the muscles tense and imagined a little ripple rolling along the outside of my cheeks.

"I mean it Joey. No time limit this evening."

"Would it be all right if we don't start at the dreams, or the accident?" I said. "I tried to tell you before, that's like starting in the middle of a story. I think we need to go back and start at the beginning."

"Not the beginning, beginning, like from the day you were born?" She smiled.

I laughed, and sat back in the chair. "No, I'd say more like starting back at, like, August."

"This past August?"

"That's right."

"And then we'll get to the car accident?"

"I don't see any way around it."

"Okay, Joey. Let's go back to August."

"Well, actually, in a way, we start in April," I said. "But April's a fast month."

She shook her head, grinning. "April, then. Would you like coffee or a Coke or something?"

"I'm good."

She sat back in her chair, crossed her legs and set her notebook down on the table beside her.

"Tell me about April."

"My wife died in April," I said. For the next fifteen minutes, I told Dr. Sanchez pretty much the same things I'd told Wayne the other night. "The toughest thing for me to deal with was being alone. I hated it. I didn't want to be in our house. It was so empty. I stopped going to church." After a while, I'd sold it, rented a one bedroom. It was the best choice I'd ever made. I didn't care about throwing money away on rent. I cared about the carefree lifestyle. No lawns to mow, driveways to shovel, rooms to paint.

"Why?"

I shook my head. "Not sure, exactly."

"Did you blame God?"

I almost laughed. "You might think I would, but I didn't. I would think He was on my side, that He wanted her to fight. I don't feel like He took her. It's like I said, she quit."

"So why stop going to church?"

"I really can't say, and in fact, I started doing the exact opposite. I started going to bars," I said. "I needed to be around people, but for some reason, I chose drunks, or people partying, over people from church."

"And that helped?"

"Nothing helped. See, I wasn't hitting clubs. I was going to bars. Not dives. I'd go in alone, have some beers, watch the groups of people having a good time and I'd leave. I ended up feeling more alone at bars than I did in my own place," I said.

"So what happened?" Dr. Sanchez asked, leaning forward.

"One night, in August, at this one bar, I met this one girl. Her name was Carissa…"

Ten

This Past August

Someone played *Daniel* on the jukebox, a live acoustic rendition of Elton John's classic, performed by Fuel. I sipped my beer sitting in a corner table. Two couples shot pool. One guy threw darts. A handful of guys sat at the bar, while a few others occupied the tables around me. Ceiling fluorescents and glowing beer signs dimly lit the place. A string of white Christmas lights outlined the windows and the bar back, where the bottles of alcohol sat stacked in rows in front of a mirror. The murmur of conversation and the crash of the cue ball couldn't compete against the volume of the song.

With the exception of a couple of ceiling fans, the air in the place was stagnant, stale. It had to be close to ninety degrees outside, still. The humidity made it feel more like a hundred. The windows weren't open, but a back door was propped open with a couple of—presumably—empty beer cases. All I could smell was beer, sawdust and cigarette smoke, even though no one was technically allowed to smoke inside.

It was almost midnight. I was almost ready to go. Despite drinking light beer, I felt full and was buzzed. Cans of cold beer waited in my fridge. If I stayed any longer, if I ordered another beer, I wouldn't be able to drive home. It was already tough focusing. My eyes felt heavy. My head spun.

But when she walked in, alone, I knew I wasn't going anywhere. As she made her way to the bar, she kept looking over her shoulder, back at the door she'd just entered. It didn't look like she was running from someone, as much as it seemed like she was expecting someone—but like maybe she wasn't looking forward to seeing them.

Her hair, so red, so long, so curly, was the most striking feature—at first. The guys at the bar noticed her as well. Like flies, they swarmed. She grabbed her drink, and tried to pay. Some guy in a t-shirt and Boston Red Sox cap slid the money back toward her and said something to the barmaid.

Although she thanked the guy, she tried to put her money back into play. Boston shook his head. He wasn't going to let her buy her own drink. Such a gentleman.

And then she saw me. I know she did. She looked at me out of the corner of her eyes. Bright blue eyes, another striking feature.

"There you are," she said. She was talking to me. Leaving her money on the bar, she lifted her glass and excused herself from those clustered around her. She walked toward me with a purposeful stride that suggested we knew each other.

Boldly, she sat down across from me.

"Please, let me sit here," she whispered, smiling. "They're watching me, aren't they?"

I smiled the best smile I could in return. Being a bit drunk made it difficult to get both sides of my lips to respond. "Yep. They are," I managed.

"Can I just sit with you, have my drink, and then I'll leave?" she asked.

How could I say no? "I was just leaving," I said, and finished off my beer in a gulp.

She put a hand on my arm. Her skin felt so cold it sent a shiver up my arm and down my spine. I shook, involuntarily. "Don't go. Please. Not yet," she said.

How could I leave? "I won't," I said. I didn't want to leave. I wanted to stay. I just didn't know what to do, how to act, what to say.

"My name's Carissa," she said.

"Joey," I said. "I'd shake your hand, but that would be a dead giveaway that we don't know each other." Oddly, I also wasn't looking forward to the chill touching her skin again.

She laughed. My heart melted. White teeth. Full lips. Even in this perpetual darkness, her eyes sparkled. Life was alive inside of her. "I don't know why I can't go anywhere without being harassed."

"They were bothering you?"

"They were rude," she said.

"Sorry," I said, on behalf of drunk men all over the globe.

"You didn't do anything," she said.

There was nothing I could say to that, and I could think of nothing else to say at all. My beer was gone. The fragments of foam slid down the glass and pooled at the bottom.

"Want another one?" she asked.

"I shouldn't," I said. "I have to drive."

"It's early," she said.

It was late. "I know my limits."

A song by Counting Crows came on next. I didn't know it. I knew it was them, though; the singer's sound was that distinct.

"You come here a lot?" she asked.

"Not really. I've been here a few times. It's never that crowded, and the drafts are cheap," I said.

"Want another—no, that's right. You're driving," she said.

The cue ball smacked into a triangle of solids and stripes. I couldn't see them from where I sat, but could picture them scatter on the green felt table.

"That's right," I said. I couldn't look her in the eyes. She was too much for me, too pretty, too dangerous. Her confidence intimidated me. I looked, instead, at my empty mug.

"So you're all right to drive now?"

"Not really," I said. "But I don't live that far away."

"I'm not ready to go home, yet," she said, after taking a generous sip from her drink. It looked like rum and Coke. "Can I go with you?"

If I'd had a mouth full of beer, I'd have spit it out the way people did in old sitcoms. "Go with me, where?"

"Where are you going?"

"Home," I said.

She nodded, looking around the bar, then back at me. "Okay," she said, as if I'd invited her to tag along.

"You want to come home with me?" I said. She was some kind of bar fly, no doubt. I wasn't against bringing her home, I just wasn't sure I wanted to. I mean, I did. It had been such a long time...

"Sure," she said.

"I don't think that's a good idea," I said. Kelly had only been dead a few months. Lonely as I was, I didn't know if I was ready for this, for whatever Carissa had in mind. "I'm not sure that's a good idea."

She puffed out her lips. "I don't want to be alone. I'm always alone."

I had a hard time believing this. "You are?"

"I am," she said. "I don't get out that often."

"You don't?"

"No. I don't."

If I spent too much time thinking about this, I'd blow the opportunity sitting in front of me. I didn't need to dress it up. We both knew what was on the table.

"You don't even know me," I said, set on ruining a sure thing. Maybe it was God. Maybe it was all those Sundays in church.

"What do I need to know about you?" she asked.

I looked into her eyes, really looked into her eyes. They were lit, alive, shining. I shook my head as I looked away. "I'm, look, I'm sorry," I said.

Goodbye, I thought, to any chance with her now.

"Do you think I'm pretty?" she asked.

I simply nodded. "It has nothing to do with that," I said. "My wife, she just died."

And the life disappeared from her eyes; the sparkle gone. "I'm sorry," she said.

I cuddled my empty glass in my hands, and concentrated on nothing but it.

"I should leave," she said, picking up her glass.

"Don't," I said. She should leave. I knew what she wanted. I knew I couldn't give it to her, not yet, not so soon. But I stopped her from getting up. "We don't have to go to my house."

She shook her head. "No," she said. "We don't have to go to your house."

I didn't want to be alone, either. I was tired of being alone. I was tired.

"Can you swim?" she asked.

"What?"

"Swim. Can you swim?"

I let out a laugh. "Yeah," I said. "I can swim. Why? You have a pool?"

She flashed a smile as life once again filled those eyes. "No. I don't have a pool."

~ * ~

Durand was far from deserted. The Lake Ontario shoreline was lined with the glow of small bon fires. We walked with shoes in hand and pant legs rolled up. Our feet sank into the wet sand, as water lapped up over them.

The sky was cloudless. The moon stood bright in a starlit sky. Most of the bonfire lights revealed litters of engaged teenagers. There was the familiar aroma of roasting marshmallows, the noise of an array of music playing different songs, different styles, all at the same time, all at competing volumes, and the sounds of laughter.

"Do you remember being that young?" I said.

Carissa looked away from the fires and out over the lake. "It seems like it's been forever since I was that young."

"Tell me about it. Not sure I miss it though," I said. "I don't know. Maybe I do miss it at times."

"I don't miss it. I like my age," she said. "The water looks inviting, doesn't it?"

"I didn't bring a suit," I said.

"Me neither," she said, as we passed the last of the small fires, and found a secluded spot to claim as our own at east end of the beach. She stood, burying her toes in the sand as she shrugged out of her clothes, down to her *delicates*.

I tried not to look as she dashed passed me, running, splashing into the lake. She looked magnificent from behind, her long hair bouncing. And then she dove into the smooth, placid water.

It was some time before she resurfaced.

"You coming in?" she asked. It was a dare, a challenge.

Hot looking women didn't hit on me. I didn't get picked up. I didn't get taken to the beach in the middle of the night for the purpose of a midnight swim. Things like this didn't happen to me. I looked at my jeans. My wallet was in my back pocket. How could I say no? I couldn't. I dropped my clothes beside hers, and wondered about all of this.

Stones and bits of broken seashells bit into the bottom of my feet as I stepped cautiously into the water. It was far colder than it looked. The sandbar lasted a few yards, and then was gone. I dove under.

When I came up, she was gone.

I looked to the beach, half expecting her to be there, grabbing my wallet, my keys, and running for the parking lot leaving me stranded.

She wasn't on the beach.

"Carissa?" I called out.

I stood up, the water just above my waist. "Carissa?"

I looked around.

If she went under, if some current had a hold of her, how would I find her? It was too dark to see into the water.

I felt it before I realized what it was.

She was underwater, and had grabbed my leg.

I jumped, pulled back. She came up, laughing.

"Scare you?"

"Scare me?" I said, trying to laugh. My hands reached for her under the water, gripped her waist, lifted her off her feet and tossed her through the air.

She crashed into the water a few feet away.

I went for her, just in case I'd caught her off guard, in case she swallowed water.

When she stood, she came at me, a different look in her eyes. She stayed low so just her head was above water. The moon lit her face. Her eyes glowed amber.

Water droplets dripped off her chin. Her hair was slicked back, making her look even more beautiful.

Her playful look vanished as her eyes shot to the night sky. They scanned from left to right as if she were watching a plane pass overhead.

"What?" I finally asked.

"We have to go," she said. "I'm sorry. But we have to go."

I wrapped my arms around her. "Are you kidding me?"

I wasn't ready to leave.

"I want to stay," she said. "I can't. We can't."

I saw it in her eyes. She did want to stay. She wasn't teasing. For whatever reason, it *was* time to go.

"Okay," I said. "Let's go."

Taking the lead, I held her hand and walked back to shore, to where our clothing was piled close in the sand. We didn't have towels. She didn't seem to care. Wet and sandy, we dressed. I kept my socks off, climbed into my pants, and dropped my shirt on over my head—all while watching her dress, admiring her free spirit. She moved slowly, elegantly, but clearly with some determination that left me feeling as if I missed something.

This time she took my hand. "Let's go," she said.

I expected us to walk back to my car. We didn't. We ran. She was bent low, as if hiding from enemy fire. I had no idea why, but I laughed as I bent low, too. "Should we serpentine?" I asked.

"What?" she asked, but we didn't stop running. And she was yelling as if bombs were dropping all around us, blowing out our eardrums.

"You know, serpentine, zigzag," I said, using my free hand to demonstrate what I meant. She didn't look back. The illustration was left for my mere amusement.

I don't know what I expected. Carissa picked me up in a bar. Sure she was beautiful, but a small part of me had to have realized she was nuts, or easy, or both. Everyone has issues. Everyone has some kind of past. But when people meet in a bar, those issues, that past, is intensified and magnified a million times over.

All I wanted now was to get her back to her car and me home. Thank goodness tomorrow—or today, actually—was Sunday. I longed for sleep. It had been a fun, wild and wacky night, but all I wanted now was to climb into bed and drift off into never-never land.

"Keys," she said, or yelled. "Where are your keys?"

I fished them out of my pocket as we reached my car. I unlocked her door. "Quick, inside," I said, playing along with her delusions.

She took my command seriously and scrambled into the passenger seat, slammed the door closed, and locked it.

If something was mentally wrong with her, I had no right to make fun. She was still a person. And for whatever reason, she trusted me.

I got into the driver's seat, closed my door.

She looked at me. "Come on, tell me that wasn't fun?" she said.

"What? Running for the car?" I said. "Dressing so quickly that I'm wet and sandy?" Was she trying to play it off like she hadn't been truly scared out in the water? Split personality? I needed to get her back to the bar and out of my car.

"You hungry?" she said, suddenly.

Okay. I needed to get this woman out of my car. I don't know what I'd been thinking coming out here with her. All right, I knew what I'd been thinking. "My life is pretty complicated right now," I said. I'd blame me. It wasn't her. She was a terrific, wonderful, sane human being. I was the crazy one, I'd tell her. Too many skeletons in the closet, so to speak. "It was wrong of me to lead you on this way."

"I want to talk about what just happened," she said.

"You know, it doesn't matter. You were just kidding around, thought it was funny. And it was," I said, I tried laughing, even managed to lightly slap the steering wheel. "But I just, I think I need to head home now. I drank way too much. It's late."

"My brothers," she said. "I come from a big Italian family. I'm the youngest. The baby. My dad, my brothers, they're so over protective."

I nodded as if I understood. "Yeah, I'm Italian. I know what you're saying." She didn't look to the bushes, or the parking lot for her brothers. She had looked to the sky.

"No, I don't think you could know. They treat me like a kid. They don't let me go anywhere. And when I'm out—they always come looking for me. Always."

I thought about when she'd first entered the bar. She'd been looking toward the door, expectantly.

"You don't live on your own?" I asked.

She shook her head. "In my family, you don't move out unless you're married."

I nodded. A lot of Italian families are that way.

"When we were in the water, I heard them. I know I heard them." She broke eye contact and looked at the dashboard.

"Did you see them?" I asked, gently. "Maybe up in the sky?"

She turned her eyes on me. Her lips twisted into an awkward smile. "Up in the what?"

I pointed up. "You were looking up into the sky right before we sprinted out of the water."

She took a moment, perhaps to gather her thoughts, and laughed. "Have you ever strained really hard to hear something? Roll down your window," she said. "Go on, roll it down."

I lowered it.

"Now, hold on," she said. "Hear that one cricket chirping, or whatever it is crickets do?"

For her sake, I tried real hard to listen for the cricket.

"Why are you looking up? The cricket's not up there, is it? It's somewhere outside in the bushes…"

I caught myself looking up as I tried to find the cricket with my ears. Point made. "So what do you want? Breakfast?"

"Somewhere that serves omelets would be wonderful."

"But I want to hear more about your family," I said.

"You'd never want to see me again if I told you all about my family," she said.

"That's the thing about families. We're always the only sane ones in them," I said.

She laughed. I pulled out of the parking lot and headed toward an all-night diner down on Culver, by Sea Breeze.

Eleven

St. Catherine's Hospital, Rochester, NY

I knew I was asleep, dreaming. I recognized this fact. When awake, I remembered the dream—what would happen first, and what would happen next—and was able to recall it with vivid detail. It was, after all, the same dream night after night. While I slept, however, I had no idea what to expect. It was the oddest feeling because I knew I was dreaming, and knew it was the same dream as the last time I dreamt it, but for some subconscious reason, it always felt like I was having the same dream for the first time.

I was in bed and under the guise of what seemed like dancing candlelight, Carissa sat beside me, her face expressionless, except for her eyes—she stared right at me—they didn't just twinkle, an amber glow that held my gaze. And then I noticed her lips, which seemed fuller as she puckered and pursed and spread them out in a smile and then moaned, and grunted and cried out.

The flickering light became more intense. I could hear crackling sounds. Carissa no longer focused on me, she stared, instead, at something behind me, something I couldn't see.

As if speaking in slow motion, I asked, "What is it?" but could not hear the sound of my voice.

Something at the foot of the bed wiggled, or twitched, or squirmed. Whatever was down there, bundled up under the blankets, moved.

I could feel my heartbeat accelerate. My breathing became quick, shallow. I felt panicked. "Carissa?" I tried to get her attention. But when I looked from the foot of the bed up into her eyes, I screamed.

Her once milky white skin had turned to something like bark. The thick, deep, dark wrinkles made her look scarred, weathered, worn—like a tree out of the Petrified Forest.

Her eyes were suddenly cat-like, changing from amber to something resembling burning embers from the belly of a fire pit. "Carissa!"

Something touched my ankle.

The thing at the foot of the bed had touched me. I jerked my leg away from it. It scared me more than Carissa's horrid transformation.

When my leg shot forward, my knee struck Carissa in the back.

Blood shot out of the center of her chest, from where her heart should have been.

"No!" I yelled…

~ * ~

"So, what do you think of Dr. Sanchez?" Wayne sat on his hands on his bed. His grin was so wide, he looked goofy—goofier.

"She's all right," I said. We were both up early. Breakfast wasn't for another half hour.

"You guys have a session today?" He stood up, while he unbuttoned his pajama shirt.

"Every day." I sat up in bed, hesitantly placing bare feet on cold tile. I needed slippers. "You?"

"Me, what?"

"You meet with her every day?" I asked.

"You know—you don't look so well," he said. Bare-chested, a ghastly sight, but especially first thing in the morning, he walked toward me. "You're so pale."

"I haven't been feeling well. Don't think I'm sleeping much." I dug the heels of my hands into my eye sockets and rubbed.

"Tell me about it." Wayne pulled a clean shirt out of the nightstand by his bed. He put it on without showering. "You spend the whole night kicking around, and talking, and yelling."

I ground my teeth. "And you just listen?"

"Well, I'd prefer to sleep. But you prevent me from doing so." He dropped his pajama bottoms. I tried to turn away, but was far from quick enough—the image forever burned into my retina.

"What do I say?" I asked, my eyes focused on the ceiling.

He snickered. "What don't you say?"

I closed my eyes. I didn't feel like pulling teeth. For all I knew, I spoke mumbo-jumbo all night long, but I needed to know for sure. It would be a shame of the secret I carried around was revealed each night through sleep-talking.

"Wayne," I said.

"I don't know," he said. "You talk about some priest, and going to the police, and some thugs that are after you. You talk about your dead wife…"

I winced.

"Sorry," he said. "You talk about her, and the Carissa woman."

"That all?"

"And fire."

"Fire?"

"Yeah. You talk about fire a lot. Or flames."

"What do I say about the priest and police, and the thugs?" I asked.

"What do you say?" He sat down.

I looked over at him, expecting him fully clothed. I gasped and turned away. "Can you finish dressing?"

"We're talking."

"Dress first," I said. I scrambled out of bed and went into the bathroom, closing the door behind me.

Twelve

Wayne and I sat at a table, our breakfast in plastic plates in front of us. Despite Wayne stabbing the scrambled eggs over and over with his fork, neither of us ate.

"When you talk in your sleep, it's not in complete sentences," he said.

"What is it then?"

"Words. Sometimes jumbled together. Like you'll say, 'tell the police,' or 'the priest won't believe me.' Those are easy enough. But when you say things like, 'fire, under the sheets, my knee went through her heart,' man, then you've lost me." He shoveled the food from one side of the plate to the other before he set his plastic fork down.

"What's wrong?"

"They look cold. I can't eat cold eggs."

"Stick them in the microwave."

"I can't eat *microwaved* eggs, either."

"They're already cooked. You'd just be heating them up." I tried my eggs. They were cold. And runny. I spit the food into a napkin. "Gross."

Wayne smiled. "What did you have to tell the police?"

"How do you know I had to tell the police anything?" I talked in my sleep. I was sure Wayne knew more than he let on. I didn't ask him to recite back everything he'd ever heard me say. Maybe I should.

"Did the priest go with you, like he said he would?"

I needed to gag myself before sleeping from now on. Stick a sock in my mouth; lock it in place with a strap tied around my head.

"They're just dreams," I tried. "I don't even remember them half the time."

Wayne cocked his head to the side, eyes on me, one side of his lips curled into a grin. "They're more than just dreams, Joey. You know that. I know that. Does Dr. Sanchez?"

"I haven't told her everything yet," I admitted.

"So there's more?"

I shivered. Did this institution have the air conditioning on in the middle of November? Morons.

"You don't have to tell me nothing," Wayne said.

"Had no intention of telling you anything," I said.

"You going to eat that?"

I pushed the plate away. "I'm going back to the room. I want to lie down for a while."

I tossed our plates in the trash and walked back to the room, and right up to the window. I looked for birds perched on the rooftop across the way. They weren't there.

I knew he was behind me. I didn't hear him as much as sense him. "The priest went with me," I said.

The bed to my right creaked under his weight.

I closed my eyes. "I was wrong to go to the police. I wasn't thinking straight." Still not.

"What happened?" Wayne's voice was soft; I barely heard him speak.

I told Wayne about going to the priest, sitting in the confessional. I'd witnessed two murders and did nothing to help the women slaughtered. The whole time I talked, I stayed by the window, faced what stood beyond the bars.

When I finished, I expected Wayne to say something, to ask questions, to egg me on to the next part of the story. What I didn't expect was the silence. It was so quiet, in fact, that I wondered if he'd left the room during my rendition. When I turned to see if he was still in the room, I caught sight of him in my peripheral vision. He was on the bed, his Bible clutched tight to his chest.

I turned back to the window. All I saw were the bars.

"You going to say anything?" I asked. "Wayne?"

"And you went to the police?"

"With the priest," I said.

"How did that go?"

Thirteen

When I stepped out of the darkness of the confessional box, I didn't leave the church. I didn't move. I stood outside of the closed confessional door, head down, and cried.

I heard the door creak, and didn't need to turn to know the priest was stepping out of the confines of his room.

My head spun. If I opened my eyes, I'd lose balance and fall for sure. I kept them closed. Even when the priest placed his hand on my shoulder, I kept them closed.

"Would you like me to drive?" I heard him ask.

I didn't trust speaking. I nodded.

"I'll get my keys. Wait here," he instructed.

I heard footfalls fade as he made his way to somewhere else.

Carissa.

I worried that she wasn't safe, wondered how she possibly could be. Her family, her brothers—they were monsters. Evil.

And I'd left her, too.

I ran.

They killed those women and I ran—first chance alone, and I ran.

She was so beautiful. Never did I expect my heart to thaw; never did I expect to feel love again. I thought that part of me had died with Kelly. I wanted that part to die with her.

But Carissa, was she any different from her family? Could she be?

I was alive.

After an accident that should have killed me, I was still alive.

It made no sense.

Or, it hadn't made sense.

The impossible, the improbable, that all changed when her brothers killed those women.

I knew what they were, then. Carissa had warned me. She'd tried to tell me.

But who believes such a tale—despite walking away from a wreck that should have left me mangled, broken and dead?

I didn't believe her.

Not then.

I believed her now, though. I believed it all.

But would the police?

Did I tell the police? Did I tell them everything? Should I? Could I?

"Ready?" The priest stood behind me. He wore a long tan coat. Keys palmed.

"Father…"

"It's best not to think about it," he said. "We should just go."

If I thought about it, I'd change my mind. He must have known that. Could he read my mind? Did he know I was a heartbeat from running, again?

I let him lead me out of church into the sunlight. I squinted, raising an arm to shield my eyes. The priest unlocked the passenger door, opened it and I climbed in. He shut the door, ran around to the driver side and got in.

"I don't know your name," I said.

"Daly."

I looked up and over at him, seeing the man for the first time. He looked young. Maybe younger than me—in his late twenties, early thirties at the oldest. Short, dark hair, clean shaven and a distinguished cleft in his chin. In a way he reminded me of John Travolta. Not at all what I'd expect a priest to look like.

I wanted to ask him why such a good looking guy would select such a… restricting vocation. The question might insult him. I refrained.

"Joey," I said, held out my hand. We shook.

Father Daly smiled before putting the car in drive.

"Why are you doing this?" I asked. I leaned my head against the glass, but paid no attention to what passed outside the window.

"Doing what?"

"This. Taking me to the police."

"It's the right thing to do," he said.

The right thing to do. He made it sound so simple. Right versus wrong. Black and white. I closed my eyes.

"We're here," he said.

I opened my eyes. We were parked between white and blue police cars. I gripped my stomach. The gut had twisted into knots on me. "I'm not sure about this," I said.

"You're not alone," he said. That voice of his was so soothing, calming. All I could do was nod and open my door.

Every ounce of instinct within me sounded alarms. I shouldn't be here, at a police station. I shouldn't have gone to a church. I should have run. To the mountains. To the south. To Canada. I should run and keep running. Never stop.

But that wasn't possible.

I couldn't run forever.

Maybe that was why I was here. Running wasn't an option.

What were my options?

I'd limited them down to one. Telling.

Like an invalid, I allowed Father Daly to take my arm and walk me to the precinct stairs. He made sure I was set before letting go to open the one of the double glass doors.

Once inside the police station, the door slowly closing behind me, I tried to take in my surroundings. Benches for people to sit on. A woman in a business suit sitting behind a glass-enclosed counter. A ticking clock on the wall. A cork board filled with wanted and missing persons posters. "Father Daly," I said.

He held up a hand to silence me as he approached the woman behind the counter. "We'd like to talk with someone, an officer," he said.

"What about?" she asked. The gold name plaque on the edge of the counter simply said SECRETARY.

"My friend witnessed two murders," he said.

I watched for the woman's reaction. She looked over at me, back at the priest. Her eyes never rolled once.

"His name?" she asked.

Father Daly looked at me. All he knew was Joey.

"Rossi," I said.

"Joseph Rossi," the priest told the secretary.

"Please have a seat. I'll have an officer come down to talk with you," she said.

Father Daly thanked her. He took my arm, led me to one of the benches. We sat.

For the first time, I noticed others already sitting, waiting. A black man sat on the far edge of the bench across from us, eyes closed. He looked like he might be sound asleep. A couple sat next to him, close. Holding hands. The guy's knee bounced, while his fingers kept re-gripping around the woman's fingers.

When he looked over at me, I looked away.

"You all right?" Father Daly sat beside me, one leg propped up over the other, hands on his calf muscle.

"I think we should go," I said. The glass double doors stood only ten feet from where we sat. I could be up and out in one swift, fluid motion. Up and out.

"Mr. Rossi?" An officer in uniform stood in a doorway, looked around the waiting area.

I wasn't going to answer him. I wanted him to shake his head and go back to where ever it was he just stepped out of, and then I could be up and out.

Unfortunately, Father Daly was with me. I saw him raise an indicating hand. The officer smiled.

"Forgive me, I meant Father Rossi."

Daly laughed. I turned away.

"I'm Father Daly, officer. This gentleman next to me is Joseph Rossi."

Fourteen

The officer explained that with so many people in the waiting area, he'd prefer to talk somewhere more confidential and private. He led Father Daly and me into the back bowels of the police station.

Not sure what I expected. What I saw was plain and simple. Desks. Filing cabinets. Cops. Coffee machine. Lots of cops huddled talking around the coffee machine.

"I'm Officer Grimes," the policeman said, offering his hand to each of us. "We'll go in here." He opened a door to reveal a nondescript room. Soft beige walls, steel table, aluminum folding chairs. "Please, have a seat."

Father Daly and I sat side by side on one side of the table. Officer Grimes lifted a notebook and pen off a filing cabinet in a back corner of the room before joining us.

"Mr. Rossi…"

"Joey," I said.

"Joey. You claim to have witnessed a murder?" Officer Grimes made eye contact with me and never let it drop. His pen tip stood poised over the pad of paper.

"That's right."

"And Father, did you witness this as well?" Grimes did not look away from me as he asked Daly the question.

"I did not."

"Are the two of you related?"

"We're not," Daly said.

"Do you go to his church?" Grimes asked me.

"I haven't been to church in a while."

"Father, respectfully, I'd like to ask why you are here."

"Moral support, you might say."

Grimes pursed his lips. "I prefer to interview people one on one."

"I won't interfere," Daly said.

"For now, Father, I'll let you stay."

"Thank you, Officer Grimes." Daly smiled and placed a reassuring hand on my shoulder. I wanted to shrug it off. It felt hot as if his flesh was burning through the fabric of my clothing. Thankfully, he removed it before we were skin on skin.

"Joey, let's start with some basic information. Full name, date of birth, address, employment—home phone, work phone, that kind of thing," Grimes said.

I gave him what he wanted. He wrote while I spoke.

"Okay," Grimes said. "Can you tell me what happened?"

I felt my neck muscles flex and strain, but could not open my mouth to speak.

"Let's start with this—where did the murders take place?" Grimes said.

"In one of the vacant warehouses on Elmgrove Road, where the old Kodak plant was located," I said.

"In Gates?" he said.

"That's right." I closed my eyes. Vivid images filled my head. "I was with two of the three responsible."

"Willingly?"

"I didn't know what was going to happen. They were going out for the night, asked me to come along. I didn't want to, not at all." Carissa said I needed to go with her brothers. No way around it.

"But you went?" Grimes said.

"I went."

"To one of the empty warehouses."

I nodded. "It was around ten,or eleven. I didn't know where we were going at the time. They wouldn't tell me."

"They?"

"The guys I was with."

"Can you tell me their names?" Grimes said.

I shook my head.

"Okay—keep going. What happened next?"

Marcus and Antonio rode up front. I sat in back, seatbelt on, memories from the last accident still fresh in my head. My senses were on overdrive. All of them. I felt electric. I could swear I heard music coming from cars passing by us, could see a deer on the soccer fields by Total Sports Experience—and would swear the deer sensed me as well as it looked up and watched us pass before darting into the woods.

"We pulled into the first entrance on the right," I said. "Took a winding road around to the back of one of the big buildings. You know where I mean?"

"I know the plant. Over six million square feet, mostly vacant," Grimes said.

"We parked and approached the fence protecting the facility. There was a turnstile thing, but we didn't have clearance cards or anything. So the fence, they jumped it." They jumped it. I climbed over it. For some reason, this made them laugh. I had no idea how they'd managed a six foot leap—but they had made it look easy.

And they kept looking at me. Watching for something.

"We followed a sidewalk up to a loading dock garage door. It was unlocked, or the lock was busted, or they busted it—but they opened and raised the door without any trouble," I said. "I followed as they led me through a maze of turns, until we reached a room."

"Were you lost?"

I should have been, but wasn't. Despite not a single light being on, I saw everything as if we walked in natural daylight. "I was somewhat disoriented."

This was not a lie. It was just the answer to a different question, one the officer hadn't actually asked.

"Please, continue."

"One of them—"

"His name?"

I shook my head. "*He* stepped forward and pulled open the door." His eyes on me the entire time. He made it all very theatrical. Bowing, as he allowed me to enter the room first.

"Inside I saw…" I almost said Dean's name out loud. "The other guy. He was already there." His eyes glowed when he looked over and saw us approach. Burning embers filled his eye sockets. Even with the absence of light, there was no mistaking his wide grin.

There was no way I could tell Grimes everything… no way at all.

~ * ~

Marcus clapped a hand onto my back. "Shall we?" he said.

I looked over at him. Like Dean, his eyes resembled burning embers. His lips parted, and I saw sharp, sharp teeth.

Only days ago, Carissa had told me everything. I didn't believe her. She had showed me things, and I still opted to discredit her tale. But right now, standing with her brothers, there was no denying the truth. They were vampires.

And, though I was still human, Carissa's bite had started my transition from living to undead. It was why my senses were so enhanced, why I could see clearly when it was dark, hear things that had to be miles away, smell things, especially blood, when it was close by. And I felt strong, very strong. She assured me that—even though I wasn't full vampire—I'd never get sick. The blood that still pumped in my veins was infected. The poison now in the blood would fight off infections, bacteria, and illnesses. Until I surrendered and drank human blood, I'd still age—but slowly, and could count on outliving everyone currently alive in this world.

Perhaps Marcus and Antonio had laughed at me when I chose to scamper up and over the chain link fence when I could have easily bound over it, as they had.

"Why are we here?" I asked Marcus.

"Why?" Marcus mused. "Do you smell it?"

I didn't have to ask what he referred to. Aside from the four of us, at least two others were in this warehouse. Women. I heard the pounding of their hearts, sensed fear and anticipation as it perspired from their pores in cold, cold sweat. And I could smell their blood. It coursed through their bodies with each quick and agitated beat of their hearts.

Marcus licked his lips. "They are why we are here. They are why you are here."

"I don't understand," I said.

"Sure you do. You've seen movies about our kind—your kind. You know how we survive."

"But sunlight…"

Marcus let out a snort of a laugh. "The myths are always mixed with the facts. But the need for blood, that is not a myth. It is a reality."

My stomach growled. Marcus smiled.

"Once you feast, your transition will be complete."

"And if I don't?" I asked.

"The longer you go without drinking blood, the more your senses and abilities will fade. You'll always be thirsty, hungry and food will not satisfy you, ever. There really is no fighting it. I'm not sure why you would want to," he said, eyes intently on me.

"I, I can't," I said. "I won't."

Marcus rolled his eyes. "The first time is not as bad as you might expect it to be. It's natural. It's right. Instinct takes over. There is nothing you need to do but relax. Your mind, your body, it will respond and react on its own. You see what I'm saying?"

This did not reassure me.

Where were the women? I knew they were close.

Antonio walked ahead of us, rounded a corner. Marcus followed, his hands clasped together behind his back.

I could turn. Run. But there was no denying the fact that I was drawn to the scent of warm blood. Slowly, I went after Carissa's brothers.

When I rounded the corner, I stopped, taking in all that suddenly surrounded me.

Dean, the youngest Tantalo, stood over two bound and gagged women, arms spread wide offering me his gifts. They looked young, late teens, early twenties. Both were thin, gaunt, with eyes wide in terror. Tears streaked dirty faces, as they tried rolling around—as if they could escape.

"Marcus," I said. "I can't."

The oldest brother hissed. "You must join the family, Joey. It's why we're here. Why you're here. It's your only option."

There were options.

"And if I don't?" I asked.

"Then you can join these ladies," Dean said.

Marcus shot his younger brother a look. Dean lowered his head and his arms to his sides.

"Our father is allowing you this opportunity, if only because of Carissa's feelings," Marcus said. "You are more fortunate than others who have been bitten, but not killed. Your soul is already lost. There is no Heaven for you, only Hell. Your choice is simple. Join us, and live forever, or die tonight and go to Hell."

Fifteen

Officer Grimes kept writing, long after I stopped talking. When he finished, he set his pen down and looked at me.

I looked over at Father Daly. He tried to offer a reassuring smile. It didn't work.

"These women were tied up?" Grimes asked.

"That's right," I said. But Marcus didn't leave them tied up. He'd torn the restraints off that bound their feet.

"And while you stood there, these men killed them?"

The women ran. It was too dark for them to possibly see where they were headed. It didn't matter. The Tantalos had no intention of letting them escape.

After playing with their food, they held the women in place and stared at me, as if silently commanding me to make the kill.

When I didn't, the brothers ripped them to shreds. "Yes."

"And you, you watched?"

"I felt frozen in place."

"You didn't run?"

"Couldn't."

"And you didn't stop them?"

I lowered my eyes, shook my head. "No."

"What happened next?"

"They started a fire," I said.

"In the warehouse?"

"That's right. They had a pile of wood pallets. They lit a wadded chunk of old newspapers. The pallets caught easily. And they tossed—" what was left "—put the bodies on the flames."

"And you?"

"They left me there, with the bodies. Locked me in the room." It had been maddening. My throat burned—felt as if I'd been wandering for weeks without water in a desert. The pool of blood surrounding the scraps and remains, an oasis.

"So how did you get out?"

"I knocked the door down," I said. After hours alone with the bodies, after contemplating whether to satisfy my urge and lap at the blood, I worked up the strength to flee. The steel door posed no problem. The adrenaline pulsing through me must have lent me enough strength to escape.

"Mr. Rossi…"

"Joey."

"Who was responsible for the murders?"

"I can't," was all I said. They would know. They would come for me—if they weren't coming for me already.

Grimes sighed and sat back in his chair, crossing his arms. "You know who is responsible."

"I do."

"But you won't tell me their names."

I shook my head.

Grimes got to his feet. "Wait here," he said. He left me alone with the priest.

"You did very well," Father Daly said.

"I haven't done anything," I said. "I told them only about the murders. Not anything specific. Not anything useful."

"I think you and I should talk some more. When we leave. Will you come back with me to the church?"

I nodded. "Sure, Father."

After a few more minutes, the door to the interview room opened. "Joey, this is Investigator Mandi Wheeler," Grimes said, standing aside to let the female officer into the room. He entered next, closing the door behind them.

Wheeler wore long, brown curly hair down over her shoulders. Piercing blue eyes met mine, and softened as she smiled. "Joey? I'm Mandi," she said.

We shook hands.

She made a show of taking off her sport coat, and hanging it over the back of Grimes' folding chair before sitting across from me. Her department-issued Glock sat snug in a shoulder holster, close to her heart.

Grimes stood close to a corner in the room.

"I understand you witnessed a murder?" she said.

"I did."

"But you're not comfortable telling us who committed the crime?"

"I'm not."

She pursed her lips into a thin smile. "Can you show us where the crime took place?"

"I explained where," I said.

"Showing us would save time," she said. "If two women were murdered, we want an investigation launched as soon as possible."

I didn't like the word *if*. I knew what was going on. They needed to weed out frivolous stories. I wondered how many people showed up claiming to have witnessed a murder, only to have revealed that the witness is a crackpot.

"I'm not sure I'm comfortable with that," I said.

"Then why are you here?" she said.

I glanced at Father Daly. "Seemed like the right thing to do."

"I see," she said. "What is keeping you from sharing the identity of the murderers with me?"

"Fear," I said.

She seemed to think about this for a long moment. I watched as her brow furrowed before speaking. "You do realize that the Elmgrove plant is huge. That it might take our crime technicians weeks of searching just to locate the exact area where you say the murders were committed. By then, any evidence could be wiped away. The families of the two dead women may never know what happened to their daughters. The killers will remain free. Does that seem *right* to you?"

"It doesn't."

"I'm not pressing you for names. I only ask that you show us the location. Please," she said.

I couldn't look away from her eyes. "I can show you," I said. "As long as Father Daly can come with us."

Mandi Wheeler nodded. "Of course he can."

"Investigator Wheeler," Daly said.

"Yes?"

"Assuming you find everything Joey has shared with you to be true—is there some sort of protection you could offer him?" Daly spoke to Wheeler, but his eyes watched me.

"Like witness protection?"

"Exactly."

"No," Wheeler said, without hesitation. "Calling through a hotline might have guaranteed anonymity. Due to discovery, if we apprehend the suspects and there is a trial—keeping Mr. Rossi's identity secret is not a possibility."

I closed my eyes. A hotline. How much more simple this could have been. Wouldn't have made much difference. The Tantalos would have known it was me who tipped off the police, regardless. I was the only *living* witness.

~ * ~

Officer Grimes drove with Father Daly and me in the back seat of his cruiser. Investigator Mandi Wheeler took point, leading us toward the Elmgrove plant.

Quietly, I sat close to the door and stared out the window. Since visiting the priest in the confessional, my mind was weighted down too heavily to concentrate on my own thirst. Trapped in the police car with the priest beside me, Grimes driving, all I could do in the pressing silence was smell their blood, and it taunted and teased my senses.

How long would it be before my senses dulled, as Marcus promised.

Natural instinct, he'd said. And I felt it. The desire to slide across the street and put an end to Father Daly's beating heart. The thump-thump, thump-thump of it grated my nerves and caused me to salivate, the same as a dinner bell being rung.

"Here we are," Grimes announced.

Once he parked, I struggled with the door. It wouldn't open. Grimes let Father Daly out first, then came around and opened my door.

"We don't want detainees making a run for it," he said, smiling.

A man in a blue dress shirt, khakis and a clipboard waited for us on the loading dock. We approached the turnstile, and one by one, were allowed to pass through. It beat climbing the fence.

Could I leap it, if I wanted?

Wheeler climbed steps I hadn't noticed before, and shook hands with the man by the open garage door. After brief introductions, the new guy's name was Bert, I led the way, my new entourage behind me.

In moments we were at the place where I broke down the door. It leaned against the wall. Bits of drywall and hardware had been swept into a neat pile by the door.

Wheeler looked at the door. "You did this?" She made it sound impossible, yet I had.

I walked through the threshold, and slowed as I came to the corner. I knew what had been around the bend. The fact that the broken door had been found, the mess swept up, led me to believe no bodies awaited our arrival. "Right around there," I said, pointing.

Wheeler and Grimes produced flashlights. They rounded the corner. Father Daly, Bert and I lagged behind.

I was in no hurry to see what the cops searched for.

"This might be blood." It was Grimes. "Can't tell."

"The area is clean—too clean. Someone took some time to clean the place." It was Wheeler.

"And?"

"And the rest of the place is dusty—as it should be. Let's get a crime tech team down here," I heard her say.

My stomach dropped.

I hadn't imagined a thing. Two innocent women had been murdered. I had gone to the police. And soon, the police would find the Tantalo brothers. It wouldn't be long before they came for me, regardless.

I needed a place to hide. Somewhere to go where I could be safe. But where? Even the police weren't planning to protect me.

Wheeler appeared, flashlight in hand. "You saw the victims?"

"I did."

"Did you know them?"

"No."

"Could you describe them for a sketch artist?"

"I might be able to."

"Let's head back to the precinct," she said. "Grimes, get this place roped off. I'll call for a team and some more uniforms when I get back to the car. No one comes in here—at all. Got it?"

"Got it," Grimes said.

"Is there any other way into this room?" Wheeler asked Bert.

"Some fire exits in back. They should be wired—only to be opened in an emergency."

"Got it," Grimes said.

This time Wheeler led the way, taking long strides through the maze back to the loading dock.

My world, the world as I knew it, had vanished.

I didn't know who I was.

I didn't know where I was headed.

If I didn't find a place to hide, I didn't know how I'd ever survive.

Sixteen

Wayne didn't move. He sat statue-still on the bed.

"Say something," I said.

"Vampires."

"Vampires."

"And you told this to the priest, Father Daly?" Wayne asked.

"It was like he suspected something. We left the police station together, and he said we needed to talk. I let him take me back to the rectory. He made coffee. We sat at the table, and he looked me in the eye and said, 'now tell me everything'." I shook my head. "When I told him—everything I just told you—I thought he'd flip. But he didn't…"

"He believed you."

"He believed me," I said.

"And you're one of them?"

I waited for my roommate to laugh, to mock me. I was certain name-calling couldn't be far off.

"Half, I guess. I've never drunk blood," I said. Thought about it. Craved it real bad at times. The desire for blood hadn't really decreased over the past few weeks, but the ability to drown the urge was more prominent. Thankfully, the distractions of being locked away and deciding whether I was actually out of mind or not helped, too.

Wayne closed his eyes. He covered his face with his enormous hands. I wasn't sure if he was praying, smothering a laugh, or suddenly lost in his own world.

I sat on my bed. My legs hurt from standing so long. My throat was dry from all the talking I'd done. Why opening up to Wayne was so easy, I had no idea. Maybe the alternative, sharing this with Dr. Sanchez was so less appealing that I understood how limited my options had become.

"And that's why you're here?" Wayne lowered his hands slowly, stretching the skin under his eyes with the weight of his fingertips, exposing blood vessels below the whites of his eyes.

"After Father Daly and I had that little heart to heart, he suggested I either stay with him in the rectory—but when I wasn't thrilled about the idea—he pulled some strings, and got me admitted in here," I said. "It wasn't what I expected."

"What do you mean?"

"I told the priest vampires killed those two girls—and that I was becoming one," I said.

"And?"

"And? And he asked me to live in his church. If someone told me they saw vampires kill people, and thought they were a bloodsucker, too—I, one, wouldn't ask them to live with me, and, two, would throw them to the curb as fast as possible!" I laughed. "Maybe that's why he picked this place as a second option for where I could hide. At least this makes more sense."

"Joey, you remember I told you God talks to me," Wayne said.

I closed my eyes.

"You don't believe me." Not a question.

I did not believe him. How could I? "I don't have to believe you. If you believe it, that's good enough for me."

"We're friends?" he asked.

I didn't have to think about it. "Of course we are."

Wayne grinned. He looked like a moron. Lips stretched wide, showing off two rows of white teeth. "So you're not crazy. No nervous breakdown," Wayne said.

"Ah—were you listening to a word I said?" I asked.

"I listened; heard every word." Wayne stood up. He went to the window. He walked to the door. Back to the window. "We have to get you out of here and to somewhere safe. I think you should live with the priest."

I should have felt relieved that Wayne believed me, but he was crazy. God talked to *him*. Of course he was going to believe me.

"Why would I leave the hospital?" I said.

"Because it's not safe. Not anymore." Wayne rolled his large fingers into fists.

"Not safe? Why not?"

"They're coming for you. The vampires."

I dropped back onto the mattress and closed my eyes. Sure, my roommate believed me. But now he thought he was caught up in some espionage film. *Bond. Wayne Bond.*

I pressed the heels of my hands into my eyes. "No one is coming, Wayne. They don't know I'm here."

"They know you aren't at work—that you haven't been to work in weeks. And they know—from someone at your law firm—that you are out on an extended medical leave."

I shot up, out of bed, ignoring bare feet on cold linoleum. "I never told you I worked at a law firm."

"Of course, you didn't." His face looked peaceful as he looked up at the ceiling tiles.

And I'd never told him I'd been out of work a while, or that I'd taken an extended medical leave. He couldn't know this. Any of it.

I looked up, too. Then got it. *God told him.*

I almost laughed. Okay, so he knew I worked for a law firm. That didn't prove a thing. He knew I was on out on Family Medical Leave. Still didn't prove anything. Maybe he'd gotten hold of my file. Not sure how he could have accomplished this, put it was possible. Probable, even.

Let's not forget, I talk in my sleep. A lot.

And yet, he was right. Not about hearing God's voice. Just his advice. Staying idle couldn't be safe. If the Tantalo family was after me, they'd—sooner or later—check hospitals, wouldn't they? Especially if they did talk to someone at the firm and were told I was out on a medical leave.

"The question is how do we get you out?" Wayne asked. His facial features all scrunched in tight around his nose. His brow furrowed, lips puckered.

"I'm considered a voluntary. It's the way the priest had it set up. I think that means I can just walk out," I said. The idea of walking out caused more anxiety than I'd have anticipated. I hated it here, being locked up, under someone else's thumb. The alternative, going back out into the world, however, seemed worse. Scary. What would I do? Did I return to work? I lived paycheck to paycheck. There was rent to pay. Insurance. If I left the hospital, my leave would be canceled. Coverage stopped. Job terminated.

Where would I stay? Should I stay at the church with Father Daly?

Sunlight didn't harm vampires. Did churches? Did God? Or was that more myths created to give mortals hope?

I went into a church—talked to a priest, but I wasn't a vampire. Not completely. I was more like a half-breed. A mutt.

"Might not be that simple," Wayne said. He appeared different, somehow. More serious. Less simple. It seemed like before—the Wayne I grew to know—was an act. For the first time I was a different man. Was it the real Wayne? Focused and intense?

"Why not?" I asked.

Seventeen

Father Daly sat in his rectory office. With a glass of orange juice cradled in his hands, he leaned back in his desk chair and stared absently at light fixture dangling from the ceiling in the center of the room.

His call with the cardinal should have been comforting. A team had been assembled and was on their way from Rome to Rochester. Skilled in martial arts and weaponry, they were the best of the best when it came to completing any objective set before them.

Have they done this kind of thing before, he'd asked.

No, was the simple answer.

The answer haunted his thoughts. He set the glass down and rubbed his temples using fingertips.

Vampires.

They've always existed. Their existence, for the most part, kept secret by the church in much the same way the government kept proof of aliens from the public.

When Daly became a priest, he was exposed to truths, and like a Mason, was expected to keep the truths quiet and confidential. Breaking the rules was not only frowned upon, but dealt with using swift, harsh punishment. He had no idea what the punishment entailed. No one ever talked about those disciplined. Aside from learning about truths in penned journals with detailed accounts of masked historic facts—given to priests like textbooks to college students—Father Daly had never heard any of his peers or superiors mention witches, the need for exorcisms or vampires.

And yet he always believed that somewhere witches were dealt with, exorcisms performed and vampires slain. This was why the cardinal's "no" left him feeling uneasy about what was headed his way.

He'd been assured that calling had been the right thing to do. The Pope needed to know what was going on at all times. It was partly why churches were set up globally. The Pope needed to keep a finger on the pulse of evil at all times.

And, Father Daly, the cardinal had said, *you will be expected to give food and shelter to the team, and work with them toward a hasty termination of the at-hand predicament.*

The words bounced off the walls inside his brain.

Was he expected to fight the monsters?

Kill them?

Human or not, with or without a soul, Daly wasn't sure he possessed the personal power, or strength, or courage to stand against such a formidable enemy, much less to strike one down.

~ * ~

Carissa hid in the shadows. If her brothers knew she was around, they gave no indication, or simply didn't care. She listened as they talked over a plan of action. She knew her father wanted Joey found. Find him, her brothers would.

She wondered if she should have kept out of family business as instructed. Her heart—what was left of it—wanted to help Joey. She never wanted him to go off that night with her brothers. She knew what they had planned. As much as she wanted Joey whole, like herself, she knew she was wrong to have bitten him in the first place.

"So we know he hasn't been into work," Marcus said.

Letting him die in the car accident would have been easier. At least for the family.

Joey had been different than other men she'd met. Mostly she associated socially with other covens in the area. It was rare that such deep feelings had so immediately attracted her to Joey.

"If he's on some kind of medical leave—we know he's not at his apartment," Antonio added.

It was his pain, mostly. That's what had drawn her to him. His internal struggle. That hot summer night when she'd walked into the bar; it was the first thing she'd sensed before approaching him as he sat alone at a table.

She never dreamed, though, they'd fall in love. Joey offered more than her kind ever could. Warmth. Sincerity. Life.

A life she'd stolen from him. Once a full-fledged vampire, would he change? Would all that had attracted her to him remain intact? Or would he, like her brothers, forget about love and feelings and emotions, and concentrate his attention on the idea of accumulating power and prestige?

The realization that this could happen, that Joey could wind up like all the other vampires she knew, troubled her. She did not want him changed in that way.

If he remained true to the person he used to be, and their love continued to grow and intensify, what a life they could lead together, forever. Bliss.

Being away from him now, not knowing where he was, knowing he was terrified of her, caused more damage to her soulless being than she ever thought possible. Even the desire to hunt had been crushed under the depressing weight she carried around.

"He's got to be in a hospital—like rehab, or something," Dean added.

And her father—with decades upon decades to accumulate such wealth—had tried to help. Love wasn't an essential in life. If it happened, so be it. If not, then not. Of course, he had wed his precious Katrina. They were happy together, even after all this time.

A part of her had wanted Joey to drink another's blood, certain the two of them could spend an eternity together—happy just like her father and mother.

"How many hospitals are in the city?" Antonio asked. "Why a hospital, though? Where else could he be?"

"Has to be somewhere where he can hide," Marcus said. "Somewhere where he thinks he's safe."

Dean laughed. "That's why somewhere like rehab makes sense. A regular hospital wouldn't waste bed space on someone, but rehab, or something like that—it's like joining a tucked away, confidential community."

"That, little brother, is worth considering," Marcus said.

Another part of her hoped he never drank blood. Doing so would damn him to Hell for certain. There was no forgiveness for the heinous crimes they, as a race, committed. There was no hope for salvation. Fallen angels is what they were. Angles cast down from Heaven, sentenced to roam the earth until the time of judgment. What wrath awaited them? Unimaginable wrath, she imagined.

"What could he be in a hospital for? If they test his blood..." Dean said.

Saving Joey seemed foolishly impossible now. Not only had he not participated in the kill at the warehouse, he had gone to the police—leading investigators right to the front door. At one time, Joey might have been considered an asset, a new member to the family. This was no longer true. Joey had become a liability. One her father would mercilessly disembowel for sure.

"I'm thinking mental institutions," Marcus said. "Think about it. He checks in. Stays anonymous. Stays hidden."

"Can you just check in?" Dean asked.

"Yeah. Tell the hospital you're suicidal, urinate in a trash can. It can be done," Marcus said.

Carissa slipped away, hopefully undetected. She ran up the stairs to her room. If Joey was in a hospital, they were close to finding him. Once they found him, she'd never be able to help, never be able to save him, never have the chance to say good-bye.

Eighteen

Cardinal David Bonsignore hated flying, but preferred a window seat. If they were going to crash, he wanted to see it coming. The rational might not make sense to most, but it he couldn't help how he felt.

Flying over a seemingly endless ocean left him uneasy. He supposed splashing into water was safer than hitting solid earth. But dead was dead, wasn't it?

How anyone could sleep on a flight was beyond him. On his left, Father Pete Cano slept soundly, arms folded, head resting on his own shoulder. At least he didn't snore. Across the aisle Father Brandon Padilla flipped through a magazine, while Sister Bri bobbed her head up and down—buds stuffed into her ears—to music only she could hear.

He'd been in touch with the priest in Rochester. The conversation hadn't been long. Vampires. A first for him, but other commissioned teams by former popes had dealt with the undead in the past—numerous times. The type of battle was nothing new. Just something new for him and his team.

Baptism by fire.

He glanced at his watch. It was still set to Rome. Twelve hours difference. He did the math. Should be arriving at Rochester International around three.

The weapons they brought were stored in the belly of the plane. He couldn't help but feel naked. Like Peter with his sword, Bonsignore preferred to have his Glock against his hip. It provided additional comfort and security, no doubt.

In movies, vampires were killed with a stake through the heart. That was movies. The journals—diaries—explained why a stake through the heart made no sense. A vampire's heart didn't beat. No blood passed through the muscle. Thrusting a stake through the heart was as effective as sticking a pin in a cushion.

Holy water worked. Fire. Silver. The Crucifix. Faith.

And dismemberment.

~ * ~

I made my way to Dr. Sanchez's office a little early. I wanted out. I was practically self-admitted. They couldn't hold me. It made sense. To me. Hopefully she'd see things my way.

"I'd like to see Dr. Sanchez," I said to the nurse behind the desk. Her eyes rose off the paperwork in front of her to look at me, but her head never moved. "I'm Joey Rossi."

Her eyes lowered. She consulted a spiral bound calendar. "Your appointment isn't until three."

"I was wondering if she was in now. I'd really like to talk to her. I'd like to go home," I said.

"I see." She set the calendar down and slowly got to her feet. "Just one moment."

I stepped back from the desk, and relaxed with hands clasped behind my back. Some of the staff seemed unnerved around me, or maybe it was just being assigned to this floor. Either way, I wanted to present a calm, non-threatening posture.

The nurse left the area and returned a few minutes later, smiling. "Mr. Rossi?"

"Joey's good," I said.

"Dr. Sanchez isn't in. She's at one of our other facilities."

"You spoke to her?"

"That's right."

"Did you tell her I wanted to leave?"

"I did."

"So what do I need to do?"

"She said she will speak with you this afternoon," the nurse said. Her lips were spread thin, making it clear that the smile was forced.

I nodded. "Do I need her approval?"

"To leave? Yes."

I closed my eyes and sighed. "Then I'll be back at three," I said.

"That would be wonderful," she said.

I walked away. Wayne said getting out would be easy. I needed Dr. Sanchez's signature was all, and I'd be out. By three thirty I'd be on my way, no doubt.

With nothing else to do, I decided to head back to my room. It was noon. I had three hours to kill.

Nineteen

When I walked back into my room, Wayne was still seated on his bed, legs folded, Indian style.

"My appointment with Dr. Sanchez is at three," I said. I wanted out. It wasn't that I didn't feel safe in the hospital anymore, as much as it felt as if the walls were closing in on me. I breathed in quick, shallow breaths.

"Tell me about Carissa," Wayne said.

Had he noticed the onset of hyperventilation, or was he merely curious? "What do you want to know?"

"Do you love her?"

I did. "Yes. And I miss her."

When my wife died, I thought I'd be alone forever. I thought I'd drink myself to death long before ever meeting someone equally as special. At first, the thought terrified me. I didn't want to be alone, but I wasn't sure I wanted to start a new relationship. They took time, work, compromise. At my age, and after all I'd been through, I didn't want to invest time, work or compromise. With that decided, I'd conceded to living a life without a companion.

And then walked in Carissa.

My plans for just existing shattered after that first night together—the swim at the beach, breakfast, and the days and weeks together that followed.

"I want to know happened after you became a vampire," he said.

It sounded surreal. I was a vampire. If it wasn't so serious an accusation, I'd have laughed. Still might have, if Wayne wasn't staring at me with such intensity.

"What happened?" I said. "I met her family."

"She took you to her family?"

"No. Not right away. She wanted to talk with them first." For the first time since I'd known her, fear was evident in her eyes. If she could shed tears, I think she would have cried. I realized confronting her father with what she'd done to me was not going to be easy.

"But, I mean, how did you take it? When she told you, when she said now you're a vampire? Did you believe her right away?"

"Believe her? No. I didn't believe her. Not for a while," I said.

~ * ~

I stood on wet brown leaves, surrounded by bare trees. Somewhere, a chimney fire burned. Although I couldn't see the smoke, I could smell the wood. I hugged myself in an attempt to contain a shiver that raced from my shoulders to the center of my back and down my spine.

Carissa stood beside me as we stared at what remained of my car: crushed metal, fallen bumper, imploded windshield, missing tire.

"I thought I was going to die," I said. I thought she was dead. She should have been. We both should not still be alive.

I cupped a hand over my neck. Warm blood gushed between my fingers. I swallowed hard, hoping saliva was extinguish the burn filling my throat.

"You were about to die," she said. She wrapped her arm around mine and snuggled in close. "I thought I was going to lose you."

I liked her close. Hated being away from her. "I don't know how—I don't know why we're here. Walking. I know I broke my legs." I shook one of them, and winced in anticipation for some kind of pain that never came. "Carissa—you, you went through the windshield. Let me look at the top of your head." I reached up, intended to part her hair.

"I'm fine," she said.

She was, too. I knew it. The proof stood and talked right in front of me. Glass shards should have shredded her skin. Purple bruises, bloody patches—something, there should have been some signs of an accident apparent on her body, on mine, but if there were any, I couldn't see them.

"We should go," she said.

"I can't," I said, and open-palm pointed at the wreck before us. "The police will be coming."

The police. I'd been drinking. I'd never pass a breathalyzer. A DUI would cost me my job. No law firm would ever hire me with a record.

What had I been thinking? Drinking and driving. That was nuts. Absolutely crazy.

"I'm going to be arrested," I said.

"Arrested? For having a car accident?" she said.

"I'm drunk. They'll nail me," I said.

"Are you drunk?" she said.

"You know I am. We both are. It's probably how we survived the crash. I've heard of things like this happening. When a drunk driver smashes into another car, the guy in the other car is killed instantly and the drunk walks away. Like us. Without a scratch," I said. I knew I was rambling. Couldn't help it. When I was nervous, I talked. It helped.

"But are you drunk?" she said again.

"Carissa…"

"Shh. Listen to your body for minute."

In the silence that followed, I heard the approaching sound of sirens. Police sirens. I realized I could focus. Concentrate. I was in complete control.

"Are you drunk?"

"Scared sober, maybe. But that won't change the alcohol levels in my blood," I said.

"Don't tell the police you were drinking," she said. "You'll pass a breathalyzer. And we'll be free to go."

"Great. Sounds like a plan." I rolled my eyes.

"And when they let us go, we need to talk."

I needed to call my insurance agent. The car was totaled. Towing it made no sense. A flatbed would be needed to deliver the jumbled carcass of metal to its final resting place in some automotive burial yard.

"We'll talk?" she said.

I gave her a kiss on the top of the head. "Sure. After the police don't arrest me, we'll talk."

Twenty

"They didn't arrest me," I said.

"I told you they wouldn't." Carissa reached for my hand. Our fingers locked together. The police called a cab for us. We were now en route back to my place.

"But how could they not? Carissa, we drank a lot tonight." I looked into bright blue, unblinking eyes. Why was I the only one struggling with this? "Dear, you went through my windshield. You were thrown from the car."

"We're okay," she whispered, one hand petted my arm.

I laughed. "We should be dead."

She didn't say anything.

I turned and looked out the window. We were almost to my place. I needed a drink.

When the cab pulled to the curb, I paid the driver, thanked him and held the door open for Carissa. The police initially wanted the two of us taken to the hospital. Carissa protested. After preliminary evaluations, paramedics on the scene didn't see a need for us to head to the hospital. Reluctantly, the police allowed us to leave.

At the complex door, I patted my pockets. "No keys. I must have left them in the ignition."

Carissa grabbed the doorknob.

"It's locked," I said. "It's a secure building."

She turned the knob. Something *thunked*. The door opened.

"That's weird. It's always locked," I said, following her into the atrium. We took the stairs to the top floor, the third floor and stopped at my door. "I know I locked this." I put my hands in my pockets and thought. "I could call the front office."

"This late, on a weekend?" Carissa said.

"They'll charge me for it, but it's that or sleep in the hallway." I looked at the worn carpet and shook my head. "We could go to a hotel, or something."

Carissa opened my apartment door.

I stood in the hall, eyes wide, mouth agape, and stared. "Come on. That was locked. I locked it. I never *don't* lock it."

"You staying out there?" she said. "I could bring you a pillow and blankets."

I entered my place, swung the door in and out a bit, and then fiddled with the door knob. "It's broken," I said. "The lock's busted. But how'd you know?"

"I broke it," she said. She curled her legs under her as she sat on the sofa. With an arm over the back, she watched me. "Joey, we need to talk."

"About?" I said. I twisted the knob left and right. I worked the lock, back and forth. The hardware was shot.

"Joey," she said.

I closed the door, engaged the chain lock and walked around to the sofa.

"Sit down," she said.

"What's wrong?" I said.

"Please," she said. "Just sit down."

I sat.

"I need to tell you something. It's important. And what I need most is for you to let me speak without interrupting me," she said.

"I wouldn't do tha—"

"You're doing it now," she said.

I closed my mouth. Twisted an imaginary key. Tossed it over my shoulder.

"There is no easy way to say what it is I have to tell you," she said.

I opened my mouth to speak. Carissa flashed me a look. I remembered I'd locked my jaw closed, and smiled.

"I went through the windshield of your car." She held up a silencing hand, perhaps anticipating my inability to stop talking. "Like you said, I should be dead. You broke your legs. Your ribs punctured your lungs. You were dying."

She was not telling me anything new. I'd been freaking out about this since stepping out of the wrecked car. We should be dead. It was that simple. I didn't need a medical degree to realize this. Maybe, just maybe, the seriousness of our situation was just setting in on Carissa. She must have been in shock. That explained a lot. Denial. She'd been in denial before, and now—after some time to deal with the situation—her world was being rocked.

"I can never die," she said. "And now, neither can you."

With lips pressed firmly closed, I let them spread into a wide smile. I kept them shut. I didn't break my promise.

"Joey," Carissa said. "I never expected to fall in love with you. But that's what happened. I love you."

"I love you, too." I held up my hands, silently apologizing for having spoken.

She took my hands and pulled me close. "Joey, I'm not who you think I am. I'm not what you think I am."

I shook my head. "So who are you? Some escaped mass murderer?" I laughed.

"Kind of," she said.

I didn't believe her. "Yeah. Right."

"Joey," she said. "I'm not even alive."

I stood up. "I need a beer. You want one?"

"Are you listening to me?" she said.

I walked toward the kitchen. "I'm listening. Keep talking. You're not alive, go on..."

When I turned to enter the kitchen, Carissa stood in front of me. I jumped back. "What the heck?"

I looked at the sofa. She was gone. Of course she wasn't still sitting there. She was standing in front of me. "I think I need to go to the hospital. I might have a concussion."

"You do not have a concussion. You're fine. Healthy, you might even say." She turned, opened the fridge and handed me a beer.

"You don't want one?"

"I don't need one," she said. "I only drank them to humor you."

"You sure went to alcoholic lengths just to humor me, then," I said, twisting open the bottle. "I'm so thirsty." I took a long swig. Swallowed. Gripped a hand around my waist. "That doesn't taste right," I said. I studied the bottle, spinning it around in my hand.

"Joey—the reason you are still alive tonight, is because I bit you," she said.

And at that point, I remembered her biting me. Reflexively, my hand went to my neck. "Why'd you bite me?"

"To save you. You were about to die. Your heart stopped beating."

I set the beer down and slid my butt into the stool in front of the counter. "I did die," I said.

"You almost died."

"But I remember that. Dying. The darkness. And then the light—the white light. The kind of light you always hear people who have died and come back to life talk about."

"You didn't die," she said. "I bit you."

"Why'd you bite me?"

"You asked that, already. And I told you. To save you." She sat in the stool across from me. Her eyes never left mine. Her hands took hold of mine. "I don't know how to explain this, not without scaring you."

"Well, now you're scaring me," I said. I had died. Almost died. My heart had stopped beating. The terrible car accident left only my car for dead. Carissa bit me. Digesting all of this, any of it, was difficult. I pulled my hands out of hers and gripped the counter, hoping it would stop the room from spinning.

"I'm just going to say it, Joey," she said.

"Then say it."

"I'm a vampire."

Laughing felt good. I didn't hold it in. "Carissa, please. I'm, it's just not the time for jokes. We almost died tonight. That's how serious this is. And I think we both should maybe go to the hospital."

"Look in my eyes, Joey. Look in my eyes and don't look away." She said. She looked sad. Scared. "And don't hate me."

"Carissa, I love you. I don't hate you. If anything, you should hate me. The accident was my fault. I know my limits, I know better than to dri—"

"Joey, please!" I'd never heard her use such a commanding tone. She had my attention. "My eyes."

I stared into the most beautiful eyes I'd ever seen. "With pleasure."

And then I shrank away from her. "What just happened? What did you just do?" In a blink, a batting of lids, her ocean-colored eyes turned crimson.

I shook my head.

"You know now what I am," she said.

"No. I absolutely do not." I stood up.

"Joey, I'm a—we're vampires." She folded her hands together, such a human gesture.

I wanted a witty retort. None came to mind. I needed a hospital. I reached a hand out toward anything for balance.

"Joey!" She took a step toward me. I stumbled back. "Don't do this," she said.

"Do what?"

"Be afraid of me," she said.

Was I afraid? "I need to go to the hospital."

"You don't. You're fine. Better than fine," she said.

"Because I'm a vampire?" A slice of sarcastic tone made its way off my tongue.

"Yes. Because you're a vampire. But not completely. Not yet," she said. "When I bit you, I started the transformation. It's up to you to take the next step."

"The next step?" The laugh I forced sounded forced, and cruel.

"We can talk about that later," she said.

"Why not talk about it now? Don't you think now would be better? You should just spill everything out onto the table. Here. Now. Let's get this over with," I said. Maybe I was yelling. I couldn't tell.

"None of this is easy to talk about," she said.

"Yeah, well, none of this is easy to hear." I needed to sit. I went back to the sofa just as my legs gave out. I crumpled onto the cushion. "So sit. Let's talk."

"You believe me?"

"Nope. But I have no idea what's going on. You seem to think you know what's happening. I figure, let's start there and see where it leads," I said, uttering perhaps the only lucid thought my brain had been able to produce all night.

Twenty-one

Wayne hadn't moved. He sat statue-still the whole time I'd talked. Now that I'd finished, I waited for him to say something. When the silence dragged on, I said, "Well?"

"I was just listening," he said.

"I know. But I've been talking for almost four minutes," I said.

"Not to you. I mean, I listened to you. But I've been listening to God," he said.

"Excuse me, then. Didn't mean to interrupt," I said through clenched teeth. Why did I bother? Here I was sharing intimate, dark secrets about myself with a crazy guy.

"No need to apologize," Wayne said. He stared at me with big eyes and a grim smile. "And when she talked to her family first—about you, what happened?"

I shook my head. "So many questions."

"We don't have to talk about it." He looked at the clock on the wall.

It was not even two. I had just over an hour before my appointment with Dr. Sanchez. "Carissa brought me to her house. It's like a mini-castle, out in Webster, up on a high hill overlooking the lake."

"Sounds nice," he said.

"Yeah. Well. Sorta." I stood with my back to the wall, and crossed my arms. "She told me they knew we were there. And I asked who? And she said—her family, that they already know we're here."

"In the driveway?"

"Yeah. It's how she made it sound. She took my hand, and moved in for a kiss, but I couldn't. I backed away from her."

"Scared?"

"A bit freaked out, you could say." I cupped my hands over my face. "She told me to wait in the car. She wanted to go in and talk with her father before introducing us. I mean, I've dated girls before and dreaded the here-meet-my-father syndrome. But Wayne, this was so much worse. Carissa thought she was a vampire—that she turned me into one. So did that mean her whole family was made of monsters?"

"Did it? Were they?"

"They were. All of them," I said. "When Carissa came to the front door and waved me in, I knew things hadn't gone well. Saw it in her face. And when I walked into the house, pulled in by Carissa, actually, they all stood in this grand marble foyer—stood side-by-side, staring at me. Three brothers, her mother and father."

"What did they look like?"

"None of them actually resembled the other—except for pale skin, and paler lips, bright eyes and the fact that each one of them was tremendously good looking. The guys looked like models—even the father, and he had to be pushing late sixty something. And the mother—almost the exact opposite of Carissa—was just as equally beautiful, and dignified. But the way they looked at me..." I shuddered. "The way they seemed to look right through me.

"I tried to be all friendly—like this was some normal boyfriend meets the family evening, you know? I said this goofy hello, and waved at them all. I mean, inside, I was like, this is nuts. What am I doing here? Meeting her family didn't convince me of anything other than I thought all of them were crazy.

"Then her father takes one step toward me. It was only one step, but he was in my face before I knew what was going on. I took like a half step back, just so my eyes could focus on his face. His features were blurred, that's how close he was to me. He didn't smile, didn't blink, he just stared.

"Carissa interrupted the silent assault, thankfully," I said.

"What'd she do?"

"She said something like, 'Daddy, if he's going to be family, why can't you treat him like family,' or something like that. I was like, half-listening. But he listened. He took a step back, and then Carissa made her introductions. Victor, that was her father; Katrina was her mother, and her brothers—oldest to youngest—Marcus, Antonio and Dean."

"And what happened next?" Wayne asked.

"What happened? Nothing, really. Victor said he wanted to talk with me, but not until after I spent some time with his sons."

"That was the night they took you out? With the girls?"

"That's right," I said.

"Tell me more about the police. What happened there?"

"If you're talking to God, He must have seen what happened. He could tell you. I'm getting tired of talking," I said.

"Well, you worked with a police sketch artist who did her best to draw the faces of the women you saw murdered by Carissa's brothers. For the most part, they came out pretty close to accurate," Wayne said.

My mouth opened wide in disbelief. "You can't know that," I said.

"Sure, I can." He stood up and moved to sit on my bed, his Bible clutched in his large hands.

I sat beside him, resting my elbows on my thighs, my head lowered, hair dangled down in front of my eyes.

"What happened next?" Wayne asked.

"The police were relentless. After they determined that no one locally fit the description of the women, they scanned that artists drawings and started emailing the pdf to police stations across the county, and state—for starters," I said. "They did all kinds of cross reference checks in all these databases. My allegations were taken very seriously."

"And a match came back?"

"Two girls went missing the night before the murder. They were college freshmen, taking film and acting courses down at NYU," I said. I sat up straight, sighed, and moved to plant my back against the coolness of the wall. I brought my knees up and wrapped my arms around my legs. "As much as I wanted it to be a nightmare, to think I'd simply lost my mind, it wasn't. They had been real people, with real names, with real worried families."

"The guilt?" he said.

"It was unbearable. I did nothing to help," I said.

"What could you have done?"

"Stopped them. Something." I shook my head and closed my eyes. "I don't know if I could have saved them, but I never tried. The way they looked at me. Their eyes pleaded with me. And all I did was watch."

"And the police?"

"Now that they had confirmed that the two victims I'd described were missing, and the fact that I attested to witnessing them die, the pressure was on."

"Pressure?"

"They wanted names. I'd told them I knew who had killed the girls. The police wanted blood." I laughed. "No pun intended."

Wayne didn't crack a smile.

"And you told them?"

"Not at first. They came to the church to see me. By this time, I'd told Father Daly everything. He stayed by my side. He told me he had a plan. For the plan to work, I needed to tell the police everything," I said.

"Everything?" he said.

"Yeah. The whole vampire thing," I said.

"And the priest's plan?"

"Since the police said they couldn't, or wouldn't provide me any protection, he came up with me staying here for a while—locked in rooms with padded walls," I said. "He thought I'd be safe this way, at least, safer than out on the streets. What amazes me is that he believed me, so easily, he just accepted all I'd told him."

"Oh, he believed you all right."

"God tell you that?"

"Yep." With a smug smile, Wayne pushed his back up against the wall. He kept his legs straight, and his hands folded over his belly, fingers laced. "So you told the police?"

"I told them. They kept looking at Father Daly, like they were expecting him to twirl a finger at his temple and roll his eyes at me."

"And did he?"

"He might have, don't know. I wasn't looking at him," I said. "Not while I was talking."

"He didn't," Wayne said.

I shrugged. I'd heard enough about the God-voice-thing. "I gave the police the Tantalo name."

"And what happened?"

"They went with it. The hauled Carissa's brothers down for questioning."

"But they weren't arrested."

"No bodies, no evidence of their having been at the scene of the crime, and only my statement," I said. "In fact, I looked more like a suspect than the vampires."

"But they couldn't prove you were there, either." He wasn't asking questions. Wayne seemed to know the answers, and was stating them.

"Right. But I think I still am at the top of the suspect list, despite having been admitted here."

"And the Tantalo family's after you—you led the police to them. They don't need the attention. Don't want it. You refused to join them, and went one-eighty on them, turning them over to the authorities," Wayne said.

"Yeah," I said. "That pretty much nails it."

Twenty-two

Father Daly loaded the last of the bags into the back of the church van and slammed the door. For four travelers, they certainly came with plenty of luggage. Aside from the suitcases, he wondered what could possibly be contained in the hockey-equipment-sized duffel bags. He was sure in time he'd see what the bags contained, he just wasn't sure he wanted to know.

Daly hopped into the driver side and buckled his seatbelt.

"Are you sure there's enough room at the rectory?" Cardinal David Bonsignore asked. He rode shotgun.

"Plenty," Daly said. "We even have a separate wing for Sister Brianna."

"Bri. Bri is fine."

Father Daly glanced into the rearview mirror, making reflective eye contact with the nun. "Sister Bri," he said.

She smiled.

"I'm not sure if you are hungry, but the church assistant has prepared a homemade stew—lots of beef and potatoes and a thick, thick gravy," Daly said.

"If I wasn't hungry, I am now," Father Pete Cano said. Daly caught sight in his mirror of Cano clap a hand onto his belly and rub.

"We'll be at the church in a moment, I'll show you around while lunch is put on the table, we can eat, and then either talk, or you can get some rest," Daly said.

"Oh, I'm rested," Cano said.

"We'll talk some," Bonsignore said. "But, not all of us slept like babies on the flight." The cardinal twisted around in his seat to glance at Cano and flashed a grin.

"I could sleep during an earthquake, no problem," Cano said.

"I don't doubt it," Bonsignore said.

"I feel rested," Bri said.

"I'm good," Father Brandon Padilla said.

"Well, I need a nap," Bonsignore said. "I'm not as young as you guys."

Laughter filled the van. Daly was envious of the bond the four seemed to share. He wondered how long they had worked together, and what other assignments they'd taken. He could almost guarantee each was filled with countless adventurous and humorous stories, that if he was lucky, and time allowed, he'd be able to hear.

~ * ~

Victor hated telephones, and hated cell phones even more. He didn't have to think back very far to remember a time when phones did not exist. If he'd known what the future held, he now relished those peaceful days and the more simplistic lifestyle.

Regardless, he was in his personal office when his cell rang, and answered it by the third ring. "It's Victor," he said.

"Victor, this is Terrance. You called?"

Terrance was head of the Buffalo territory. His coven was twice the size of Victor's. "I appreciate you calling back," he said.

"It sounded important."

"It is. We have a situation." Victor considered himself self-sufficient. He did not like calling for help. He would rather be called on to help others. "I'm thinking we may need to gather."

"That bad?"

"Not necessarily." Victor wandered around his office, and stopped by the window. The outdoors instinctively called to him. And yet, more times than not he found himself locked away inside his home. Not like a prisoner as much as like a hermit.

"Then why call?"

Victor sighed. "It's Rome."

Silence came from the other end of the phone. Victor let it fill the space between them.

"What's that mean?" Sawyer said. "What are you saying?"

No one liked to admit mistakes. Victor even more so. "We've had some problems here."

"Problems?"

"My girl. Carissa. She met a boy," he said.

"Ah geez. This ain't good, Victor. You know what I'm saying. I don't even know what you're going to tell me, but I can already tell, this ain't good," Sawyer said. "And then you start the whole thing off mentioning Rome? What's that about?"

"It's why I said, I think we need a gathering."

"Before I go *anywheres*, I want to know what we're talking about. This ain't like back in the day when all we could do was send a quick message—and gatherings happened. You see? Either you tell me what's going on, or I'm out."

"You're out?"

"Out."

"Just like that? You'd do that to family?"

"What's your family done to me? To my family? Victor, Carissa's yours to control. If you had troubles, you should have handled it before anything happened." Sawyer was yelling.

"Let's not turn this into a shouting match," Victor said, speaking softly.

"Then put it out there, Victor. What's going on?"

"My Carissa. She bit a man. Turned him."

"Ah geez. Recently? She did this recently?"

"Yeah. She did."

"What happened? He out of control? I haven't seen anything in the papers." When vampires are new it takes time for them to learn the rules. They forget they can't kill all the humans in the area when they hunt, despite the desperation of constant thirst that fills them. Many times they go on a killing spree. Police and media suspect a serial killer is on the loose. And for the most part, they're right. When that happens, the newly turned vampire must be eliminated, and a human must be set up to take the fall. Son of Sam was a perfect example. Once captured by a coven, he is tortured to the point of insanity—brainwashed to believe he is responsible for countless murders, and released for the police to pick up, and the law to prosecute.

"He's a half breed. Hasn't killed. Won't."

"So what's the problem then?" Sawyer asked. Finally, he used a much calmer tone of voice.

"He's gone."

"Gone?"

"Took off."

"Took off. And you can't find him?"

"That's what I meant when I said 'gone.'" Victor closed his eyes. "My boys have a lead. We think he's holed up in a hospital, or some kind of rehab facility."

"Smart boy," Sawyer said. "Tough to confirm with all those privacy acts in place. You think he's still in your territory?"

Victor opened his eyes and stared out at the water below the bluff his house was perched on. "I can't be certain."

"This is not the best time for something like this to happen. I don't think I need to tell you this," Sawyer said.

"No. You don't. But it's happened."

"Have you contacted Miguel? No. Of course you haven't. It's why you've called me." Sawyer went silent for a moment. "And what's this about room?"

"The half breed brought the police to my door—a few weeks back. The officers are investigating the disappearance of a two missing women. They suspect my boys are involved," Victor said. He hissed between clenched teeth.

"Police. Not good. Not good at all."

Sawyer continued to state the obvious, to repeat all that was said to him, and it grated on Victor's nerves. "He also apparently went to a priest," he added.

"How do you know this?"

"Because I got a call from a family in Rome. They said something was going on. The Vatican was acting abnormally. And then, yesterday, the Pope's team of vampire hunters boarded a plane bound for Rochester. They landed not long ago," Victor said.

"How big a team?"

"Four. As far as we know."

"Four? That don't sound so bad. What are you? Six?"

"Six, yes." Victor knew that his family held the advantage, number wise. But that wasn't good enough. Although his family was not related by blood, he still considered them his actual family, and didn't want to see any of them harmed—even if they won the Pope's inspired battle. "There is safety in numbers, Sawyer. You know this. As a strong front, we can overpower the hunters. Easily. We could possibly avoid a single casualty to our families."

"Our families? Victor, I've not agreed to anything. You know that."

"It's why I called. To convince you to join with me."

"And who else have you called?"

"Theron, in Syracuse."

"And what did she have to say."

"She hasn't called back, yet." Victor hated begging. If it was what doing to ensure the safety of his family, he'd do it. But Carissa, dear Carissa, was going to find herself in some serious trouble when this was all over.

"I'll tell you what, Victor. You talk to Theron. If she agrees to stand with you and your family, then so will I," Sawyer said.

"And if she doesn't?"

"Then I wish you and your wife all the best," he said.

"Just like that? You'd wash your hands of this, just like that?"

"Just like that," he said. "This isn't my mess. I don't need to draw attention to my coven. You know that. We are on the brink of something huge. Huge. And the timing of this is horrendous. But you know this already. It's why you haven't gone to Miguel," Sawyer said.

"And will you?"

"What? Go to Miguel? Not my place. I'd wager a guess if you make enough phone calls to other covens, he'll find out soon enough. Which is another reason why I'm not interested in getting involved with this. Miguel is *not* going to be happy. Not at all," he said. "I've got to go. Call me when you hear back from Theron. I'll be curious to see which side of the fence she takes."

"Thanks for your time, brother."

"Hey, it's what family's for. No?"

Twenty-three

"It's almost three," Wayne said.

My appointment with Dr. Sanchez started at three. It was time to be discharged. "Wish me luck," I said.

"I'll pray for you," he said.

"Yeah, or do that," I said.

"You know, I may have an answer for you," he said.

"And what was my question?" I asked.

"Not now. We'll talk later," he said.

"About your answer?"

He nodded as I left the room and walked the hall down to Sanchez's office. The same nurse sat at the desk outside the office. "I'm back."

"Dr. Sanchez will be with you shortly," she said. "Have a seat."

I sat in a chair outside the doctor's door. Magazines were on the small table next to me. It seemed more like a doctor's office than a wing in the psychiatric ward. I picked up a magazine and flipped through it to take my mind off the scent of the nurse's pumping blood, and did my best to ignore the intense thirst it caused.

It seemed like an eternity passed before the phone on the nurse's desk rang. "She'll see you now, Mr. Rossi," the nurse said, hanging up the phone.

"Thank you," I said. "And it's…ah, forget it."

I set the magazine back on the small stack on the table and quietly opened the door.

"Hello, Joey," she said. "Come in. Please."

I entered the office. She sat behind her desk and looked at me over the rim of her glasses.

I shut the door behind me and sat in the chair across from her, assuming a calm and professional demeanor. I hoped.

"I understand you stopped by earlier?" she said. "Is something wrong?"

"I did. And no, nothing's wrong. It's just, you see, I'd like to leave now." I wasn't sure how else to put it.

"Leave?"

"That's right. I want to go." I crossed my legs and folded my hands in my lap.

"And you believe you are ready to leave?" she asked. She removed her glasses and set them down on the papers she'd been looking at.

"I do. I appreciate your help, and the chance I've had to stay here. It's helped, but I'm feeling much better," I said. It was time to lay it on a little thick. Give her the things she wanted to hear. Say the things that would convince her I understood my illness—the way she saw it—and had conquered it. "The accident messed me up. The death of my wife played a big part in all of it, too. I was searching for me. Drinking too much. I'd been lost. But since I've been here, I haven't had a single drink. Haven't needed one, either."

"Have you thought about drinking?"

I'd be lying if I said no. "No."

"And what about Wayne, your roommate?"

"What about him?"

"Can you tell me a little more about what he's like, about the kinds of things the two of you talk about?" she asked. She rested her elbows on the desk and pressed the tips of her fingers together.

"You want to talk about—*Wayne*?"

"Do you not want to talk about him?" she said.

"I mean, no, sure. We can talk about him. If that's what you want to do." It took tremendous control not to roll my eyes. "What do you want me to say?"

"Well, earlier you told me he liked to read the Bible. Is that true?" she said.

"Seems like he's always reading from the Bible," I said. I smiled.

"And does that bother you?"

"Bother me? I don't think so. It's what works for him. I don't hold things like that against people. He's a decent enough guy."

"Do you believe in God?"

"I did. I do. Yes." When she didn't say anything, I continued. "When my wife died, I kind of cooled my relationship with him."

"Did you blame God for your wife's death?"

"I thought you wanted to talk about Wayne?" I asked.

"In a way, we are," she said.

"I didn't blame God. No. I just, I felt cheated. My wife gave up. She died. I just wasn't—maybe still aren't—in a place to worship God, and give thanks."

"So you blame Him?"

I shook my head. "No. I don't."

"Have you and Wayne talked about this?"

"Some. He's pretty easy to talk to," I admitted.

"That's good. I'm glad that he's been there for you. Nothing wrong with that," she said. "What else do the two of you talk about?"

I was not going to tell her about vampires. That would be a one-way ticket to isolation, padded walls and a straitjacket. "He says God talks to him," I said, taking the focus off me. "We talk about that."

"I see. And how is Wayne as a roommate?" she said.

"More sane than I could have hoped for. If I had to room with anyone, I guess I got lucky with him," I said.

"So you get along?"

"For the most part, yeah." I had no idea how talking about Wayne had anything to do with my release. If it was what she wanted to discuss before letting me go, then I'd talk about him.

Dr. Sanchez picked up her phone. "Yes, please," she said, and hung up.

The office door opened. Two male orderlies walked in.

"What's going on?" I asked.

"I need to tell you something, Joey," Dr. Sanchez said. "These men are here, just to observe."

I twisted in my seat looking at the orderlies, and back at Dr. Sanchez. "What's going on?" I repeated.

"It's about Wayne," she said.

"Is he all right? I just left him, just two seconds ago," I said.

"Joey, Wayne is not real," she said.

I laughed. What else could I do? "What kind of game is this?"

"Joey, there is no Wayne. You do not have a roommate. No roommate has been assigned to your room. There is no Wayne in this ward," she said. If she didn't look so serious, I'd have sworn she was kidding, pulling my leg.

I got to my feet. Hands grabbed my shoulders, pushed me back down to sitting. "Dr. Sanchez, this isn't funny."

"It's not meant to be funny," she said. "You came here wanting to talk about being discharged. I'm trying to explain to you why you are not ready to leave."

"And you think I made him up, that Wayne is some figment of my imagination?" I said.

She stared at me.

"I'm not crazy. I didn't make this guy up. Everyone's seen him. Everyone has talked to him," I said.

Hadn't they?

"Remember that first time we met, when you had me removed—the orderlies took me to my room—I'd said, so I got a new roommate."

"And what did the orderly say?"

I turned to look at the culprit.

"I told you to take some time to cool down," he said.

Yeah. That's what he'd said. Not a word about my new roommate.

And in the cafeteria—that crazy woman—she'd ignored Wayne, and had stared at me the entire time.

But when the crazy guy stabbed me with the plastic knife, I'd looked to Wayne for confirmation that it was stuck into my arm. He'd agreed. The orderly that time had merely said, well it looks fine now. He didn't look, or even talk to Wayne.

"This can't be," I said. It can't. There had to be some other explanation. Was it some kind of psychotherapy? Was I some kind of medical guinea pig?

"Joey," Dr. Sanchez said in a voice so soft, I barely heard her speak. "Joey?"

"I don't know what's going on," I said. If Wayne wasn't real, if he was a figment of my imagination, then was Carissa real? Had there been a car accident?

Did vampires really exist?

Was I even one of them?

Or was I just insane.

"How long have I been here, Dr. Sanchez?"

"A week," she said.

Not longer? Not since birth?

"I want to go back to my room," I said.

"I think that would be a good idea, Joey. And tomorrow, we'll talk more. Okay?" Dr. Sanchez stood up, her hands together in front of her. She looked sad. Was it because I'd slipped? Was it because instead of making progress, I'd gotten worse?

We weren't going to talk anymore about my release. Not today. And surely not tomorrow.

I was certifiable. I knew it. No doubt. Forget the old saying that if you question your sanity, you're sane. I was questioning mine, and now I knew for certain, I was loony, and belonged right where I was.

"Gentlemen," she said.

They didn't grab me, as much as help me to my feet. "Thank you," I said, wondering if I'd-have been able to get up on my own. My legs felt boneless, as if I'd collapse under the weight of my head and torso.

Allowing the orderlies to lead and half-carry me back to my room, I wracked my brain for proof that Wayne existed. I searched my mind for some memory of someone else actually talking to him—someone other than myself. Reluctantly, I had to admit, I could think of no one.

Once at the threshold to my room, I stared at the empty bed across from mine. No sheets. No blankets. No pillow. No...

"There," I said, pulling away from the men holding me as I dashed into the room. I lunged for the nightstand by my bed. The thick black Bible with gold framed pages... that was proof. "What about this? This was Wayne's. He read it all the time. This proves I wasn't imagining him, that he's real."

"Mr. Rossi," one of the orderlies said. "That's yours. You came here with that."

I laughed. "Are you kidding me? Are you serious? This is Wayne's. It was his."

I thumbed through the pages, working my way to the front, to the first page. "Right there, look," I said, and stopped. My finger rested on the handwritten words:

To Joey
From Father Daly
"This Book will keep me from sin,
Or sin will keep me from this Book"—D.L. Moody

No. No. This wasn't right. It couldn't be. It was Wayne's Bible. Not mine. Not mine!

Twenty-four

I was in the woods, lying on my back on the cold, hard ground. I could see my breath in plumes as I exhaled, and feel the burn in my lungs as I sucked in frigid air. Through the canopy of skeletal fingers of leafless branches sat the glowing sight of a full moon. I couldn't smell or hear a thing. But I could feel and…

Hands touched my shoulders.

I twisted my head around to see Carissa.

She knelt beside me. She looked at me hard, as if trying to look into me, as if staring into my eyes might actually give her passage to see into my soul.

If I still had a soul.

If I'd ever had one.

Like a clash of thunder, my hearing returned. Something boomed. Out of the corner of my eye, I saw flames. Spreading flames. The trees around me were quickly engulfed by fire. I placed my hand on the top of my head—my hair felt hot, and now the back of my hand felt hot, too. How close was the fire?

I tried to move, to get up. We needed to leave, to run.

Carissa, who had just been watching me writhe on the ground, looked up and back toward where the fire was. Her features slowly changed. Her skin became dark and wrinkled and thick—it looked rough, the way dried mud looks after four-wheel trucks barrel through it, rutted and tracked in all directions.

"Carissa, what is it?" I said. I thought I said. I couldn't hear me speak. Was the hungry fire speaking louder than I could talk?

She looked at me—beauty gone, and then her eyes closed and opened. And when they opened they were crimson, fierier red than even her hair, and the pupils were diamond-shaped. When she smiled, lips parted, I noticed her teeth. Fangs. Long and sharp. As her mouth opened wider, strands of saliva stretched from bottom to top teeth before snapping away, and running down the sides of her mouth.

"Carissa… Carissa," I said.

Something behind her moved in the dark, a shadow made whole by the fire light opposite it . . . And when I tried to move, to pull Carissa away, her chest exploded…

"Carissa!"

~ * ~

"I'm here, Joey."

"Carissa," I said. The woman in the woods shimmied and swayed and slowly dissolved, allowing me to see through her, to the trees across from her, to the flames making their way closer to where we were in the woods. "Carissa!

"I'm here, Joey. Open your eyes."

I opened my eyes. I was lying in my hospital bed. Carissa sat beside me, her hands on my shoulders.

Had I awoke from a nightmare, only to find myself still in a dream?

"Carissa?" I said.

Her skin was pale. Milky. Her lips, red. Her eyes vibrant. She leaned down, lips parted. As we kissed, I kept my eyes open, as did she.

"I'm still dreaming," I said.

"No. You're awake," she said. "You're in your room in the hospital. I found you."

Found me. "Your family?"

"Their close. They're checking hospitals, too."

"How'd you know I was here?" I asked.

"We're connected. I felt you. The sensation increased the closer I got," she said.

I sat up. She kept her hands on my arms. "Why are you here?" Was she mad that I'd gone to the police? Was she here to bring me to her family? I'd betrayed them all.

"We have to leave. It won't be long before my brothers find you," she said. "Marcus can sense me. Just like I can sense you."

"Built in vampire GPS," I said. The joke fell flat. Neither of us even smiled.

"They're coming."

"They won't let me out," I said. "I'm crazy."

She stood up. Her movement was smooth, elegant. Her arms drifted to her sides. Dressed in low cut tight leather pants and a white blouse, red hair draped over her shoulders, she looked stunning. "I've missed you," I said.

"Have you?" She couldn't mask the tone of insecurity. "Didn't you run from me? I'd have come with you. I'd have gone anywhere you wanted. But you never asked. I thought you weren't just hiding from my family, but from me, too."

Maybe I had been. "I'm messed up," I said. "I don't know what's going on—I mean, I do—but none of it makes sense."

"It takes time."

"I couldn't kill those girls."

"I didn't think you would."

"What does that mean? Will I turn back to normal, into a human?"

"You're a half-breed, Joey. You'll always be one, unless you make a kill. The kill—the drinking of human blood—is what completes the transformation," she said.

"So what happens to me?"

"You will live on forever, but with little to comfort the constant thirst you'll feel. Blood will always call to you, always demand your attention. It will get quite maddening at times—and at other times, you may be able to control it," she said.

"Did you fight it?" I asked.

"I didn't. I embraced it. Then. But I'd give anything to change that, to be half-breed, or human—and long dead by now," she said.

"Long dead?"

"I'm a lot older than I look," she said.

"How old?"

"Please, Joey. Not now. We have to get out of here," she said.

"And go where?"

"South, north, somewhere," she said.

"I don't know if I can do this without you," I said.

"You won't have to," she said. "I'll stay at your side as long as you want me around."

Did I want her around? She would have to hunt, kill and drink. Would that be tempting? "I don't know what I want."

She turned to face the window, pressed her palms on the glass. I stared at her reflection, her downcast eyes and pouting lips. "Then I'll get you out of here and you can disappear."

"If you came with me, wouldn't they always be after us?" I said.

"I won't come with you. You made it clear. I scare you. I should scare you." She threw her hands in the air. "I scare me."

In movies, vampires seemed heartless, cold, like Carissa's brothers. But Carissa, she was different. Trapped. Reborn into a life she perhaps hadn't chosen, but had clung to for some means of survival.

"Can you live on any blood, or does it have to be human?" I asked.

"Any blood—it's just, well, human blood is more nutritious, more satisfying. But it doesn't have to be that way," she said. She slowly turned to face me. "Is that what bothers you?"

"I can't be with you if you are killing people," I said.

"I don't need to do that," she said. "I can adjust my diet. I've always wanted to, actually, but never had a reason. Not while living home with my family—and it has been a long time since I've… No one like you has ever been part of my life before. And, Joey, you're an important part."

I desperately wanted a cigarette. My hands shook. I rubbed my palms up and down my thighs. "Will things like animal blood turn me, transform me?"

"No. It's like a ceremony. The kill and the blood of a human. It's the only way. It's sin that is involved in the ritual. It's is a final nail in the damning coffin," she said. "When God forced Lucifer out of Heaven, many other angels followed Lucifer's fall. These fallen angels were the first, original vampires. They fed off humans, stealing souls for Lucifer. Our bloodline is traced all the way back to him."

"Our bloodline?"

She nodded. "In a way, all vampires are only half-breeds when compared to the fallen angels. You more than most."

Sin is the key.

"Joey, you are not crazy, but you do need to accept what's happened." She knelt in front of me, looked up at me. A flash-memory of skin like tree bark filled my mind. I closed my eyes and shook my head. When I opened them, the grisly image was gone.

"I'm trying," I said.

"You have to quit trying and just accept," she said.

If only it were that simple. And yet, what other options were before me? None. If I was crazy, go with it. If I was part human, part vampire, what was there to fight? "So how do we get out of here?" I asked.

"We walk out," she said.

I laughed. "This is almost like a prison, Carissa. It's why I'm here. We're locked away."

"And yet, here I am." She smiled up at me.

"And yet, here you are," I said. "So you have a plan?"

"I have better. I have the way," she said. She stood up, held out her hand. I took it. She helped me to my feet. "Put some clothes on. You won't get very far in pajamas."

I grabbed clothes out of the nightstand by my bed and rushed into the bathroom, closing the door to block out Carissa's snickering.

Twenty-five

"Sin is the key."

I spun around, dropped my bundled clothes to the floor. "Wayne—you scared me," I said.

You're not real. You're not here.

"I'm sorry. Didn't mean to." He sat on the closed toilet lid.

"You're not here," I said. "You only exist in my mind." I reached out a hand, waving it, and leaned toward him, expecting the action to shatter his seemingly solidified existence.

Like a coiled snake, his arm shot forward. His hand locked around my wrist. "I'm real, Joey. I'm here."

I couldn't pull free of his grasp. "They told me I never had a roommate; that I made you up. And you were gone. When I got back to the room, you weren't here. The Bible—it's mine. Not yours."

"I never said the Bible was mine. I was just reading it. Maybe I should have asked," he said.

"That's why, that first night you kept asking me if I read the Bible," I said.

"Figured you must, if you carried one around with you," he said.

I laughed. "Can you let go, please."

"Oops. Sorry." He released my wrist. "But, in a way, they were right."

"They were right about what?"

"Me not being your roommate. I never was."

"So what are you, a doctor?"

"In a sense, I suppose," he said.

I hated the cryptic, secretive way in which Wayne now preferred to talk. "Look, I'm leaving. I'm sneaking out. Carissa's here. She came back for me."

"I think that's a good plan," Wayne said. "Where will you go?"

"Still not sure."

"What happened to going to the church? Back to Father Daly?"

"Yeah. We might go there. At least for now," I said.

"Joey?" Carissa knocked on the door.

"Be right out," I said.

"I have the answer for you," Wayne said.

"The answer?"

"How you can beat this," he said.

"Beat what?"

"Being caught between human and vampire."

"God told you?"

"God told me." He stood up and leaned against the sink.

"Mind if I change while we talk?" I stripped out of my pajamas.

"Please. Feel free." He laughed. "No pun intended."

"What's the answer?"

"Sin."

Again. Sin.

"Look, Wayne, I don't know if you're real, or in my head, but I have to hurry. Carissa's brothers are coming for me. If they find me, I'm dead," I said.

"More dead than you are now," he said.

"Right. Whatever."

"Lucifer and the rest of his group chose not to follow God. They were thrown out of Heaven, cast down to live forever on earth—and to one day burn in the lake of fire," he said.

"Yeah, well, right now—he's not getting much sympathy from me."

"But you have a choice still. If you kill, and drink human blood—you damn your soul," he said. "That's right. You still have a soul. You haven't walked completely away from God. As long as you stay in His good graces and do His will—you can be redeemed."

"You mean go to Heaven when I die?"

"I mean the whole package. God. Jesus. Love. Eternal life."

"I have eternal life now. It's not so great," I said, zipping up my jeans and tucking my t-shirt in around the waist.

"You have something perceived as eternal life. Vampires are not immortal, as they claim. They age one year for every hundred years they live. And although it may not seem like it, old age can kill them—same as it does everyone else," Wayne said. "And when judgment day comes—and it's coming—they'll be judged. You'll be judged. Will it be Heaven, or the lake of fire with Satan and his minions?" Wayne used his thumbnail to scrape the gook out from his middle fingernail. "People, real people, have the same choice. Follow Jesus, or don't. They will face judgment on judgment day, too. No one escapes that day. No one. Everyone sins. No way around it. As people, we're flawed that way. But recognizing sin, and turning from it, turning to God—it makes all the difference in the world. You are in a unique situation. There is a plan in place for your half-breed existence. A purpose."

"God knew this was going to happen to me?"

"Of course He knew," Wayne said. He planted both hands on the sink and stared at his own reflection in the bathroom mirror. His eyes veered to the right so that they locked onto mine. "Don't give in to the temptation of drinking human blood."

"Shouldn't be hard," I said. It was a lie. That night in the warehouse, despite fear and disgust, a part of me wanted to kill, wanted to feast. Carissa promised the desire would always exist, and taunt until I either gave in to it and drank, or went insane . . .

"It won't be easy," he said, as if speaking from experience.

"And how am I supposed to know God's plan? My purpose?"

"He'll make it known to you when He's ready," Wayne said. "The time is soon."

"Wayne, who are you, I mean, really? Where did you come from?"

"I'll be seeing you around, okay. You don't have to be alone if you don't want to be. Know this, He is always there for you. Always has been, but He won't call on you to see if you need help. It's up to you to call on Him. It's the way it works," he said, and shrugged. "You dropped a sock."

I bent down and picked up the sock. "Wayne—"

I was alone in the bathroom.

"Nah. This isn't happening to me. Not to me," I said. I stumbled into the door as I stood on one foot to put the sock on the other.

"You okay?" Carissa said through the door.

"I'm wonderful," I said. I put on the other sock. "Things couldn't be better."

~ * ~

It was ten when I stepped out of the bathroom, dressed in jeans, t-shirt and bent over to put on my sneakers. "How is this going to work?"

"We're going to walk out the front door," Carissa said. She sat on the edge of my bed, hands planted on her knees. "Joey—I've missed you."

"I know," I said, tying laces. "I've missed you."

The words felt flat before I said them, but tasted stale as they passed over my lips, like morning breath.

"What's wrong?"

What's right, I wanted to ask. "Once we get out of here," I said, thinking, if we get out of here, "then what?"

"We hide. We run."

"It will never be easy," I said.

"But we'll be together. That's more important to me than immortality."

"Immortality is important to you?" I asked.

"You get used to it," she said.

There was no need to share Wayne's take on immortality with Carissa at this moment. Instead I thought of my own longevity. I wasn't sure I wanted to be alive today. I couldn't imagine how much worse I'd feel a hundred years from now.

"Come here," I said, standing up straight.

Carissa rose, and glided toward me. We held hands, a foot of space between us. I looked into her eyes. "I'm scared," I said.

"I know." She smiled. "We'll figure things out. You'll be fine."

"You don't get it. I'm not worried about me. It's you. You're turning your back on your family," I said.

"I just live with them. I don't consider them family. I was never treated as a family member. My father is all about his boys. The dynasty is theirs to inherit. There is no plan for me. No purpose. I can't live forever without direction, without an objective. Can you understand that, Joey? And in you, I have found both," she said.

"You have?"

She nodded. "A plan and a purpose."

I wanted to tell her about the conversation I just had in the bathroom with the apparition I had called Wayne. She'd think I was crazy. Or would she? "I'm waiting to see what my plan and purpose are," I said. I didn't want to hurt her feelings. The right response would have been that I felt like she did, as if my plan and purpose revolved around her, too. It would be a lie at this point. In the future, that might change. But right now—for some insane reason— I wanted to place my faith and trust in Wayne's theory, that God was out to help me.

"We should go," she said. She kissed me with soft lips, our eyes open.

I squeezed her hand, hoped it provided reassurance. "I'm right behind you," I said.

"No. Beside me. We're in this together," she said.

I smiled and pulled the door open. "Ah, wait a sec." I ran to the dresser and picked up the Bible.

The hall outside was quiet. All the lights were on, an illusion of comforting normalcy, as if swimming in the depths of warm ocean waters on a hot summer day, unaware of the threat of jellyfish pooled just under your kicking feet.

As we approached a nurse seated behind the desk at the nurses' station, I focused on just beyond that desk, seeing the doors that exit the ward and enter into the pulsing heart of the rest of the hospital. She did not hear us approach, her face buried in a paperback novel.

I didn't dare speak in case the plan was to simply make for the exit undetected. Maybe Carissa had turned us invisible? What did I really know about vampires, anyway?

We weren't invisible. The nurse dropped her book and jumped up to her feet. "Miss, who are you? How did you get in here? Sir, please go back to your room."

"We're leaving," Carissa said.

"You're leaving," the nurse repeated.

"You don't see Joey. And you don't see me. We were never here," Carissa said. I watched her speak. Her lips moved methodically, enunciating each syllable with patient efficiency. "When we reach the door, you will let us out. And when asked about Joey in the morning, you will state that you were at your desk the entire shift, and nothing out of the ordinary happened at all."

The nurse looked around. Brow furrowed. Eyes scanning. She clapped a hand over her heart and slowly sat back down. She shook her head, as if trying to shake loose the dangling webs of sleep. She yawned, picked up her book and went back to reading.

This time, Carissa gave my hand a squeeze. Still staring at the nurse, I allowed Carissa to lead me to the double doors. The nurse—without taking her face out of the book—reached and depressed a red button by her computer. The doors swung open.

We walked out of the psycho ward, out of the hospital—despite odd stares from staff who must have assumed we'd managed to keep hidden from wardens when visiting hours ended—and into the night.

Twenty-six

"Ok," I said, as I stole a glance over my shoulder. "I have no idea how you pulled that Star Wars stuff on that nurse, but Carissa, that was incredible. I mean, what just happened? How did we get by that nurse? Was that some kind of trick?"

"I guess. We call it a psyche-pus, getting humans to do as we say. It doesn't work on all people. But you'd be surprised just how many it does work on," she said. "I'm pretty sure you can do it, too."

"Can I?" I said. I didn't have a coat. I felt cold. Lately, I always felt kind of cold. I didn't shiver, but hunched my shoulders as a shield against the brisk night air.

We approached her car. She fished keys out of a pocket, and disengaged the alarm. *Chirp! Chirp!*

"I'm pretty sure you can. You have lots of new… talents. You just don't realize it."

"Why?" I asked, and pulled open the passenger door. The parking lot was pretty empty. Carissa car sat beside a light pole, illuminated under its circle of light.

"You ran. You weren't trained," she said.

"There's vampire training?"

"Mentors. You would have worked with me, or one of my brothers. Shadowed us. Learned the dos and don'ts, and the how tos and stuff," she said, and climbed into the driver's side.

Inside the warmth of her car, I set the Bible in the back seat and rubbed my palms on my knees. "I have so many questions. The dreams I've been having," I said.

"Normal."

I laughed. "They're too bizarre to be normal."

"And yet, they are." She started the engine. I switched on the heat. "Have you noticed anything strange, or odd about yourself—excessive strength, speed, vision, hearing?"

I shrugged. "Just the opposite. I'm tired but can't sleep."

"The nightmares?"

"Always there waiting," I said.

"Have you had any blood to drink?"

"No. None." I shook my head. "I'm not going to do that…"

"I'm not referring to human blood. I mean, any blood, animal, rodent…"

"Rodent?"

"Excellent source of fiber," she said.

I stared at her. She laughed. "You pulling my leg?"

"About the fiber? Yeah. But you need blood. Your body needs it. To be honest, how you've not killed by now is beyond me. There are vampires who, once they've transformed fully, have never again touched human blood. They sustain their life from drinking blood from sources other than people."

"And that works?"

"Sure. It's like—having Spam, instead real food," she said, still smiling.

"It's not funny," I said.

"No. But it's true, and at least it's an option."

"And if I drink blood, what, I'll get stronger?" I asked. The excitement heard in my tone caught me off guard. I closed my mouth quickly, tightly.

"Even for a half breed, with blood you'll see a considerable difference in all your senses, and abilities."

"I mean, how much blood do you drink?"

She looked at me, eyelids fluttered. "We need very little. A pint will last months. The thing is—we're like alcoholics. Why stop at one beer, when a six pack will give you a buzz?"

"There's a buzz?"

"Blood is life. When we absorb it, it fills that emptiness that is within us, making us feel alive again. Because, Joey, we are technically dead."

"But my heart still beats," I said.

"Well, not you," she said.

I thought I could hear her last word lost on her lips. *Yet.*

"We've been at this a long time, our kind. Little is new. The nightmares while you're asleep. The nightmares while you're awake. It happens to us all at first."

I thought about my teeth falling out of my mouth in the bathroom the other day. I'd been awake. Not asleep. I knew it. "I still don't get how," I said.

"How what?"

"How do you, we, get away with it. I mean, Carissa, vampires murder people," I said. I knew it sounded harsh. It directly reflected against her, her family, her brothers.

"She smiled a thin smile. "We're careful. The homeless, the runaways, the isolated. We're careful. Mostly," she said.

"Mostly?"

"I'm thinking back to the nineteenth century," she said.

"Thinking back to then?" I shook my head. "You mean, remembering?"

She didn't answer the question. "The coven for New England crumbled. The head of the coven was executed by his family. A coup. It was the leader's fault. He showed weakness. The family sensed it. Like wolves, they shredded him to pieces," she said. "And for a while, what was left of the family went wild. They ignored the basic rules of indiscretion and caution."

"What happened?" I asked. She pulled out of the parking lot, shifting gears, and picking up speed.

"The medical world said that consumption was killing people."

"Consumption?"

"Um. It's what they called it then. Now it's called tuberculosis," Carissa said. She stopped at a red light, at the edge of the hospital campus. She signaled a left turn, and waited patiently for the light to change.

"I don't get it. Tuberculosis is a real disease, right?"

"Sure it is. But it wasn't what was killing those people in the late eighteen-hundreds."

"Vampires?"

"A rogue coven. Some people caught on, suspecting us. Most refused to believe, despite the evidence and facts staring them in the face. The entire coven blatantly attacked people, killing and turning them. It was a nightmare. The covens all around New England waited anxiously for some kind of resolution. If the world found out that vampires existed—the hunt would be on, again," she said.

"But you said some people figured out vampires were responsible?"

"Mercy Brown was a kid. Nineteen. One member of the Southern Tier coven bit her. Her heart stopped. She was pronounced dead."

"But she wasn't it?"

"No. She was like you. A half-breed. Only, unlike you, she went into a coma," she said.

"Should I have gone into one?"

"You could have. If you did, I'd have been ready to carry you home," she said. "And we would have fed you human blood to wake you."

"Would that have turned me?"

"You need to make a kill, and drink the blood. Not one or the other. It's a rite of passage," she said. She kept her eyes on the road. I couldn't look away from her, from her profile.

"What happened to Mercy?"

"After she was buried, after the funeral, the girl's father and the family physician went back and broke into her tomb. She was alive and well at that point, and hungry. They fought her, pinned her down and cut out her heart. They burned it," Carissa said.

I swallowed hard. "That killed her?"

"Fire bad," she said, as if trying to lighten the mood. "It wasn't just happening here. It was happening all over the world. In Europe, especially."

"More rogue covens?"

"Just a different world, on that side of the ocean," she said. "They called it the Eighteenth Century Vampire Controversy."

"They did not," I said. We laughed. "That sounds so made up."

"It's true." She slapped the steering wheel with a hand, still laughing, smiling. White teeth—fangs—shone as we passed under street lights and faded as the interior became dark again. It didn't matter. She looked beautiful.

"The empress, Maria Theresa, sent her personal physician to investigate the rumors of vampires. When he returned, he claimed vampires did not exist, that people were in hysteria and panicked and needed to blame something for the sickness that killed so many people. And Maria Theresa passed laws protecting corpses in graves from being dug up and desecrated."

"And that stopped it?"

"Yeah. For the most part," she said.

"But if this physician…"

"Gerhard van Swieten," she said.

"Him. If he looked into the validity of vampires…"

"He was one," she said.

I fell silent, and nodded.

"Are we not immortal?" I asked.

"Yes. And no. Things like bullets, and knifes and stakes—they can't kill us. But some things can. Fire, for one. Beheading."

"God."

She hissed. "Sorry," she said. "But yes. Him."

"But, can't God also save you?"

"We have no souls. What is there to save?"

"What about me?"

She was silent for a moment. The world passed by us as we turned onto 104 and headed west.

"Carissa, what about me?"

"You have your soul, Joey."

"What if I told you, you have yours, too. That only the true vampires, the fallen angels, are without souls. Would that make a difference?" I asked.

"I don't know. It's not true. So supposing makes no sense," she said.

"There's got to be a better way," I said.

"I am who I am."

"But you are willing to stop drinking human blood," I said.

"If I can stay with you, I would give up anything, everything," she said.

"You're taking me to a church, you know."

"I know."

"I've been inside this church, I've talked with a priest. Those things didn't affect me. I mean, when I mentioned God, you hissed."

Her jaw tightened, lips spread, mouth opened.

"Like that—right there," I said, pointing.

"Say you'll stay with me," she said.

"Say you'll give this a try," I said. I wasn't sure I knew what I was talking about. Things Wayne had said, and didn't say, spilled through my mind. Jumbled. Distorted. It just seemed like a picture was forming. A picture with sound. I couldn't hear anything in particular, as much as sense it. I sensed explanation. Was God talking to me? Is this what hearing Him sounded like? Static, white noise? "Will you trust me, and try?"

"I'm scared," she said.

I put my hand on hers, which rested on the gear shift. "So am I."

Twenty-seven

Victor Tantalo stood in his study by the window, lights off, tumbler of chilled blood in hand. The calls had been made. Some would show for the gathering. Others refused. No matter. Something needed to be done, and it all rested on his shoulders. All of it. Because of Carissa. She'd been careless, but under his keep, and therefore it was his responsibility to set things right. Like it or not, all eyes were now on him.

Well, hopefully not all eyes. Miguel, who ran all of New York, did not need to know what was going on. He did not forgive easily. If informed, he might not allow Victor the chance to rectify the situation. And it could be guaranteed that punishments would be dished out.

Victor knew the wrath Miguel unleashed. He'd never be able to protect Carissa. He wasn't strong enough to stop Miguel.

He laughed as he realized the truth. Miguel might not be interested in Carissa. Miguel might have his eyes set on Victor.

What a mess. What a terrible mess.

The rolling lake waves did little to calm his mood. He thought of Katrina, always so mellow and trusting and confident. The perfect jewel. Finding her had been his blessing. Her falling in love with him had changed his life—or lack there of.

The smile that formed was short lived, as his lips crushed against each other. Katrina was who she was because of her faith in him. She'd never said as much, but always sensed it, took pride in that fact.

What good wife didn't expect security from her husband?

Security. For all these years they had been safe. Secure. Tucked away. Living seamlessly side-by-side with humans. Always undetected.

He closed his eyes tightly as one thought, one name, filled his mind. *Carissa.*

When his cell phone rang, he answered it. "Victor," he said.

"It's Theron," she said. "I've talked with Sawyer, Demitri, and Candace, from Albany. Today's Thursday. We'll arrive Saturday for the gathering."

Victor swallowed. "Thank you." He sat in his leather chair, letting relief flood through his body as his tense muscles relaxed. "I will have rooms made up for you, assuming you'll be staying with us."

"Wouldn't have it any other way," she said. "But I insist on a room that looks over the lake. Nothing that refreshing in my neck of the woods."

"Of course, my dear," he said. "And Theron, again, thank you."

"Don't thank me for anything. Not now. Not yet. This is far from over. We realized burying our heads in the sand is a technique that will get us nothing but killed. And despite how much I loathe this wretched life, being taken out by the church is not something I look forward to," she said.

"And the others?"

"They feel the same. Sawyer took some convincing. I worked on him a bit. Not an easy guy to talk to when his mind's made up," she said.

"I can send my boys out to pick you up."

"No. Not necessary. I look forward to the drive. We all agreed to show up on Saturday, though. Each of us is bringing one lieutenant. Will that be a problem?" she said.

"My home is plenty big," he said.

"And Victor, I'm serious."

"Serious? About what?"

"A room with a view."

He laughed. "I already have the room picked out for you. It's the least I can do."

"We have a lot to talk about."

"We do."

"As much as I look forward to seeing you and Katrina—it's been so long, too long—this is not a social call."

"You don't need to remind me." Victor held up his tumbler and held it up toward the window. The moon behind the glass made the crimson drink look like diluted wine.

"I didn't think so, but just in case, I wanted to put it out there."

"Consider it out there," he said, and closed his phone.

Nothing had been resolved. The threat still existed—from both ends, the Pope and Miguel—but for the first time in a while, Victor breathed slow, even breaths and shifted his weight, finally getting comfortable in his chair.

Twenty-eight

Cardinal David Bonsignore was as settled in as possible. After waking from a quick nap, he unpacked his things into the nightstand and hung some of his stuff up in the small closet. He belted his holster around his waist, removed his Glock from the case, checked to ensure it was loaded and slid it in place. The presence of heavy metal pressed reassuringly against his thigh caused some of the anxiety to subside. The loaded silver bullets were what made the difference.

Aside from a bed with a lumpy mattress, the nightstand with missing knobs, a lamp with an askew shade and a wooden crucifix on the wall, the tiny room was bare. Cool gray walls, a linoleum floor—this was a culture shock compared to his room at the Vatican.

He thought of the Apostle Paul who spent most of his life in prisons and realized his room would have looked like a suite at the Ritz. Humbled, he sat on the bed and spent the next few moments in prayer.

The scent of fresh-brewed coffee infiltrated Bonsignore's senses. He opened his eyes as he thought, *Amen.* As he stood up, a portion of the uncertainty he felt drifted down his spine with a shudder, but with a casual glance around the room, eyes locked on the eyes of his Savior nailed to the cross, Bonsignore could not shield the doubt, questions and fear filling him.

Using the handrail, he descended the staircase slowly, and smiled as he listened to the banter his team engaged in.

"Sequels are never as good as the original movie," Padilla said. "Look at the *Jaws* films."

"*Jaws Two* was as good as one," Cano said.

"But not better," Padilla said.

Bonsignore noticed the empty and discarded duffel bags in a corner of the room as he reached the kitchen in time to see Cano shrug his agreement. He knew weapons had been strategically placed around the rectory. While he'd napped, the team had done its job. This caused an equal portion of guilt and pride to fill him.

"And what about *Jaws Three*?" Bonsignore joined the conversation, and smiled at his team.

Bri laughed. "Three-D, no less."

Now they all laughed. "That was horrible," Cano said. "Horrible story, horrible effects."

"And they didn't stop there," Padilla said. "What did they make, two more?"

"Something like that."

"I liked all of the Rocky movies—well, except three. Where he fights Mr. T.," Bri said. "What is it with the third films?"

"*Return of the Jedi*—same thing," Padilla said.

"*Friday the thirteenth*," Bri said. "Part three."

They all groaned, and then simultaneously added, "Three-D."

Father Daly walked into the kitchen, and smiled as he looked at everyone sitting around the table talking, laughing. "What did I miss?"

"Absolutely nothing," Cano said.

Bonsignore made his way to the coffee pot. "Would you like a cup, Daly?"

"It's too late for me. I'll never get to sleep," the priest said. "Well. Maybe half a cup. I have the feeling we're not going to get to bed too early, anyway."

Daly sat at the table, between Bri and Padilla. Bonsignore added cream and sugar to his coffee. "I know you and I talked on the phone," he said to Daly. "But I want you to tell us everything, again. From the beginning."

Daly sighed. "I can do that."

Bonsignore hoisted himself up onto the counter by the coffee pot. He held the cup with both hands and blew on it before taking a tiny sip. "We're going to interrupt you—asking questions, all right?"

"That's fine," Daly said.

Bonsignore watched the priest's hands fidget with each other on the table top. "Whenever you're ready," Bonsignore pushed.

Daly let out an anxious laugh. "It's just not real. We learned about witches and exorcisms and vampires in seminary, but you know, a part of me didn't really believe any of it. Maybe it wasn't that I didn't believe it ever existed, but I guess I couldn't believe such things still existed."

Daly's eyes flitted about the room, focused on everything for a mere split second—on everything except for making eye contact with anyone, Bonsignore noticed. "Most parishes will never encounter a supernatural force," the cardinal said.

Daly nodded, but did not look comforted by the thought. Why would he be? The "most" was not part of his parish at the moment. "He came to see me in the confessional," Daly said.

"Joseph Rossi," Bonsignore said.

"Joey. He prefers Joey," the priest said. "He told me about witnessing murders and felt guilty for not helping, not trying to prevent the deaths. He talked about lost souls and…"

"Father, Father," Cano said. "Can you try to recite back to us the exact conversation between the two of you—as best as you can remember?"

Father Daly nodded. "I can try. From the beginning?"

"Best you can," Cano said.

"I slid open the screen to the confessional Joey occupied. He said, 'Bless me Father, for I have sinned…'"

~ * ~

"Have the police found out much of anything?" Bonsignore asked after listening to Daly's rendition of events and a long silence ensued. He shivered. A draft made its way into the house. The window over the sink at his back rattled as wind whipped about outside, howled.

"They don't talk to me. But I haven't seen anything in the papers. Nothing. No reports of any crime. Nothing. But I know for a fact the police went to see the Tantalos," Daly said.

"But you don't know what happened."

"I don't."

"And where is Joey now?" Bri asked.

"He didn't want to stay with me. I don't know if being around God upset him, or what, but he wanted to hide somewhere else," Daly said.

"Hide—from the Tantalos?"

"That's right. And I'll be honest. I wasn't thrilled about a vampire living here," Daly said. "He seems like a good enough guy. It just made me a bit apprehensive."

"I should think so," Padilla said. He stood up, dumped his coffee in the sink and rinsed the cup. "Father—do you have milk?"

"In the fridge," Daly said. "Help yourself."

"And so Joey went where?" Bri said, bringing the conversation back on topic.

"I called some people. We had him committed to the psychiatric wing in a hospital. It sounds harsh, but—well, to be honest, it might be good for him. And with all the privacy laws, I figured he'd be hard to track down. Maybe not hard, but if the vampires were looking for him, it might slow them down—and getting to him wouldn't be so easy."

Bonsignore crossed his ankles, letting his feet swing out and back against the lower set of cupboard doors. The *tap, tap, tap,* helped him concentrate. "Nah, that's clever. I like it. Have you been up to see him?"

"No. We both thought, in case the family was watching me, we didn't want to risk my leading them right to him," Daly said.

Padilla stood with the fridge door open, leaning on and chugging milk. The white mustache was wiped off with the swipe of the back of his sleeve. "So now what? Do we get him out?"

Bonsignore jumped down from the counter. "Shut the fridge—you're wasting energy," he said. "Joey may seem like a good enough guy, but he can't be trusted. He's still one of them. Getting him out makes no sense. Truth is, if we get him out of the hospital, we'll have to kill him. No way around that. He's part of our mission, not a member of our team. No. We leave him in the hospital. Let him think he's safe. And when we're done with the Tantalo coven, we'll check him out, and then, well, finish the job."

Daly pursed his lips and shut his eyes.

"I understand you like the guy," Bonsignore said. "But he's not human. He's a vampire."

"Half."

"Same difference. He's not human. The Pope wants him dead. He wants all of them dead. It's not murder. It may sound like it. But it's not. You know it's not. They don't have heartbeats, or pulsing blood. They are already dead. We just need to make them stay that way. You see what I'm saying?" Bonsignore said. He leaned against the counter, arms folded across his chest, fingers rolling over bulging biceps.

"I suppose," Daly said.

"We need some help from you, Father. Some information. Nothing more. You are not coming with us. You are not going to be expected to do more than provide intelligence. Understand me? What takes place over the next several days is not a sin, and should not weigh on your conscience." Bonsignore hoped he spoke with enough conviction to convince the priest. He knew it was all easier said than done. He did not want guilt hacking away at the priest's faith and trust. Faith needed strengthening at a time like this. Encouragement.

"I'll do whatever is needed," Daly said. "You don't have to worry about me. If that means we have to kill Joey, that I have to kill Joey—then so be it. I know God has a plan, and like it or not, I'm thankful to be doing His will."

"Amen to that," Cano said.

Twenty-nine

Through the window over the sink, headlights roamed over the kitchen wall. Despite the wail and howl of the wind, the sound of loose gravel crunching under tires, and the squeal of brakes was heard. All head in the priest's kitchen turned to the window at Bonsignore's back.

"Expecting company?" the cardinal asked with arms at his side, muscles flexed.

"Here? Rarely. And this late at night, almost never," Daly said.

Everyone got to their feet in one fluid motion. Daly stood still as the team around him moved stealthily, disappearing from the room as if they were part ninja.

"Go upstairs," Bonsignore barked the order. "We'll see who's here." Daly didn't move. "Now!"

Bonsignore turned to face the window as Daly shuffled out of the room. He listened as the staircase creaked under Daly's weight. With the lights in the kitchen on, he could see only his reflection in the window glass. Taking a nap had been the wrong thing to do. Upon arrival, he and the team should have familiarized themselves with the layout, should have put a defense into place immediately. Their first big assignment, and already he'd made irreparable mistakes.

"Bri? Cano? Padilla?"

"Front door," Bri called back.

"Front window," Cano yelled.

"Back door," Padilla said.

Bonsignore looked around the kitchen. There was a door. He went to it. Chain locked, dead bolted.

"Coming toward the front door," Cano said. "Two people; male, female."

Bonsignore removed his Glock 37 from the holster, confident the pure silver, .45 GAP ammunition, with extended 19 round magazine, should stop anything, human or otherwise.

The soft, *knock, knock, knock,* echoed through the silent home. Bonsignore wished they'd had radios on. Keeping in contact while spread throughout the rectory is vital; without radios, they were essential in the dark. Bonsignore stepped away from the door, the barrel trained on the knob, ready to unload rounds if the knob turned. In the threshold between the kitchen and the front room, he saw Bri crouched alongside the front door, and to her left, Cano with his back pressed flat against the wall, finger parting the back half of window drapes.

Reverting to hand signals, he told his team to be ready.

More knocks, a bit louder and quicker this time.

"Yeah, who is it?" Bonsignore yelled. "Do you know what time it is?" He wanted to sound . . . normal. He hoped he'd just said something anyone would say to unexpected visitors.

"Father Daly? It's me, Joey."

Bonsignore locked eyes with Bri. Again, he used his hands to delegate direction. Bri backed away from the door. She took cover by the wall, deep in the shadows. Cano readied his pistol with a two handed grip.

"You alone?" Bonsignore asked.

"Where's Father Daly?" Joey said. The knocks came again. Loud. Hard. "I want to talk with Father Daly."

"I'm here, Joey."

It was Father Daly who had spoken. Bonsignore scanned the kitchen, the front room, but nothing. The voice had been muffled—distant.

"Upstairs window," Cano whispered.

Bonsignore deflated with a sigh.

"I'll be right down," Bonsignore heard the priest say.

The priest came down the stairs and into the kitchen. Just for the shock value, Bonsignore leveled his gun, aiming for Daly's heart. "Are you out of your mind, Father?"

"But that's Joey." Daly pointed at the kitchen window,

"And who's with him?"

"I don't know," the priest said. "Carissa?"

"But you don't know."

"No. I don't."

"And Joey was bitten, right?"

"But he's not one of them, he's not a bloodsucker." Father Daly took small steps forward, inching his way closer to Bonsignore, despite having a weapon pointed at his chest.

"You haven't been with him in a while. He's been locked away, surrounded constantly by the sweet aroma of warm, pulsing blood. He may have cracked, broke down, and had himself a feast. I thought he was locked away in a hospital?" Bonsignore said, shaking his head. "He must have broken out. And now he's here, perhaps to take out the only other person who knows his true identity. That, of course, being you."

"How do you know he escaped the hospital?"

"It's late. You think he was discharged this late at night?"

The telephone rang. Daly's eyes drifted toward it. "That's assuming he came right here."

"Let it ring," Bonsignore said. "Father, Joey is a vampire. The woman he's with—if it's Carissa, then we know she's one, and if it's not her, then we still have to suspect she's undead. They both need to be dealt with."

"Let's let them in, first. Talk to them." Daly's body trembled. "Please, let's talk to them first. There's four of you—five, if you count me. Just two of them. One's a girl. You're armed, you're ready."

Bonsignore shook his head.

"Father?" Joey yelled. Something hard banged the door. Could it have been the guy's fist?

"You've seen some vampire movies, Daly. I know you have. One vampire has the strength of ten men. They're fast when they run. Fast when they fly—oh yes, they fly—and even faster when they attack," Bonsignore said. "We're not here to listen. We're not here to take depositions and report back findings to the Vatican. We are the jury, judge and executioner."

"Then let them talk before you execute," Daly said, a thin lipped smile overtaking his mouth.

Bonsignore gave hand signals to Cano. He ducked down low and crossed under the picture window on his belly. He reached up and unlocked the front door, and then slithered back into position.

"Door's unlocked," Bonsignore called out. "Open the door slowly. Walk in one at a time, hands up, fingers laced together behind your head. Got it?"

Silence. Bonsignore nodded at Cano.

"Looks like they're talking about it," he whispered, and shrugged.

"Joey, it's okay," Daly said.

Bonsignore grit his teeth. "You, Father, will either stop interfering, or we'll have you stationed at some no-name church in some no-name town in the arctic. Got it?"

The front door opened slowly. Joey stepped in first, hands behind his head. "Don't shoot."

"Wouldn't matter." It was a woman's voice. The thick sarcasm was meant to be heard. She stepped into the room, hands folded across her chest.

"Silver ammo, honey," Cano said and snickered.

When she hissed, she caught everyone off guard. With weapons raised, safeties off, complete chaos exploded.

Thirty

Why'd she hiss?

"Down! Now! On your knees, both of you," one of the guys with a gun pointed at me shouted. The tight fitting t-shirt revealed bulging, twitching muscles in the forearms, biceps and pecs. He looked like a marine, complete with cargo-style pants.

As I dropped to my knees, I pushed Carissa out of the rectory. I scanned the room for Father Daly. How could I help him now? I'd been caught. Was he all right? "You better not have hurt Father Daly," I said.

"I'm right here," Daly said. The lights came on. The priest's hand hovered over the light switch.

The marine eyed the priest with disdain. "Lady, I'm not telling you a second time. Down. Now!"

"Carissa, get out of here!" I shouted. "Go!"

"Cano!" Marine shouted.

Although I could smell more than one person in the room, could hear the rapid beating of several hearts, I had no idea Cano was behind me. He stepped over the backs of my legs and ran out the front door in pursuit of Carissa.

He might be fast, he might be trained to hunt, but unless he was a vampire, he'd never catch her.

"David, this man is not a threat," Father Daly said.

"Bri—take the priest to the church," Marine said.

A woman crept out of the shadows. Our eyes met. She looked young and was very pretty. She kept her gun locked on me, apparently aimed at my skull. She held the thing with both hands, finger against the trigger.

"I'm not going to move," I said. "I'm not going anywhere."

"That's right, you're not," she said. "Father, please come with me."

"Anyone else with you?" Marine asked.

"It was just us," I said.

"Padilla?"

"We're clear back here," a man shouted.

"Join us up front," Marine said.

I don't know why he insisted on yelling.

"Bri," Marine said.

"Father," Bri said. "Take me to the church."

"Please, Bonsignore, let him talk," Father Daly said. Bri turned the priest around. As he led the way, she walked backwards behind him, her gun—steady in those hands—still trained on me.

Another marine came bounding into the room. No surprise—his gun drawn. Padilla. He quickly looked around the room, and then focused on me. His eyes. The barrel of his gun.

"Sir?" Padilla said.

"Secure him," Bonsignore said. "Don't move, Mr. Rossi."

"I haven't," I said. I'd never been handcuffed. Padilla stood behind me. I felt cold metal wrap around one wrist, that arm lowered and twisted around behind my back. I lowered my other arm, slowly, and reached back so he could secure the wrists together. "Why don't you let the priest go? I'm guessing it's me you want."

"Why do you think we want you?" Bonsignore asked.

"Why would you want him?" I asked.

"Get him to his feet." Bonsignore did not lower his gun. Instead he took careful aim, one eye squinted shut. "Don't mess around here."

Assisted, I got to my feet. I turned to look at Cano. "Thanks," I said.

Where had Carissa gone? How could she have left me? These were her people, here to kill me, and she just fled. Nice.

"Where you want him?" Cano said. He had one hand clamped firmly over my arm.

Bonsignore looked puzzled. "Must be a basement, somewhere secure," he said. "Padilla, ask the priest."

Padilla ran out the room.

There were Cano, Bonsignore and me. "Let's not draw this out," I said and puffed my chest some.

"In a hurry?" Cano asked. Something poked into my side, just under the ribs. My puffed chest, deflated.

"I want…"

"You want?" Bonsignore said. "You're in no position to *want*."

His eyes looked dark under a brooding caveman-like brow. Steroids did that to people, and explained the hulking size, as well as the moody demeanor. "I want," I said, placing emphasis on *want*. "I want you to let Father Daly go. He doesn't know anything. He's innocent. You don't have to do anything with him." I didn't want to place ideas in their heads. I didn't want to tell them not to kill or harm the priest, just on the off chance that they hadn't thought of doing so already.

Tantalo's men were defiantly intimidating. Trying to act courageous, brave, strong, was difficult. Their weapons and very presence were enough to make me more than a bit apprehensive, if not downright scared. My fate, no doubt, rested in their calloused hands.

"I'm not sure why you think we're going to harm the priest," Bonsignore said.

I had no answer. Keeping silent made more sense.

"Basement's this way," Padilla said, after galloping back into the hall. "Come on."

"Follow him," Bonsignore ordered.

I did as commanded. Cuffed hands behind me, the barrel of Cano's gun pressed into the small of my back. I didn't know a thing about guns, but hoped the trigger wasn't sensitive and, instead, required physical finger strength for pulling.

Padilla led me through the dark kitchen. Just outside it was a door on the left, a parlor on the right. He opened the door and felt along the wall. Lights came on in the staircase.

Without hesitating, Padilla padded his way down the stairs. I followed. Cano and, presumably, Bonsignore in tow.

As far as basements go, this was as creepy as they get. Wet, moldy cinderblock walls; naked bulbs hung from ceiling rafters, casting little light, not doing much to chase darkness back into nooks and crannies. Involuntarily, I shivered. I suppose if I were completely undead, the effect might be different. As far as I knew, I was still mostly alive, at least according to Carissa and according to Wayne.

I think I expected a laundry area, piles of dirty clothes, boxes, pipes. Not a narrow passageway. History was never my strong suit, but what I could recall about the Inquisition is what filled my head. Holding cells, torture chambers, dark and dank dungeons.

Certain thoughts that crept to the forefront: Why are they prolonging this? Why not just kill me? Why not just turn me over to Carissa's family? Why didn't they come for me themselves? Why hire mercenaries?

"Guys," I said. I laughed.

"Something funny, Rossi?" I knew it was Bonsignore. I didn't need to see his lips move to recognize the voice.

"Funny? Yes. This is funny. If you're going to kill me, then get it over with. I promise not to bleed on the carpet," I said.

"Wiseguy," Cano said.

"I'm not trying to be a wiseguy, okay? But the theatrics—they're overkill," I said. "And the priest…"

"Stop worrying about him. Start worrying about you," Cano said.

Any grin I was sporting vanished. "Father Daly's in the dark. I didn't tell him anything. He was just helping me out. It's his job. I came to him. I wasn't sure who else to go to. He doesn't know a thing."

I still didn't want to say too much. Not specifics. I didn't know how much these guys knew. The fact their ammo was silver said they knew something.

We came to a break in the cinderblock walls. A room on the left revealed a washing machine, dryer, and mounds of laundry. On the right, a sofa, tables, boxes. Nice and normal like. I almost sighed in relief.

We went right. I was thrown onto the sofa. "Sit," I was told.

I righted myself. Sat. Obedience might be the only resource I'd have to call on. If it meant the possible difference between life and death, and saving Father Daly, I'd comply. No pride issue here.

"Why do you care so much about what happens to the priest?" Bonsignore asked.

"He was just helping me out. Nothing more," I said. I don't think I answered the question. If I gave up too much, they might look more closely at him.

Bonsignore and Cano stood in front of me. I'm not sure what happened to Padilla. He might be standing behind me. Or doing laundry. Just not sure.

I closed my eyes. I could hear him breathing back there. Could hear his heart beat. He was behind me.

"You know why we're here?" Bonsignore asked. "You know what we want with you?"

"The Tantalos sent you. You're here to kill me," I said. "I didn't mean to cause them this much trouble. I just can't, I can't be like them. I didn't ask for this, you know. I didn't want this. Carissa thought she was doing me a favor." I swallowed. Death at the scene of the accident would have been so much easier, so much more peaceful.

"We're not *with* the Tantalos," Bonsignore said. "Quite the opposite. We're from the Vatican."

I couldn't help but laugh. "What does that mean?"

"We're here to extinguish your existence." Bonsignore was all business. Square jaw, lips so pursed they seemed nonexistent, and eyes that looked blacker than any of Carissa's brothers.

"The Vatican, you mean like, the Pope?" I said, shook my head. "He knows about all of this? Vampires and stuff?"

"It's nothing new," Bonsignore said.

Why were they telling me this? Why bother?

And it hit me. They didn't want me dead. Not yet. I was a hostage, a link to the Tantalos. The Inquisition suddenly seemed very real, very frightening. Maybe it was good thing I didn't know many specifics about that timeframe. Ignorance is bliss, right?

"You expect me to believe the Pope hires mercenaries?" I tried to laugh. It sounded like a trembling grunt. If their scent of smell were as keen as mine, the fear billowing from my pores would overpower their senses.

"How about we ask questions from now on," Bonsignore said. He was not looking for permission.

"I was just filling the gaps. No one was saying much," I said.

"Enough with the wiseguy attitude," Cano said. "You're in trouble here. You know it. We know it."

"Any chance of getting out of this—give you what you're looking for, you let me and the priest go?" I said.

"Priest's not in trouble," Bonsignore said. "You're not getting this. He called the Vatican. He sent for us."

This shut me up. They must have known it would. Part of the interrogation process, no doubt. Break me.

"We want to know everything," Bonsignore said.

"Everything?"

"Everything. Don't leave anything out."

I took in a deep breath. "It's a long story."

"We've got time," Cano said.

I looked around the room. Padilla came and stood between Cano and Bonsignore. The way they stood with weapons aimed at me, I felt like I was on the losing end of a firing squad. Where was my blindfold? "My wife died," I said. "I spent a lot of time alone, in bars…"

Thirty-one

Victor told his boys to meet him in the study. There was business to discuss. Despite the size of the house, the study was always considered a place for business. With a fresh glass of blood on ice, he sat patiently behind his desk and stared for a good long time at each of his sons before lifting the tumbler to his lips and taking a soothing sip.

"Marcus?" Victor set his glass down, folded his hands, and leaned back in his chair.

Marcus cleared his throat. "We haven't found him yet."

Victor closed his eyes. If blood pumped through his veins, a throbbing headache would be upon him for certain. Instead, he welcomed the darkness that came from shutting out the light.

Losing his temper made no sense. His boys were doing what they could. He had been hoping for a different outcome, what with everyone showing up tomorrow for the gathering.

"We did find him, he just wasn't there," Dean said, leaning forward in his chair.

Victor zeroed in on the baby of the family, shooting him a look with eyes ablaze.

"Sorry," Dean said. "Sorry, Marcus."

He never learns, Victor thought. Never.

"He was in a hospital. Checked in to a psychiatric ward. We did find him," Marcus said, and turned to look at his brother. "At least, we found where he had been. When we went in to search for him, he wasn't around."

"This was when, tonight?" Victor said, still staring at Dean.

"That's right," Marcus said. "But there's more."

"I'm listening."

"Carissa had been there," he said.

Victor jumped to his feet. "When you got there?"

"No. She'd been there, though. We smelled her. In his room."

"And he's gone?"

"That's right. She must have gotten to him an hour ahead of us— the scent was that fresh." Marcus let his eyes drop to look at the floor, but not before Victor caught the shame that filled his expression.

Victor locked his hands behind his back and walked slowly toward the window. Despite the beauty outside, he could see only black thunderclouds, clouds that matched his darkening mood. "She is going to have to be dealt with," he said. "I didn't want it to come to this. Her involvement makes her guilty. That guilt can't be overlooked. Not by me, and it certainly will not be dismissed by the other covens. She's gone too far. Turning Joseph Rossi at the critical moment between life and death was one thing. It could have been regarded as admirable, if presented properly, even if Mr. Rossi turned tail and ran. She couldn't have known. But this, her helping him escape, that's something else altogether. Unacceptable."

Silence filled the large study.

"Dad?"

Victor turned around. Marcus was on his feet, hands in front of him, head bowed. Humbled. "I did not mean to fail you."

"And you haven't," Victor said. "You've done all you could have, considering. Unfortunately, we need to step things up a bit. We need to take some kind of action. There needs to be discipline and order for peace to be restored." He thought of Miguel. Wrath would be unavoidable at this point. Unthinkable pain and suffering was just off in the near distance. Who would be the recipient still remained to be seen. Clearly, two candidates were in the forefront. Carissa. Himself.

"I'll make this right," Marcus said.

"Find your sister. Bring her to me," Victor said. "As far as our Mr. Rossi, he's around. If he were going to flee the state, he'd have done so by now. No. The man is here. And I believe I might know exactly where he is."

"Should we go get him?" Marcus said.

"If I'm right, then he's unreachable. Safer now than he had been in the hospital," Victor said, although he had to admit, the hospital had been a rather clever hiding spot. "So go now instead, and find your sister. I want to talk with her. Marcus—you stay a moment."

Antonio and Dean left the study.

"Sit, please," Victor said, pointing to the chair. As his son sat, Victor planted himself on the edge of his desk. "We're having a gathering tomorrow evening."

"Yes, Dad. I know. I'm sorry it's come to this."

Victor nodded. "Aside from each coven head, a lieutenant will be present. I want you to be my lieutenant at the gathering."

Marcus lowered his head. "Thank you."

"Marcus, we need to find your sister."

"We will."

"What happens to her may not be pleasant. It may not be blood that binds you as siblings, but you've been together for a long time," he said.

"I know what needs to be done, Dad. I'll do whatever you ask of me."

"I know that. And, might I say, even if you were not the oldest, you would still be my lieutenant."

"Thank you."

"Dean speaks his mind too freely. He refuses to learn his place. I want you to keep him busy tomorrow—away from the house. I can't be worrying about what he might say or do, not with everything else going on," Victor said.

"I can keep him busy," Marcus said.

"Join your brothers. Find your sister."

Marcus got up and walked out of the study. Victor reached for his tumbler. In a gulp, he drained the blood and smacked his lips together when he finished.

There was a quick knock on the study door before it opened. "Dad, sorry to bother you," Marcus said. "We have company."

Victor felt it at that moment. His senses blazed. There was no mistaking the smell, or the tingling sensation that ran through his neck and along his shoulders, causing him to shudder. "He's here?"

"Downstairs," Marcus said. "He don't look happy."

"Can't imagine he would. Take your brothers. Go out the back," Victor said.

With fresh blood coursing through his body, he felt strong, but far from courageous. Working his way toward the study door took effort. He'd rather close and lock the door, instead of walk through its threshold. But there was nowhere to run. Nowhere to hide. In a way, he'd brought this on himself.

At the top of the staircase, leaning on the rail, Victor looked down to the front vestibule. He thought about acting surprised. That would be futile. "Ah, Miguel! I thought you might pay me a visit."

~ * ~

Katrina brought in refreshments, set them on the coffee table between her husband and Miguel and silent excused herself with a nod.

"Thank you, dear," Miguel said. Always polite. Always charming. He appeared to be in his thirties, light blond hair one length, pulled back and tied off in a tail. Blue eyes, white teeth and a killer smile made the hearts of ladies—any age—melt.

"I was going to contact you," Victor said. Regretted it as soon as the words were spoken.

"When?" Miguel's demeanor changed to hostile as soon as Katrina was out of the room. "Your gathering is tomorrow. How much notice were you going to give me? None, I imagine. You weren't going to call me. You hoped to keep this from me. Secrets like this, Victor, never stay secret long. They're too juicy. Word gets out, gets around, and there's nothing you can do to contain them. But lying to me," he said.

"Forgive me," Victor said. The blood he'd drunk early turned sour in his gut. "You're right. I wasn't going to call you. I was," he thought to tell another lie, but thought better of it, "hoping to avoid involving you, afraid of what the consequences might be."

"For yourself?"

"Yes. And for Carissa."

"Carissa," Miguel said and sighed. "You're in the center of a mess now, aren't you?"

"You could say that."

"And what's being done to fix it? Start at the beginning. Bring me up to speed, if you will." Miguel lifted his tumbler and swirled the fluid inside around so that it splashed over the ice cubes. He took a delicate sniff before taking a tentative sip. "Nice. Smooth. I never used to like this on ice. I believe it was you who introduced me to the delicacy of serving it chilled."

Victor knew better than to sugarcoat any of it. Miguel would see through such artificial flavoring, and call him on it. He did the best he could to give Miguel the entire truth, as best he could.

"I see," Miguel said, after an hour of listening silently to Victor's rendition of events. "And so now your boys are tracking down Carissa? You believe this Rossi character is holed up in a church? My guess is he's at the same church as the Pope's commissioned team. He's either a prisoner by now, or an alley. Prisoner would be better. Either way, we don't know him, so we can't trust that he'll keep his mouth shut. In fact, he's already brought the police to your doorstep, so I think it's safe to assume he'll talk, giving the storm troopers your name and address, and offering up anything else he may know."

Victor had no idea what to say. He had no idea what to do. Miguel seemed to be talking out loud, using himself as his own sounding board. Keeping silent seemed like the best path. He'd follow it for as long as he could, and speak only when required.

"Are you confident your boys will find Carissa, that they can capture her and bring her back home to you?" Miguel set his tumbler back down, and leaned forward on the sofa.

"I'm confident they can, yes." Victor sat forward on his sofa, too, hoping to appear to match Miguel's intensity.

"Then I think getting our hands on Rossi won't be too difficult," Miguel said.

"Oh? Why's that?"

"You're in love, Victor," Miguel smiled. "You'd die for Katrina, wouldn't you? Of course you would. Love is funny that way." The smile widened as he laughed.

Thirty-two

Antonio drove. Marcus rode shotgun. Dean kept silent, head down, sitting in back.

Catching Carissa's scent would be impossible in the SUV; even driving with the windows down, her scent would be masked, saturated by the smells of oil and gas. They needed to head back to the hospital. Pick up her scent and track her from there. It wouldn't be difficult. Just time consuming.

Marcus chewed his lip. He knew his father expected him to set Dean straight. Keeping him away from the members at the gathering wasn't the punishment, but merely a precaution.

"Brother," Marcus said.

Dean grunted, as if he knew it was he being addressed.

"You need to learn your place. Speaking out of turn is not acceptable. You know this. It's nothing new, and yet you refuse to submit." Marcus looked out the window. Looking back, and making eye contact, would turn this confrontational. They needed unity, not division. Still, Dean's actions could no longer be overlooked.

"Gotcha," Dean said.

Marcus ground his teeth. "Gotcha don't cover it. Never covered it. It's that kind of answer that illustrates exactly what I'm talking about."

"Oh, I'm sorry. Forgive me," Dean said, his words dripped with sarcasm and spite. "If I weren't sitting back here, I'd bow, or curtsy to your highness."

Marcus felt his fangs drop, eyes change, and stopped controlling the built up anger inside. He pivoted his head and torso around. "That's enough!"

Dean transformed—skin darkening, rutting, eyes ablaze, fangs sporting strings of saliva. "Is it, Marcus? Is it enough?"

"You know it is!"

"Guys, I'm driving," Antonio said.

"If you want to remain in this coven, you must obey," Marcus said.

"Obey who? You? Father? What wrong have I done? Talked? You going to kick me to the curb for talking?" Dean sat forward, hands—claws—planted on the leather seat. "Does that really make sense, brother?"

"Not for talking. For forgetting your place."

"Hierarchy?" He laughed. "This isn't the Dark Ages, or haven't you noticed? We're in America. Home of the free."

"You want freedom?" Marcus spat.

"I want respect!" Dean said. "No. I demand it. You, I'm afraid, are not better than me. If anything, I'm stronger, more powerful and hungrier. But Father remains glued to ancient rules and rituals that prohibit me from shining as I should, and why? Because you have seniority. That's demented and sad."

Dean's features softened, anidirias eyes returned, fangs receded.

Marcus hissed. Dean snorted out a laugh, and waved him off as he turned his attention to what passed by outside the window. "They are not the goldfish," he said. "We are. It's foolish for us to consider ourselves free when it is *we* who are trapped, contained and unable to walk the earth without fear of discovery and repercussion for being who and what we are. *We* are the bowled fish. Don't think for a moment that we are the ones in control. We clearly are not."

"Wonderful speech, little brother," Antonio said. "But you're wrong, wrong and you know it."

"Right. Gotcha," Dean said. "Turn around Marcus—your ugly face is annoying me to death!"

The hospital parking lot was mostly empty. Cars of staff, and visitors who refused to go home, littered the lot. Antonio pulled into an unlit spot alongside another vehicle, hoping to blend. He shut the engine and pocketed the keys as they got out of the vehicle.

Antonio and Dean stood on one side, Marcus on the other. All three remained silent, eyes closed, noses turned up. Filtering the scents of sickness and outdoors in order to lock on Carissa took patience, concentration.

Dean opened his eyes first. "Got it," he said.

The others opened their eyes, smiled. "Me, too," Antonio said, and thrust his hands into his pockets.

Marcus came around to their side, his eyes scanning the parking lot, looking for people, anyone who might be outside, anyone who might witness the transformation.

As one, they changed. Faces wrinkled, hardened, teeth elongated, eyes glowed.

Dean hissed first. Regardless of protocol, he launched himself into the night sky. Marcus followed, with Antonio taking up the rear.

Like seagulls they soared, climbing higher and higher in the air, out of range from the parking lot lights, and quickly out of sight to anyone who might have thought they saw flying people.

They didn't need the lights to see. The dark did not penetrate their vision. Even on a moonless, cloud-filled night, it would be so bright it would resemble mid-day. This was why, during the day, Marcus and the others like him, wore sunglasses. Actual sunlight made it feel like staring directly into the sun. This was the stuff folklore was made of; insinuating vampires could only come out at night. Truth was, most vampires preferred to live by night. No one really wanted to deal with the sun. It didn't burn flesh from the bone, the way it might to vampires in movies. It just felt that way.

With arms at their sides, they flew. No one talked. They directed all attention on honing in on their sister's scent. Her body, as if decaying, emitted such a distinct odor, there was no mistaking which way to go.

Once passing the hospital campus, they flew lower to the ground, staying as close to the trail as possible. She had not flown away from the hospital, must have driven. Her scent was not as strong the farther they got from the parking lot. In the parking lot, she would have gotten out of the car in order to walk into the hospital, and when she left, walked back to her car. Once in her car, driving to wherever, the scent faded considerably, became close to nonexistent. Close. But it hadn't disappeared completely. After decades of being around each other, Carissa's scent was as unique as a thumbprint.

"See why lowjack would be nice," Dean said. "I've said it before. I'll say it again."

Marcus hissed, gritted his teeth. "We're not slaves. We don't need shackles."

Traveling at close to fifty miles an hour, the wind whistled in their ears. Luckily, their hearing was so supernatural that whispers from miles away were easily heard.

"Just saying," Dean said. "We'd know where her car is. No problem. Instead, we're flying blind."

"Far from blind," Antonio said.

This time Dean hissed. Marcus felt a slight swell of pride. Antonio was always so quiet. Seemed to listen. Take things in. Rarely spoke up. Talking back to Dean was the last thing Marcus expected. Perhaps Antonio was as fed up with Dean's constant shenanigans as everyone else.

Cars, homes, businesses passed underneath the brothers unnoticed. If people saw them, it wouldn't matter. Reported or not, who would ever believe claims of flying people? No one. Marcus grinned. He loved his life. Loved it. Dad making him lieutenant. How awesome was that? Awesome.

"It's what I thought," Dean said, pulling Marcus out of his thoughts. He looked over at the youngest brother, who pointed west and down.

"A church," Antonio volunteered.

"It's not right. Something…" Dean slowed, stopped, stood suspended upright in the air.

Marcus and Antonio circled back around, stopped and stood beside Dean.

"She's not here," Antonio said.

"Was," Marcus said.

"Maybe she dropped Rossi off—sanctuary and all that," Dean said.

"Let's fly in closer, see where the scent goes from there," Marcus said.

Thirty-three

Why'd I run, why'd I run?

Carissa tried to think straight. Leaving Joey was a mistake. So used to fight or flight, instinct kicked in. Leaving Joe—that was inexcusable, unforgivable.

She needed to go back. No doubt. Joey was in trouble. Captured. God.

He scared her. Scared her terribly.

Going back might mean certain demise.

Living without Joey was equally as devastating.

She turned, flying high, looking down on the city of Rochester. She followed the Genesee river.

How could she have left him?

What a coward!

He'd never have left her. Never.

Only he had. When he fled. When he went into hiding. He never told her where he was headed.

There was no way to blame him. Had she been in his shoes, she'd have done the same thing. Ran. Hid. No. She wouldn't blame him.

But he could blame her.

She'd left him.

Abandoned him. He didn't know his vulnerabilities.

God. Truth.

But she did.

And he needed her. He needed her guidance. Said she'd mentor him, and then left him alone at the first sign of trouble.

She cried. Her tears fell off her cheeks and plummeted.

She hated this life, all it entailed.

So many times, so many tear-filled nights, she welcomed death. Peace. Eternal rest. It seemed so much more appealing.

Waking up each morning to a world that offered nothing was draining. The life she was now forced to live was worse than anything she ever could have imagined. Forever cold, unfeeling. . .

Unfeeling, that is, until she'd met Joey.

She saw it with her father and mother. Love. Compatibility. Enjoyment. It gave them something more, so much more, to look forward to than the insistent nagging of thirst, and keeping hidden from the eyes of the rest of the world. They had something. It was special. Real.

Never did she expect to experience such joys. Never. For how many years had she looked, hoped, longed? Too many.

And then along came Joey. A stranger in a bar. And by strange chance, it happens. Unexpected. Wonderfully unexpected.

She turned around, a sharp right, and headed back toward the church. Going back was decided. How to help Joey was something else altogether. She had no idea who those men had been. They weren't family. They weren't hired by her family—her brothers on the hunt was guaranteed to accomplish plenty without the need to involve outsiders.

Under normal circumstances—whatever constituted normal, that is—she'd go to her father, her brothers for help. They'd devise a search and rescue. Joey would be plucked from enemy hands in the beat of a heart.

Unfortunately, a search and seizure was underway—complicating things even more.

Some army-thugs had Joey holed up in a church building. Carissa's brothers were looking to snatch Joey out of the night. She needed to find and save Joey before her brothers attacked, and before the army-thugs tried to hurt him.

Time was short. She knew her brothers well. They would retrace her steps, steps that would lead them directly to the church. Directly to Joey.

She flew as fast as she could, arms tight at her side, chin to chest for better aerodynamics and concentrated her strength on the flying. Although she had no idea how flight was possible, she knew the harder she thought about flying faster, the faster she flew. It was like levitation with motion, and completely mind boggling, and yet, it was her favorite part of being undead. Flying. The freedom that came with rising above the world and soaring over problems and persistent pain was amazingly satisfying.

She remembered the first time she lifted herself off the ground. It was at night. In bed. She woke from a nightmare where she thought she'd been falling. She woke before splattering on asphalt. When she sat up, eyes open, body caked in cold sweat, she knew something was wrong. Her bed was on the ceiling. So had been her dresser, nightstand, everything in her room. And then she noticed her bedroom door. The knob. She was the one on the ceiling. Panicking, she dropped. The mattress cushioned the fall. She did the only thing she could think to do. She screamed, waking everyone in the house.

Instead of sympathy and reassurance, everyone laughed. Even her father. His laugh, however, was different. Not mocking. He'd clapped his hands together.

Not every vampire could fly. Most. But not all.

Their entire family could. Her father took pride in that fact, sure it was part of his DNA, contained in the virus he'd infected Katrina and Marcus with, and in turn as Marcus infected Antonio, Dean and Carissa, it was also inherited. The flight gene was passed down, generation to generation.

Concentrating on flying and memories was one thing, forgetting to focus on her surroundings was something else altogether. And that was exactly what'd she'd done, forgot to pay attention to her surroundings.

As soon as she smelled them—all of them, it was too late. They were on her fast, hard, knocking her from the sky. With arms flailing, she plunged toward the sully brown, fast flowing Genesee.

Thirty-four

Father Daly ran into the basement room where I was being questioned. Sweaty, breathing heavy, eyes wide—he looked scared, suddenly old.

"He won't stay upstairs." Bri came in behind him, huffed, puffed, like she'd chased him twenty miles.

"Father—you okay?" I asked.

He nodded. "How are you?" He'd dismissed my concern, inserted his own.

"I'm fine. So far," I said.

"I didn't want this to happen," Daly said.

"That's enough, Father," Bonsignore said.

"It's not your…" Someone slapped me—hard. My head twisted to the right so fast, so hard, I thought I heard bones in my neck snap.

"Stop that!" Daly ran at Cano. "He's not the threat."

"And how do you know that, Father?" Bonsignore asked.

Bri locked her arms through Daly's, a restraint he'd be hard pressed to slip out from.

"Let him go…"

This time I saw Cano's hand come at my face—as if in slow motion. Everything slowed. As if in a dream, when you can't run from the monster, feet stuck in gooey gunk… everything moved in such a way that it didn't seem to be moving at all.

I studied Cano's hand. Each finger. Looked at the palm and his knuckles. I thought about biting him, but stopped from acting on that thought. The virus. I didn't want to turn him. I didn't want to harm him, but neither did I want to be slapped.

So I stood. Walked around to stand behind Cano, and sighed.

With the sigh, things speeded up to normal speed.

And Cano slapped air, fell forward and landed on the cushion I'd been standing on.

Everyone looked around the room.

"My Lord," Daly said.

Bonsignore cocked his gun and pointed it at me. "What was that?"

I shook my head. "I don't know. I—everything moved in slow, slow motion."

"It did not," Padilla said. "It was you, Rossi. You moved at the speed of light. That's what happened."

I laughed. "Now who's crazy," I said. But had he been right? Had I moved at the speed of light? Was such speed even possible for a human being?

But that was the point, wasn't it? I wasn't a human being. Not completely. "Try that again," I said, without thinking.

Cano's muscles tensed. He raised the butt of his gun over his head, ready to deliver a bruising blow. And time froze again. I laughed. It was too surreal to be happening. I took the gun out of his hand, looked around, and decided to take all four weapons.

Then I sat back down.

Cano's fierce swing sliced through nothing but air. I laughed out loud, hard laughter. It was silly. Was I that fast? Was that possible?

"He's got the guns!" Bonsignore screamed. It jerked me out of the moment. I wasn't holding any of the weapons in any kind of threatening manner. Startled, I tensed and squeezed and the guns slipped from my grasp.

"Sorry," I said, held my hands up, their guns in my lap.

They retrieved them, snatching them up.

My display put them on edge. Rightly so, I supposed. "I moved at the speed of light," I said. "Like a bullet."

"Father," Bonsignore said, pleading evident in his tone of voice.

Daly seemed speechless. He stared at me. "Joey," he said. He turned to Bonsignore. "He can help us. I know he can."

Cano snickered. "Father—that's ridiculous. Our mission is to exterminate vampires. Not make allies."

Bonsignore was silent, fingers caressing his chin, as if he were considering the possibility. But then his hand dropped away.

"I've never had human blood," I said. I thought about Wayne, the only proof I possessed proving I was crazy and that none of this is real.

"Then we can kill you before you hurt real people," Padilla said.

That cut deep. "I'm not going to hurt people. And I don't ever have to. Wayne said…"

"Who's Wayne?" Bri asked.

I lowered my head. "Part of my story I guess. I left him out."

"On purpose?" Bonsignore asked.

"Yeah. On purpose." I closed my eyes and ran my hands like a comb through my hair. "He was my roommate while I was at the institution. Only, I didn't have a roommate."

Cano grunted and spun around. "Dave, we don't have time for this. This vampire's girlfriend is out there. She is going to get reinforcements and come back to save him."

"That's not going to happen," I said. "She's on her own." Maybe I shouldn't have volunteered that information. Not yet, anyway. I trusted these mercenaries about as much as they trusted me. I wanted them to know Carissa was not a threat. I might be faster than them, but they had guns, and experience, and strong as Carissa might be, four on one was rarely considered a fair fight.

"You might not understand this," Cano said. "But we're not listening to you, Rossi. What you say means nothing. Get what I'm *saying*? You are dead. Dead. You're not on our team. And your soul is damned."

"Please," Daly said. He held his hands up, palms out, as if he could will Cano to keep his mouth shut.

"My soul is not damned," I said. Not yet. Not ever, if I could help it.

"It's damned," Cano said.

"Wayne says it's not."

"And Wayne, your psycho roommate, knows this how?" Padilla asked.

"Because God talks to Wayne," I said. They all laughed, all except Bri and Daly. "I didn't believe him at first either. Thought he was more nuts than me. More insane, thinking God talked to him, than I felt thinking I'd been turned into a vampire. Only, when I talked about Wayne with my shrink—she told me I didn't have a roommate. She proved I'd been alone—talking to myself the whole time I was at the hospital."

"Well, now I feel better, like I can trust you with my everything," Cano said. "Because Wayne didn't exist, and you are wacko, I have no problem letting you join our team in this fight against the undead." He held his gun out, butt first, as if asking me to take it.

I reached for it.

He pulled it away. "You are crazy." Cano laughed.

"That's enough," Daly said. "Wayne might be some kind of angel."

Even I laughed when Daly said this. My laughter joined in with Cano, Padilla and Bonsignore.

Daly pursed his lips and furrowed his brow. "He's a vampire! His existence is something of fiction novels, and legends and yet, here he is. Sitting before us. He's real. You know he's real. The Pope knows he's real, that his kind lives, flourishes. You're ready to accept that reality, but not the existence of angels?"

"You misunderstand, Father," Bonsignore said. "I believe in angels. With all my heart I do. I just can't imagine one appearing to a vampire. Call me crazy, but that seems a little blasphemous, wouldn't you agree?"

"No," Daly said. "I wouldn't. God has always worked miracles through the most unlikely of subjects. When He chose kings, he picked the littlest of brothers, shepherds forgotten by both older brothers and fathers. Jesse didn't even think of David when Samuel showed up at his door. David, tending to the flock, was absent from Jesse's thoughts, and yet God wanted him. Not his bigger, older, braver warrior-brothers."

"Certainly you are not comparing Joey to David," Bonsignore said.

"How about Moses? A murderer. God spoke with Moses. Ordered him to lead his people out of Egypt," Daly said.

Bonsignore appeared speechless. He did not look like he believed the priest, but like he thought Daly was mad. As mad as me, as off the wall as Wayne.

"God never spoke to me," I said.

Daly shushed me. "David," he said. "God might have sent an angel to Rossi. We're not giving Joey a chance. If we let Joey talk, let him explain, then we can decide what happened. Who Wayne is. An angel? A figment of this man's imagination? But to stand here and pass judgment? It's not our call to make. Is it? Is it?"

I looked at everyone's face, hoping Daly's little speech impacted them. It didn't look good. It didn't seem like they bought the spiel.

"Joey, tell us about Wayne. Everything about him. Please. We're listening." Daly sat next to me, hands folded in his lap. His posture showed he felt safe next to me, as if he wanted to prove I was not a threat.

I wasn't.

But I could smell them.

And I felt suddenly hungry. "Can I have some water or something?"

"After," Bonsignore said. "Tell us about Wayne."

I sucked my mouth dry and swallowed. "Wayne… where to start," I said. "Where to start…"

~ * ~

Bri brought me a glass of water, only after I finished telling everyone about my stay in the hospital, about my interactions with Wayne, God's angel, my roommate.

"Thank you," I said. I didn't really want the water. Wasn't sure I needed it. My mouth felt dry, as if I'd been sucked cotton balls thinking them hard candy. The cold water moistened my tongue, but did little to kill the thirst.

"And you never saw Wayne... after you talked with the doctor, Wayne was gone?" Bonsignore sat on an old bar stool, legs crossed at the ankles, arms folded behind his head. I'd watched him the most while retelling my tale. I watched his eyes. He might work for the Pope, but there was no mistaking such cold eyes. Soft, he was not. "And the Bible in your room…"

Father Daly shook his head. "Wasn't mine. I didn't give it to him."

Cano laughed. "You didn't give it to him? It was inscribed. Isn't that right, Rossi? The author wrote in the Good Book."

"I saw the writing," I said. I closed my eyes. I have no idea why, but when I needed to concentrate, closing my eyes helped. I played back as many memories as possible, but came up empty. "But, I don't remember Father Daly giving it to me. And I sure don't remember bringing it with me to the hospital."

"You still have it?" Padilla asked. He was on his feet. Paced. His arms crossed his chest. The gun's grip snuggled in his palm.

"I took it. Yeah. It was in Carissa's car. Back seat. But—she ran," I said, shrugged.

"Yeah. She ran. She didn't drive away. Her car's still out there." Padilla planted his hands on his hips like Superman. Superman with a gun.

"Padilla, Bri, check it out," Bonsignore said. "Father, you're positive you did not give Rossi a Bible?"

"It sounds like something I should have done. To be honest, everything seemed to happen so fast. No," he shook his head. "I did not give him a Bible. I didn't give him anything."

"A place to hide," I corrected him. Bonsignore raised an eyebrow at me. "Well, he gave me that. And I appreciated it."

"It was the least I could do," Daly said.

Bonsignore sighed, stood up, stretched, reached for the low ceiling. "I don't get this. I'm just, this is so not what I expected."

"You expected black and white, maybe?" Daly said.

Bonsignore ignored the priest. "Cano, we need to secure Rossi for the rest of the night. We can't leave him down here unattended. Won't do."

"There's got to be a better way," Daly said. Sitting beside me, he placed a reassuring hand on my shoulder. I knew he was looking out for me. I felt the same bond. How it became so solid, so quickly, I have no idea. Sometimes people just hit it off.

I thought of Carissa. "I'll be all right," I said. "Do your worst, Cano."

Cano let out a growl of a laugh. "If I did my worst, we wouldn't be faced with this conundrum."

"Conundrum. Great word," I said. "Lots of syllables." While Daly and I connected immediately, on an array of levels, polar opposites worked between Cano and me.

Thoughts of bullies in elementary school filled my mind. Mike. Can't forget him. I liked the kid all right. No doubt, he'd been a bully. Never toward me. It didn't matter. Watching his reign of terror over less physically able kids used to leave a taste in my mouth, same as taking a swig from a milk cartoon long after its expiration date. Mike liked to wait for the teacher to leave the room. Usually before the classroom door even closed, Mike began the torment. Who can hit the hardest? A favorite game of his. Brian. Poor kid. Brian always seemed to be seated next to Mike—or at a minimum, within striking distance. This was why alphabetical seating arrangements were not a diverse enough way to organize students. Not always.

So when Cano knocked me in the back of the head with the butt of his gun, I grinned.

"That funny, Rossi?"

"You know what it is, Cano? It's expected. How's that?"

This time Daly laughed. "Father Cano, that's not necessary?"

My jaw dropped. Eyes popped open wide. The way Bonsignore looked at me; I realized it must look like my eyeballs were trying to escape from the sockets. "You're a priest, Cano? A priest?"

"And Bonsignore is a cardinal," Daly added.

"Padilla? Bri?" I asked.

"A priest and a…"

"No. Don't say it. A nun? Bri's a nun?" My ears must be filled with wax. Tons of yellow wax, blocking my ability to hear clearly. The way Daly smiled and nodded, I knew it wasn't wax that caused the disconnect but my own inability to properly process the information. "The Pope sent you guys?"

"To kill you."

"Cano!" Bonsignore shook his head. "That's enough. Now, find something to tie him up."

Thirty-five

She wasn't ready for the cold. When her body pierced the frigid river water, she gasped, sucking in water. Her hands grabbed at her chest. It felt like it might be caving in. She didn't need air. There was no way she'd drown. Because her heart did not pump, and hot blood did not flow through her veins, she was more like a cold-blooded reptile than she was human. The drastic temperature change sent her body into spasms.

Having fallen from so high, her body dropped like a boulder, taking her deep into the murky depths. All she could think to do was kick her feet. Once she let go of her chest, she used her arms. The current was strong. She felt weakened by the icy water. She concentrated on reaching the surface and launching herself out of the river and onto a bank. Although, once out of the water, she knew she would not be allowed time to warm herself; her brothers would be right there. Waiting.

And they'd expect her to come splashing up to the surface. They'd laugh and tease and drag her back to her father, soaking wet and shivering.

That's what they'd plan to do.

Everything was different now. So different.

She knew she needed to do the unexpected.

The only unexpected thing she could think to do would be to stay not only in the water, but under it.

She stopped kicking her way up toward the surface. She brought her legs up, stretched out and swam with the current.

Her keen vision was useless. The darkness around her made it impossible to see more than a few feet in front of her. A few feet felt better than not being able to see at all. She kicked her legs and parted the water with big, broad strokes.

The current felt strong. Carissa knew she was stronger. She needed to slow down. Not just to save her strength, but because the ripples she caused would lead her brothers right to her, making her extended stay in the river futile.

How long had it been since she'd last had any nourishment? She tried to remember. The fridge at home was always stocked. A pint every few days was plenty. There was rarely a need to hunt. There was never a need to kill. It wasn't like they lived in the Dark Ages. With hospital blood banks and vagrants, it seemed like blood supplies were limitless.

Vagrants. She sometimes felt bad for them. Sneaking up on a passed out bum and extracting a pint or two was simple. If they ever caught on, if they ever noticed track marks, what difference did it make? Who would believe them if they claimed someone was stealing their blood? No one. That's who.

Looking up, Carissa hoped she could see something besides bleak water. She couldn't. She swam closer to the surface, slowing down her speed considerably. The closer she got to the surface, the more she could see. She saw the moon as it wavered against the watery ceiling and no sign of her brothers.

That didn't mean they weren't there, flying off to the sides, or high up in the sky knowing that the water would obscure her vision and they could take refuge, shielded by the night.

She couldn't smell or sense them. Again, it had to be the protective river, what with its pungent stench and gloomy disposition, that prevented detection the same way a lead wall stopped Superman's x-ray vision.

She knew where she needed to go. Back to the church. Back to Joey. She'd get him out of that place. The two of them could fly somewhere far, somewhere unexpected.

She shivered while she swam, and thought maybe Alaska would be a good state to run and hide in.

No. Too many vampires live in Alaska. From one to six months of darkness in parts of the northern state—it held the same appeal as Florida did for retirees.

Mexico. Sunny. Hot. Not too many vampires that far south. Some, and they were an ornery clan, but much fewer than in North America. With Mexico as desolate as it was, she and Joey would be able to find a parcel of land far from anyone and, if they were smart, could live undetected for decades and decades.

Mexico.

It has a nice ring to it.

The current increased. Carissa stopped kicking. She wanted to be pulled the rest of the way, an insurance policy that might prevent her brothers from following her. Soon she would be dumped into Lake Ontario. Once in that large body of water she could head anywhere and would be virtually untraceable—she would simply dive down deep, head toward Canada, double back in a roundabout way and then head for the church.

If fish swimming around her could see the smile she wore, she'd bet they'd be smiling right back, even though they didn't have a clue what all the smiling was about. She folded her arms in front of her and, despite the cold that numbed her inside and out, she enjoyed the ride. Her body coursed, moving up and down and around submerged rocks and debris.

The ride ended suddenly. Something grabbed her shoulders, her legs and her hair. She was plucked from the water like a tuna caught in a net.

Once in the air, the wind threatening to make icicles out of the water on her skin and clothing, she saw Dean. He held her hair in fists, flew backwards, and wore that smile of his—crooked, half cocked.

"Thought we lost you, sis."

Dean thought he was funny. Always had. Problem was, he wasn't. Except maybe to himself. "I demand to be let go!"

"Marcus, can you hear her? She *demands* to be let go." Dean chortled out a wicked laugh.

"You can't make demands, little sister. Never could. But can't, especially now."

"You're not taking me back to father," she said.

"Ah, yes we are."

She was tired of talking to Dean. He was the baby. His voice didn't count. "Marcus," she said.

"You're going home, Carissa." Marcus must have her legs. That means Antonio had her arms.

"You're hurting me, Antonio," she said. "You break my arms or my shoulders, and I'll wreck you!"

Dean laughed.

"I'm going to wreck you, regardless," she said.

Dean raised his eyebrows and grinned. She knew her threats didn't affect him. What he didn't realize was, she wasn't threatening. She was making him a promise.

"Let's set her down."

Marcus. The only voice of reason. She suspected Antonio would have set her down, too. It was Marcus' call. No one would do a thing unless Marcus ordered it. He knew how to lead. Antonio was her favorite brother. He knew how to listen, how to open up to his own feelings, but he'd never lead. Too quiet. Too unsure of himself. Too soft.

Once she looked around, she sighed. They were at Charlotte. Just at the beginning of the pier. Freedom loomed just a few hundred yards out.

The beach was closed. No one would have seen their descent and landing on the sand.

"You can't bring me back, Marcus. I belong with Joey," she said.

"That why you left him?" Dean snickered.

She shot him a look, knew her eyes had turned red. She opened her mouth, baring elongated teeth, and from the back of her throat growled. "Can you talk without being instructed to do so, doggy?"

Dean advanced on her. Pushing buttons might be considered her extra special ability.

Marcus's arm shot out, stopping Dean. "Carissa, we have to take you home. You know that. The clans are stressed out enough. The economy has taken a massive dive. You know this."

"It's just money," she said.

This time Marcus snickered. "We spent centuries accruing wealth. Without money, we're lost. I know you get this. It's not complicated."

"I don't care," she said.

"Luckily, the rest of the family does," Dean said. "And then we can spend the rest of our days taking care of you. Unless, sis, you want to work. Feel like going to the mall tomorrow and filling out applications?"

"Carissa, money lets us keep hidden. It allows us to buy enough blood so that we never have to hunt, so we rarely have to kill."

"Shame," Dean said.

Marcus placed a quieting hand on Dean's shoulder. "Carissa, this is not a game. We're not in some Romeo and Juliet play. Joey refuses to become one of us. But that's not our fault. It's yours. You chose to start the transformation. Not us. We can't allow him to walk around as some half breed. You know this. Tell me you get this."

Carissa sighed.

"He needs us around him at all times. The smell of blood will drive him crazy—or to kill. It's bound to happen. No one can resist the temptation for long. The desire is like a fire inside. It's burning in him. Even now. Without family, he'll never survive. And if he's caught, if the police get their hands on him, then what?"

"Then we're all exposed," Dean said. He shook Marcus's hand off his shoulder. "He's already involved the police, Carissa. He's already messed up the sanctity of our existence. In a few months he's caused more trouble than we've seen in decades."

"Dean's right, dear," Marcus said. He spoke with a soft, tender tone of voice.

"Antonio?" I said.

He looked at me. His eyes silently asking, what?

"What do you think? Do I just come with you? Do I help you capture Joey, let you turn him over to father and sit idly by and watch my family kill the man I love? Is that what I'm supposed to do? Am I supposed to just accept all of this, just let this happen?" She waited for him to answer. She expected Marcus to stop her from asking her questions. She expected baby Dean to cut her off. Maybe they were equally anxious to see what Antonio would say.

"Maybe we could give him another chance." Antonio stuffed his hands in his pockets and shrugged. "Don't know, been thinking by now the smell of blood has to have his nostrils constantly flaring. He might be ready. Before might have been too soon. But now, who knows?"

Carissa smiled. She leapt forward. She wrapped arms around Antonio's neck, kissed his cheek. In his ear she whispered, "I love you, brother."

Her whisper was as loud as a shout to the rest of her family.

"Are you kidding me?" Dean bent forward, his breath a plume of exhaust. "Antonio, you kidding me, man? That like a joke or something? You trying to be funny? It didn't work."

"I'm not trying to be funny," Antonio said.

Dean stood up straight. He pointed at Antonio, but talked to Marcus. "See that? Now that's funny. Him not trying to be funny; he's hilarious."

"Marcus?" Carissa asked.

"I don't know, kid. We'd have to talk to Dad about this. He might go for it."

"Yeah, right," Dean said. "He might agree to make me the older brother, too."

Carissa did not miss the intensity in Marcus's stare. "Stop, Dean."

"Marcus?" she said, again.

"I'll talk to him. It's all I can promise."

She nodded. "Thank you."

Thirty-six

Carissa flew home. Dean followed. Marcus and Antonio went back for their vehicle.

"You don't have to fly behind me." Carissa slowed. She didn't like her little brother flying back there, not without being able to see what he was up to.

Dean flew up alongside her. He looked over, smiled. "Father's never going to go for this, you know. Ain't no way he's giving Joey another chance. You know that?"

"Marcus is going to talk to him," she said. "Dad listens to Marcus." She couldn't avoid the dig. It was always in her back pocket, ready to use. When the opportunity arose, like now, she merely pulled it out and shoved it in.

"He might listen to Marcus, but that doesn't mean he'll do what my brother says." His words seemed to slip from his mouth effortlessly, but Carissa wasn't fooled. She'd hit a nerve. With Dean, you rarely had to aim.

It wasn't pleasure she got when she needled her brother, as much as a sense of revenge, or retaliation. Their relationship had been strained from day one. Dean did not like having a sister. He never tried to hide his feelings, either.

219

Although her mind was filled with memories of his constant verbal, and sometimes physical, lashings, one day in particular stood always at the forefront in her mind.

On her way to her room, she'd come across her father's study. She heard noise coming from inside. She knew her father was not home. Instead of knocking, she just pushed open the door.

"What are you doing?" Carissa asked, standing in the doorway to the study.

"Nothing." Dean spun around. He stood behind Father's desk. There was no hiding the bundled bills in his hands, despite his efforts to conceal the theft by dropping everything onto the ground. "What are you doing in here?"

"I was looking for Dad."

"Well, look around. He's not here," Dean said. His eyes went left and right. The open safe behind his head could not be dropped to floor next to the money.

"I'll ask again. What are you doing?"

"That's none of your business." The temper. The grinding of teeth when he talked. He came around the desk, finger pointed at her face. "This is not what it looks like. I have a reason for why I'm here."

"And that reason is?" Carissa was not about to back down. Outside, on the streets, down some dark alley, she'd never challenge Dean. To say he was unstable would be like saying New York City is home to some talented dancers.

"You think I need to clear this with you?" He laughed, shook his head. "You've got to be out of your mind, Carissa. You know that? What I do, that's my business. Mine. Got it? I don't discuss my stuff with you. I'm not looking for your approval. Don't need it."

"Okay. Fine," she said, turned.

"Whoa. Wait. Where you going?" Dean grabbed her arm. The grip was tight, but she could easily shrug out of it.

She knew his thoughts, even if she couldn't read minds. He was scared, didn't want her blabbing.

"Thought I'd go see what Antonio was up to," she said. She fought to keep her wicked grin contained. She wasn't sure she succeeded, nor was she sure she really cared. Let him see her smile. He loved flashing his half-cocked grins when she was in hot water. If it's good for him, then it was certainly good for her.

"Yeah? Antonio? What for?"

"Dean, that's my business. You think I need to clear my calendar with you before doing things? Ah, I think not," she said. Staring hard at him, never breaking eye contact was difficult. The intensity behind his pupils, in his cornea, was more like a hurricane brewing out on the Atlantic. She couldn't deny Dean was dangerous. Toying with him would one day get her into trouble. The realization did nothing to curb her desire to mess with his mind. "But, so you know, Antonio and I love chatting. We talk about all kinds of things. With Antonio, I feel like I can tell him anything. Secrets. Anything."

If Dean could sweat, his body would be covered in beads of perspiration, no doubt. Instead, she watched as he licked his lips. Those eyes of his never stopped roving.

"Carissa, sis, come here. Sit down, okay? Sit." He led her to Father's chair. He forced her to sit, pressing her shoulders until she bent.

She never saw him move. In a flash he was by the study door, easing it closed, careful not to make a sound. He sauntered back toward her, chewing on his lower lip.

"So what's going on, Dean?" She looked out the window. She watched the rolling waves. She did not want to appear even mildly interested. She was, though. Part of her wanted to leap up, grab his arms and shake him until the truth fell from his tongue.

"The money," he said.

"Dad's money?"

Dean snickered. "I'm headed up to Seneca," he said. "I know how Dad's always worried about money, always trying to find more and better ways to increase our portfolio and stuff."

"And you thought using his money at the casino would help him meet his financial goals for this family?" Carissa had to look at Dean. She needed to see his eyes. Did he even believe a word he said? Or was he just lying.

The half-cocked grin. He knew he was lying.

"Not just the family," he said. "I've got a system. I know a sure fire way to win, and win big. We'll be able to tuck our share away, throw it in IRAs and CDs, and investments and stuff, and give shares to other families, too."

"That's generous."

"I know it is. Don't think I don't know it."

"And Dad was good with this, said here's the combo to my safe, help yourself?" Carissa folded her arms.

Dean made a fist. He bounced on the balls of his feet, as if about to launch himself at her. He settled down, stuffed hands in his pockets. "Carissa. Dear. Dad didn't say—he didn't say, Dean, here's the combo, go make the families rich."

"He didn't?" she asked.

He shook his head.

"But you asked him? What did he say when you told him about this brilliant plan of yours?" She didn't want sarcasm to seep into her tone of voice. It was essential not to push too hard, too fast, or he'd clam up. Now that he'd started his tale, she needed to let it play through. She was dying to hear the end.

Dean sat in mother's chair, across from Carissa. He even crossed his legs, folded his hands over his knees. "You doing this on purpose to me, or what?"

"Doing what on purpose?"

"This. What you're doing. It's on purpose, isn't it?" Dean stuck the edge of his thumb into his mouth and chewed on the skin as he looked out the window.

"Nice night, huh?" Carissa said.

Dean slammed his hands on the armrests and shot to his feet. "You know what? Okay, fine. I didn't tell Dad about this. You think he'd go for it? You think he'd let me try out any new plan? Na. No. Of course not. But let me tell you this, if Marcus—if it had been Marcus who came up with this plan, you know Dad would be all for it. You know that, don't you?"

"Of course I do," Carissa said. Dean raised his eyebrows, cocked his head to one side. "Dad likes Marcus."

The blow was low. She saw the rolling, treacherous waves within his eyes, and worried she'd gone too far, pushed too hard. "But you never took this idea to Dad, so who knows what he'd have said."

"I know. I know what he'd say. You do, too. Don't pretend like you don't."

"Not pretending," she said. "Can I ask you something?"

"Yeah. Sure, why not." Dean sat back down.

"Why Dad's money? Why not use your own?" And she got it. Ensuing silence stretched on and on. "You've used your money."

Dean lowered his eyes, dropped his head, chin to chest.

"All of it," she said.

"I've got a system," he said.

"Then where's your money?"

"I used it developing the system. But it's perfected now. A sure thing. I was only taking enough to make back some of the money I'd lost, enough to give Dad back what I was taking, and then I'd set those winnings aside, and make a fortune for everybody to share," he said.

Carissa had had enough. Play time was over. She placed a hand over her stomach. His lack of reality made her sick. She stood up.

"Where are you going?" he asked, again grabbing her.

She shook his hand off. "Away from you."

He struck her, a backhand across the face. The power behind the blow knocked her off her feet. Thankfully Father's chair caught her. With legs splayed over the armrest, one arm dangling toward the floor, she reached and wiped blood from the corner of her mouth.

His nostrils flared. "I'm sorry, Carissa. Ah, man, I'm so sorry."

He knelt in front of her, tried to caress her arm.

"Dean, you're out of your mind. No joke, bro. Nuts," she said. She pushed him over, got up and walked heavily toward the study door. Before she reached for the knob, he was in front of her, blocking her escape.

"You better not go see Antonio, or Marcus, or anyone for that matter. This, what was going on here tonight, stays between us. We get each other?"

"I don't need to tell anyone. You'll be found out. Dad's not dumb," she said.

"Maybe not. He finds out, he finds out. I'll deal with that then. But if I hear he found out because you have a problem keeping your mouth shut, that's different. Then we have a problem."

"You've already got a problem," she said. She pushed him aside and pulled open the door.

Again, he planted a hand on her shoulder. "You keep your mouth shut. Got it? You get it?"

Carissa walked into the hallway and up the stairs toward her room. She wanted to go see Marcus. She wanted to tell him everything that had just happened. He'd deal with Dean. He'd go to Father, and then Father would deal with Dean.

But what if, just by chance, they didn't deal with Dean?

Then Dean would make good on his promise. He'd deal with her. As much as she ever hated feeling fear, Dean scared her. No way around it.

Thirty-seven

They left me down in the basement. Lights off. Cano found and used towing chains. He wrapped them around my legs and arms and secured me to a steel support pole that probably ran all the way up to the attic.

Father Daly had been kind enough to toss old couch cushions onto the floor, at least giving me something comfortable to rest my behind. It was leaning against the pole that promised a long, restless night.

"Joey?"

I must have fallen asleep, but didn't realize it. The room seemed bright. Brighter than it had been a moment ago. But that's not what led me to believe I'd been asleep. It was Wayne's voice I'd heard.

"Joey?"

Was I still asleep? "Wayne?"

"Right here," he said.

I looked around as best I could. I didn't see anyone, but especially not my old hospital roommate. I had to be asleep. I shook my head. If my hands weren't bound, I'd pinch myself.

"I'm behind you," Wayne said.

I felt the tug and pull. "Ou-ouch!"

"They got you wrapped in here tight." Wayne laughed. The chains fell off my body and clanged softly as they landed on the cement basement floor. "There. How's that? That's got to be better."

I rubbed my wrists and got to my feet. Wayne looked the same as he had in the hospital. Big, like a giant. Dumb grin on his lips. "How'd you know I was here? How'd you get in here? What are you doing?"

"I'm here to help."

"Me?" I asked.

"You. Father Daly. The cardinal and his team."

"Who are you, Wayne? I mean, for real? What's going on here?"

"You're ready for it all now, aren't you?"

"Ready for what?"

"The truth. Are you interested in a story?"

I looked around the basement. No doubt Cano was perched just outside the basement door, armed with silver bullets and Holy Water. "Don't think I'm going anywhere too soon," I said.

Wayne lifted the couch cushions off the floor and put them in place. "Let's sit. This may take a little while to tell. Might as well get comfortable."

"And in this story, Wayne, you're going to tell me who you are?"

He smiled. "I'm going to reveal who I am, what's going on, and what needs to be done to set things right. That is, if you're interested in setting things right."

We sat down. "I want to set things right, Wayne. I do."

"It's what I thought."

I waited. Wayne pursed his lips, furrowed his brow and inhaled a deep breath and held it for a moment before letting it out in a long sigh.

"Lucifer was God's anointed one, the most powerful and beautiful angel in heaven. God gave Lucifer exceptional powers and abilities. God had created Lucifer in likeness to Himself. Lucifer abused that power and it wasn't long before he wasn't happy with what God had given him, and eventually desired more. Lucifer thought he should be worshipped, that he was better, stronger than God," Wayne said.

"How's that possible? Didn't God control the angels?" I asked.

"God gave angels the same thing he gave humans. Free will. God has never forced anyone to follow Him. He's never forced people to worship Him. God wants you to want to worship Him. He wants you to want to follow Him. Same holds true for his angels. The same was true of Lucifer. Only Lucifer decided he wanted to do things his own way, believing he was a deity of equal power and position," Wayne said.

I wanted a cigarette. I chewed on my lip. "So what happened?"

"God wanted Lucifer for a specific purpose. To protect earth," Wayne said.

I laughed.

Wayne raised an eyebrow. "Not funny. It was perhaps this assignment that led Lucifer to such illusions of grandeur."

Nodding, I puckered my lips to remove the smile. "Was Lucifer cast out of Heaven before Adam and Eve were created?"

Seemingly satisfied, Wayne continued. "Some like to think so. Gap Theory experts teach this. But no. That's not true. Lucifer was banished from Heaven after Adam and Eve."

"And how would you know this?" How did Wayne know any of this? "It's not like you were around at the beginning of time."

Wayne cocked that eyebrow again, offered up a half smile.

"Get out of here," I said. "You can't expect me to believe you've been alive that long."

Wayne stood up, slapped his hands on his thighs. "I think we're done here."

"No. No. Please. Sit, I'm sorry. Tell me the rest," I said.

"Accepting Jesus on faith alone is challenging for most. There was a time, Joey, when you did this. You accepted Christ into your life. Is it so hard to believe I'm an angel? God made us before making humans. He doesn't make angels anymore."

"He doesn't?"

"No. He doesn't." Wayne looked at me in a way—eyes wide, lips tight—that made me feel sad.

"Please tell me the rest," I said.

Wayne sat back down. "After God created man, He said His creations were good. Very good. How could that be a true and accurate statement if Lucifer and his demons were loose at the time? It couldn't be."

Made sense. "So it was after?"

"Shortly after. Lucifer was so smug and vain and jealous." This time Wayne laughed. He covered his mouth. "Excuse me. That was rude."

"Why?"

"Well, when God gave Adam the authority to name the creatures, and Lucifer saw the love in God's eyes when He looked at Adam—heard the love in God's voice when spoke of Adam—the jealousy Lucifer felt was like a separate entity. You could almost see jealousy in Lucifer like a shadow attached to his feet, and following him around anywhere, everywhere he went," Wayne said.

"It was jealousy?"

Wayne nodded. "Jealousy. It put Lucifer over the edge. He wanted to be God so bad, he even considered himself a god of the earth, perverting the role God had given him as protector."

"And what happened? What did Satan do to get kicked out of Heaven?"

"He wasn't Satan then. He was Lucifer. That was the name God gave him. It was only after he was cast out of heaven that he became known as Satan. And what happened exactly, no one knows. God doesn't talk about it. It's not our business; it's between them. But whatever Lucifer had done, it was enough to anger God to such drastic measures. When he kicked Lucifer out of Heaven, a third of the angels followed. Think about that. The other angels, they hadn't been kicked out of heaven. Just Lucifer. But they followed Lucifer, perhaps blinded by his glowing beauty and empty promises. At this point, Lucifer became Satan. The other angels became demons. It didn't take them long to begin their evil tasks. Satan moved right in. He tempted Eve, introducing sin into the world."

"I don't know. I don't get it. Why not just kill Satan and the demons?"

"An easy solution, so you or I might think. But God, He's always looking at the bigger picture." Wayne smiled, eyes briefly looking toward the basement ceiling. "Being a just God, if he killed Satan for his sins, wouldn't He have to kill Adam and Eve as well? They sinned, too. No, God had a better idea, a plan for salvation and redemption."

"Jesus."

"Sending Jesus. That's exactly right," Wayne said.

We sat in silence for a moment. I knew the opening chapters of Genesis. I knew the story of creation. Adam and Eve and the forbidden fruit. The serpent—Satan. The introduction of sin. Never had I had it explained to me like this, never in such a clear and easy to follow rationale. "But the vampires," I said. "How do they fit in?"

"You call them vampires. Pop culture, movies, books—call them vampires. But really, the creatures that suck the soul out of man are none other than Satan's demons. They are your original vampires. They fed on human blood, infecting the body, the mind and stealing the soul. What's left is a new race of undead beings. But like I tried to explain in the hospital, it all comes down to choice."

"Whether I make a kill or not."

"You all sin, Joey. It's human. But for you to make the mistake and kill, to drink another human's blood, that would be devastatingly bad."

"So right now, have I still got a soul?"

He nodded. "And it's why I'm here."

"Why?"

"Because. God has a plan for you," he said.

"And what is that plan?"

"It's not my place to tell you. And in fact, I do not know what the plan is. What I know, right now, is that He wants you to help Father Daly, and Cardinal Bonsignore," Wayne said.

"And kill vampires?" It didn't sound right, not like something God would want me doing.

Wayne laughed and shook his head. "Not kill. Save."

"But you said if a half-breed like me takes a life, drinks human blood…"

"If you kill someone, Joey, if you murder a person, there is hell to pay. Right? But if you are sorry for that sin, if you ask God's forgiveness, will He give it to you?"

I shrug. "It's what I've always been taught."

"And do you believe that?"

"I have to. It's what my faith is based on. Otherwise…"

"Otherwise Christ's death on the cross was for nothing," Wayne said. "So if a vampire repents, asks God's forgiveness and turns from their sin, do you believe God will forgive them?"

"Yeah. I guess He would."

"Absolutely He would."

"But, once a vampire has human blood, how can they just stop drinking?"

Wayne was silent.

"They'll die, won't they? They stop drinking blood and ask God's forgiveness, and then die. Is that what you're saying?" I asked.

"God wants you to help the Pope's team."

I laughed. I didn't apologize. "Do you think vampires will listen to me? They're hunting me right now. They want to kill me. They won't listen to me—I'll sound like some lunatic asking them to give up blood and follow Jesus. And then they'll kill me. It's crazy."

"Moses said the same thing, you know. When God spoke to him through a burning bush, Moses told God He was asking for the wrong guy's help. God wanted Moses to go ask the Pharaoh to release His people," Wayne said.

"That's not the same thing," I said. I pounded a fist into the couch cushions.

"It's not? Moses was a murderer, on the run. The Pharaoh needed his slaves to do work, to build his city. You think Moses thought he had a chance at all of convincing the Pharaoh to let the slaves go free? But you know what happened, don't you?" Wayne asked.

"It worked."

Wayne smiled. "It worked, yes, but because God never left Moses' side. He performed miracles through Moses, convincing Pharaoh to let the slaves go."

"I'm going to be able to do miracles?"

"Never said that." Wayne held up his hands. "I'm just saying you won't be alone. And, believe it or not—despite the cliché—He does seem to consistently work in mysterious ways."

I groaned. "But Cano and the others, they aren't going to let me stand side-by-side with them."

"Let God worry about the semantics. That's His job."

"Right. I'll let Him take care of the semantics."

"It's all I'm asking."

"Are you my burning bush?"

"Apparently. No bushes in the hospital. None in here. Guess God figured flames inside would be hazardous. That was a joke."

I didn't feel up to laughing. Not anymore.

Thirty-eight

With her senses heightened, Carissa sensed that more than just her father and mother were in the house. She landed in the front yard, between trees, and glanced to her right as Dean set down beside her.

She hugged herself, eyes down. "Miguel," she said.

Dean's breath spilled out of his nostrils. He tilted his head back some and scanned the house. "He's here because of you, dear."

It was either from being dripping wet and cold or out of fear that she shivered. The sky looked black. She couldn't see the moon or the stars. She took tentative steps forward, pulling her weight along, worried she might have to ask Dean for help.

"Scared?" Dean smiled. He inhaled a deep breath, sucking in the crisp night air, nostrils flared. "Should be."

"Well, I'm not," she said. She forced her hands down to her side.

"You're a liar."

"You're an idiot." She planted each foot down hard on the frozen ground. Long, purposeful strides brought her to the door too quickly. If her heart beat, she knew it would be pounding behind her rib cage, the thud-thud-thud would fill her ears.

The door opened. Carissa gasped. "Father."

"Come in, Carissa. We've been waiting for you." Victor stepped aside, clearing her passage into the house. He did not smile, did not look at all glad to see her. The creases in his skin told her that he was worried, scared, perhaps.

"I'm sorry…"

He held up a hand to silence her. "It's not the time."

She mouthed Miguel's name.

"In my study. Go on in. I'll be along."

Carissa pursed her lips. The house felt cold. "I'm wet."

"Go and change, but don't waste time. We have lots to talk about."

Carissa turned around to see her brother bounce on his feet, tips of his hands tucked into his pockets.

"Wipe that stupid grin off your face, Dean. You might think this is a game, all some sort of ploy. It's not. This is serious. By now, I shouldn't need to explain all of this to you, and yet, I know if I don't you will continue not to get it." Victor spoke quietly. The edge in his tone of voice placed harsh emphasis on the last four words. "Carissa!"

Startled, she stumbled back a step. "I'm going."

She ran to the stairs, took them two at a time. In her room, she closed the door. She wanted to change into warm, dry clothes, but not so much that once done she'd have to return downstairs.

Donned in wool socks, jeans, tank top and sweater, she knew she could no longer delay the inevitable. Downstairs, it wasn't just her father who waited, but Miguel.

Dean had said he was here for her.

Dean said lots of things. Most only contained half-truths, she knew. He talked. A lot. Oftentimes it seemed like the only reason he said a word was to cause trouble, stir the pot, or to create doubt and chaos.

Miguel was downstairs. There was no denying that.

Joey.

Was he safe?

Marcus would help her, would help him. He said he would. He'd talk to Father. Things would work out. Had to.

But time… there couldn't be much left.

Those goons at the church had him. They could be hurting Joey, torturing him. They could have killed him by now.

"No," she whispered, her hands clasped together and pressed against the center of her chest. I'd know, she thought. If anything had happened to him, if anything bad had happened, I'd know.

As she descended the staircase, she concentrated on sounds. She hoped to pick up voices. Conversation. She heard nothing. When she entered her father's study, she understood. Both her father and Miguel sat in chairs across from each other with faces that looked chiseled out of stone, as if opening their mouths would crack the rock and their faces would crumble.

"Carissa." Victor sat in Katrina's chair.

Mother. Where was she?

She looked around the room, hoping to see her. Knowing that she was absent made her stomach drop. It confirmed Dean's threat—Miguel was there for her. What mother could stand to be around and witness the punishment she was sure to receive?

Rubbing her thumbs along her other fingers, Carissa managed to find the strength to walk farther into the room, up to Father and their guest.

"You remember Miguel, I'm sure." Victor sat stiffly, fleet planted on the floor, hands on his legs, eyes never leaving Miguel.

"Of course," she said, tried to smile. If she'd had a mirror, no doubt a grimace would have been all she'd delivered. She held out a hand. "How have you been?"

Miguel was on his feet before she knew what was happening. He stood behind her, took a fistful of hair and pulled her head back, exposing her throat.

"Where is he?" Miguel's breath was hot. She smelled his blood—or the blood from others that kept his body alive, although the rest of him was ultimately a long time dead.

She opened her mouth to speak.

Miguel released her hair. Her head shot forward. She cringed as teeth crunched, severing the tip of her tongue. When she screamed, he let her fall to her knees. She spit the pooled blood and piece of tongue onto the highly polished hardwoods.

On all fours, she twisted her head to look up at their leader. Miguel's face was contorted—hideous. Yellow and red eyes, black and corroded fangs dripped with strands of gooey saliva. Like a panther, he crouched and hissed in her face. Spoiled breath like the pungent odor from a corpse left rotting for weeks under an August sun sprayed from his mouth.

She refused to look away, or to cower.

If everything that went wrong was her fault, she'd accept whatever discipline was handed out, even if the degree of punishment equaled her death. But she would not surrender an ounce of self-respect. Not to Miguel, nor to her father, not even to Joey. If the alternative to keeping her head high was termination, then she'd go out with some dignity and pride.

"Where is he?" Miguel stood. In that instant, his transformation disappeared, as if he hadn't become a monster in the beat of a human's heart. He circled her father's chair once, and then stood behind it, hands planted on the high back leather.

"He's at the church."

Miguel shot Victor a look. Carissa went from staring at Miguel's eyes to his hands. Long, green and sharp finger nails grew, puncturing the chair's upholstery. "I did not ask you."

Victor rolled his lips into his mouth. "We don't have time for this. Dean has told us what we want."

Carissa lowered her head. She wanted to cry and wished she were capable. Why was he sticking up for her? Miguel would not tolerate it. In the end, they'd both suffer. Surely he knew this as well as she.

White chair stuffing billowed out from eight slash marks when Miguel ripped his hands away, spun around and stood pressing his head against her father's bookcases.

Speaking out of turn, when not spoken to, was not acceptable. Her father knew this. He'd made Dean aware of this rule countless times.

When her father stood, she stared at him. She did not have the strength to stand beside him, so with her eyes, she silently pleaded with him to sit, to keep his mouth shut. She shook her head, no, no, no.

Her father looked at her with a softness to his eyes like she'd never noticed in them. He nodded, and smiled a thin smile. "Miguel, Joey Rossi is at the church. He's holed up in there with the priest, and the Pope's team. It's only a matter of time before they work answers out of the half-breed, that's if Rossi didn't tell them everything all on his own, which wouldn't surprise me. He has no loyalty to us, to the family. . ."

Miguel laughed. With his back to them, he tipped his head and laughed a second time. "Loyalty? What an odd word to use at a time like this."

"Miguel, I spoke out of turn. For that, I'm sorry. Right or wrong, she's my daughter."

"She is not your daughter." He spoke with venom. Spittle sprayed from his curled lips. "Those wild boys out there, they are not your sons. When we say family, it is about blood, but not parental and maternal blood. You have no ties to the creatures you've created. You have no family. You have nothing."

Carissa lowered her head. She didn't want her family taken from her. She thought of her brothers. Her mother. Her father. This was her fault. All of it.

"Miguel, she is my daughter."

The silence that filled the room lasted for minutes. Miguel stood like a mirror statue to her father. Both refused to move a muscle, or to even blink.

She wanted to scream, pull hair out of her head, something, anything, as long as it shattered the silence. She couldn't move, not even an arm to wipe away the blood and drool that dripped from her lips.

"She's my daughter, Miguel. And those boys, wild as they might be, they are my sons. And Katrina, she's my wife. You might not consider that a family. They are my family. I will do whatever I have to to protect them. Whatever it takes," Victor said.

Miguel let the silence linger for several more seconds. It felt like minutes. Hours. "We need to get Joey out of their hands!" Miguel pointed at the window, as if Joey were just on the opposite side of the glass.

"And we will."

"And your daughter—she'll help."

"Absolutely." Victor sat in Katrina's chair. He crossed his legs. "Carissa, go get cleaned up. Come right back. We have lots to discuss."

Wanting desperately to see the look on Miguel's face, Carissa used every last bit of energy to refrain and push herself onto her feet. Her legs trembled. She wondered if her father sat down when he did because his legs felt the same. She wrapped an arm around her stomach, hoping she wouldn't puke before making it to the bathroom.

Thirty-nine

Lying on my back on snow staring up into a moonlit sky, all I can see are bare branches from the surrounding trees. Behind me I can hear fire crackling, smell smoke, hear whistling screams, something like live lobsters being dropped into a pot of boiling water.

"Carissa?" Did I speak? I can't feel my mouth moving.

And she's there. Beside me. She's on her belly, her chin on my outstretched arm. Her blue eyes look at me. Fangs drip blood onto my sleeve.

"I can save you," I said. "Can I save you?"

But what does that mean? If I save her, I lose her.

She smiled. "You can't save me, Joey."

Something is in the trees. Watching. Approaching. I can't look around, can't look away from Carissa.

"I can," I said.

She shakes her head as she pushes herself into a sitting position. On her knees, she looks back toward where I am certain a fire burns.

Something is snaking its way up my leg.

"Carissa—help me," I said.

She laughed. "Joey, Joey, Joey—you just said you could save me. You can save me, but you can't save yourself? If you are any kind of a hero, save yourself, then maybe I'll believe you can save me."

"It doesn't work that way." Teeth sink into my thigh. I strain to move my arms, to kick my legs. Nothing moves. "Carissa!"

Her laughs turn into cackles like something a wicked witch might spew.

"No!" I shut my eyes against intense pain; it burns. When I open my eyes, a giant serpent has snaked itself around her body, her neck, and its head is poised a few inches from her face, mouth open, fangs bared. "Carissa!"

She continues to laugh—cackle. Can't she feel the snake wrapped around her? Can't she see it? Doesn't she know it's about to bite her cheek off?

I'd been able to move fast in the church basement, like lightning. I wanted to grab the snake and throw it into the woods, or into the fire. My limbs didn't respond. I'd never given much thought to movement. If I wanted to stand, I stood. If I wanted to run, I ran. I didn't know how to make them move. It always just happened. Always, except now.

I tried thinking about my arm, stared at it, to no avail.

Like a shadowy blur behind Carissa, something walked toward us. Slow, stealthy steps, as if they thought they were invisible, approaching unnoticed. But I saw them. I couldn't see a face, but a form. I recognized the shape, but that did nothing to help my memory. I knew who it was, but didn't.

I tried opening my mouth to shout a warning, but my lips felt connected by gooey strands of glue. Speaking was impossible as the goo seeped into my mouth, slid over my tongue and down my throat.

I couldn't swallow. My esophagus was backed up. The goo filled my mouth, oozed from the cracks in the strands that bound my lips.

Like always, similar to all the dreams before, Carissa's chest exploded, chunking away the center of the snake, as well.

My arms shot out. "Carissa!"

I caught her shoulders, pulled myself up and laid her down.

Her facial features kept twitching and contorting. "Carissa?"

"You saved yourself?"

"I want to save you," I said.

Her lips curled and puckered, but never managed to form a smile, if that had been what she was trying for. "It's too late for me. It's not too late for others."

"What others?"

Blood gurgled in the back of her throat. Her head bounced on the ground. Her blue eyes lost their sparkle. She didn't blink. They didn't close. I knew she was gone. Finally dead.

"Carissa? Carissa!"

~ * ~

"Good. You're up. I wasn't looking forward to waking a dreaming vampire." Bri stood near the stairs, weapon raised, barrel locked on my head. I knew if I made a sudden move, she'd have no problem blowing me away.

"I'm up." I slowly brought my legs around and set my feet on the ground.

"How'd you get on the couch, out of the restraints?"

"Cano ties a terrible knot," I said, leaned forward and ran my hands through my hair.

"You didn't run?"

"Run where? Where am I going? I came here of my own free will. You just wanted to keep me here. Joke's on you guys. I'm not looking to leave." I stood up, watched Bri's body tense as I stretched, arms up, fingers pointing at the ceiling.

"Sleep well?"

"I don't sleep much at all," I said. I felt tired almost all the time. A pint of blood might cure the insomnia. Or, at the very least, feed me the energy to keep going. I suppose living as a half-breed might be comparable to suffering from a serious case of anemia. Can't imagine describing my condition to a pharmacist, looking for a blood protein supplement?

"He up?" Cano sounded like he was standing at the top of the stairs, all the way at the opposite end of the basement's hallway.

"Yeah," Bri shouted back.

"He send you down to get me?"

"Get you? No."

"Keep an eye on me, then," I said. She kept quiet. "So what's your plan? You all here to wipe vampires off the face of the earth?"

"Something like that." Bri held her assault rifle with both hands, stood with feet shoulder width apart.

"And you work for God?" It sounded sarcastic. Wasn't meant to be.

"Got a problem with that?" she asked.

"None at all." I shook my head. I wanted to tell her we had the same boss. Don't think my saying so would have gotten me open-arm welcomes. "So how does a nun end up in Rome working on special teams for the Pope?"

"We're done talking," she said.

I sat back down. I did not want her thinking me a threat. I wanted to build trust. Confidence. "I'm just saying, is all."

Tight-lipped, she kept locked eyes on me.

"I went to a Catholic school growing up. Great school. Loved it and the other kids. Even the classes weren't so bad. But the nuns—not all of them, all right, but most of 'em—they were the worst. Not like when my father was a kid and the nuns whacked his knuckles with rulers, and the priests threw punches—times were different when I was in Catholic school. The staff couldn't get away with hurting the kids, physically, that is. Mentally, that was another story," I said, shook my head, remembering.

"I had teachers like that," Bri said.

"You went to a Catholic school, too? Ah, right. Dumb question." I watched her, tried to get a read on her eyes. Wished I could climb into her head and listen in on her thoughts.

"Only, most of the nuns were cool. It was the old-school ones, they caused students the most grief," she said.

"They wore the old uniforms?" I asked, my hands flowed over my head, drawing a habit. For a minute, I'd thought my conversation would take this in the wrong direction. I was just looking for common ground. Agree or disagree, I knew if I could find that similar denominator maybe I could get some footing on my way up and out of the basement.

"Not the young nuns." She smiled, as if some memory flitted about inside her brain.

"When my dad was in high school, my grandmother worked in the cafeteria. So when my dad went through the line, she'd slip an extra burger into his bun. She thought she was taking care of her son, you know? But at the end of the line, by the register, a nun rang out the food, and a priest stood watching over her shoulder. My dad said he'd sweat bad, worrying about two things. Getting caught, and getting beat up in front of his mother," I said, laughing.

"You make us sound like monsters." Bri lost her smile. I'd crossed the line, pushed too hard, gone too far. The sarcasm was not lost on me.

"Sorry. Just talking," I said. "So what's the plan? Gonna kill me now, or later?"

Bri's eyes never left mine. She saw how fast I could move. If I wanted, I could take her gun before she realized a thing. She must have realized this. I know I'd thought about it. "I want to help," I said. "I think I can help."

Stonewalled. She wasn't having it.

"If you think about it, I'm the one they're after. I'm your bait. I'm willing to be the bait. Can't ask for more than that in a plan, can ya?" Nothing. Not a crack in her demeanor. "Tell Bonsignore. I'm not running. I'm not giving you a hard time. I'm staying right here."

I smelled Cano. He was coming down the stairs. I don't know if my senses have been this acute the whole time and I was only now recognizing the heightened awareness, and if maybe the ammonia and urine smell in the hospital confused smells—or if, over time, the ability to distinguish scents has become enhanced the longer I'm a half-breed. "Cano, I want to do what I can to… change the way things are."

He stepped around the corner, gun raised and stood beside Sister Bri. "Oh, and what way are things?"

"You want to take out the vampires," I said. I want to help them. "I can lead you to them."

"We know where they are, where they live." Aside from blood, I heard quick beating hearts. They acted tough. I scared them. Cano stood in such a defensive way I knew he just needed a small excuse to shoot me full of silver. I stayed still, not wanting to give him a chance at execution.

"So what about me?"

"What about you?"

"Why keep me around?" I asked.

Cano made a face and nodded. "No reason I can see, half-breed."

Forty

Victor knew the meeting would no longer be his. Miguel would run things. Trying to mask deflation, Victor led the others into the boardroom. With Miguel present, there was no need for lieutenants to accompany the clan heads.

They chatted as they sat in chairs around the long mahogany table. Sawyer sat by the window. He wore his hair long, like Victor's sons. Despite running most of Buffalo for just over half a century, the vampire was in his early twenties and liked to show off his solid build in tight t-shirts and baggy jeans.

Theron, who sat next to Sawyer, was pure elegance. Long, dark hair framed opaque skin and radiant green eyes. Her athletic build could not be covered, despite the wool sweater and ankle-length skirt.

"Please, help yourselves to drinks," Victor said, pointing at the pitcher and glasses on the tray at the center of the table.

Candace sat across from Theron. Although the two nodded a hello, the animosity between them was obvious. Victor thought their differences stemmed from jealousy. While Theron's presence exhibited beauty, Candace's brought about the perception of brute force. Tall and thick, Candace kept her hair short, cropped tight to her scalp. With pitted skin, dark beady eyes and a gravely voice,

Candace learned early to use her more masculine qualities to gain respect and authority.

"Ice?" Sawyer said, pouring blood into a tumbler.

"It's an acquired taste," Candace said, using tongs to drop cubes into her glass before pouring her drink.

Sawyer grimaced and sat back in his chair. "Think I'll pass on the ice."

Candace shrugged. "Why try something new, right?"

"Ah-geez," Sawyer said. He plopped two cubes into his glass.

Candace smiled. "Let it chill for a minute before taking a sip."

"Right," Sawyer said.

Victor watched Miguel, Demitri and Marcus enter the room, with Marcus closing the doors behind them.

"Miguel, would you like to sit here?" Victor said, indicating his chair at the head of the table.

He held up a hand. "Wouldn't think of it."

Victor would have preferred Miguel sit in his place. If the man was going to run things, he might as well do it from the head of the room, instead of like a representative seated between clan representatives.

While waiting for Demitri and Miguel to sit, Victor made eye contact with his son, and then looked at the seat at the far end of the table. Marcus sat there.

Demitri, a five foot four Puerto Rican, made his way to the chair next to Candace. "Why is Marcus here?" he asked.

Victor winced. "He's my son." He didn't need or want hostility. Everything had changed with Miguel showing up. The most he could now hope for was unity.

Demitri looked at Miguel. "And our lieutenants?"

"Marcus is fine," Miguel said, sitting down next to Marcus. "He can consider this an educational field trip of sorts."

Demitri *humphed*, but left it alone.

Victor avoided eye contact with Marcus, who watched him intently.

Miguel didn't pour a drink. Instead, with elbows on the table, fingertips touching fingertips, he sighed. The signal was clear. Forget the small talk.

"First," Victor said. "I want to thank everyone for coming."

"Why aren't the other New York families here?" Candace asked.

Victor tried to smile. "I thought it best to hit surrounding cities, not the entire state. I chose not to call them."

"The way you chose not to call me." It didn't take long for Miguel to speak up. Victor wasn't at all surprised.

"We've discussed that, Miguel. I wanted to handle the situation without involving you," he said.

"What you mean is you wanted to clean up *your* mess without getting caught." Miguel planted his palms on the table. Victor expected the man to leap out of his seat, maybe jump on the table, run at and tackle him in front of everyone.

"Perhaps," Victor said. No sense denying the truth. Miguel saw through lies, was able to pick up even the slightest infliction in person's tone of voice. "Regardless, I wanted to make things right, while attracting as little attention as possible."

Marcus looked like he might speak. Victor shot him a stern look. "For what it's worth, I'm sorry."

"Save your 'sorry.' Not interested," Miguel said. "What solution do you have in mind?"

"One, we need to get Joey Rossi."

"Which, from what I understand, you've tried a few times and have failed." Miguel wanted this to be difficult, no doubt.

Victor nodded and chewed on the flesh inside his cheeks to keep from saying something he'd be sure to regret. "We know where he is," Victor said.

"You knew where he was," Miguel said.

"My other sons are watching the church, from a distance. I checked in with them just before we closed those doors. Rossi is inside the church with the priest and the Pope's team," Victor said.

Miguel slowly looked at the faces of those seated around him. His roving stopped when his eyes fell on Marcus. "And the police?"

"Haven't been around," Victor said, a lame response. "With no bodies, there is no way to match descriptions to missing persons. It's just Rossi's word against, well, it's just his word."

Miguel closed his eyes, sat back in his chair. "And the money?"

Victor wanted to stand, pace. He shifted his weight in his chair, leaned forward and rested his elbows on the table, fingers laced. "It's not good. The market's a mess. We've lost a substantial amount the last few months. It isn't just the U.S. dollar that's failing, it's currency across the globe. I'm monitoring everything, shifting money and completing transactions to ensure security."

"And can you ensure our security?" Miguel drummed fingertips on the mahogany and raised an eyebrow.

"We're not in any trouble right now," Victor said.

"You're good with numbers. Always have been. It's why you run the finances for my families. I don't want you to think I'm unhappy with your work. I'm not. I see what's going on. I check your activity daily. You seem on top of the trends, a step ahead in many cases." Miguel pulled his hand from the table, caressed his chin. "We need to control spending. Essentials only from here on out. Blood costs are constantly on the rise. It's a commodity. Our suppliers know this. They've jacked up prices by a couple hundred percent."

"I didn't get a shipment last week." Candace swirled her drink. Ice clanked against class.

"Demitri, make a note of that," Miguel said. "My point, we need to tighten our belts. All of us. Victor, I want you to cut each stipend payout by ten percent."

Sawyer was the only one to groan out loud.

Miguel got to his feet. "Problem?"

"No, Miguel. No problem." Sawyer smiled, thin lips resembling an equals sign. He placed a hand on his stomach, as if to indicate the pain came from the belly and not the wallet.

"Victor?"

"Yes?"

"You are on your own." Miguel stuffed his hands in his pockets and twirled around, stepping to stand behind his chair. "This is your mess. Yours. Your… family's. Not ours. And you were out of line to include the other families. Out of line!"

Victor winced. He'd heard Miguel raise his voice at others, never had it been directed at him. "If we stand together…"

Miguel waved a hand. "We're not standing together. Your daughter messed up, bad. Your incompetent sons have failed repeatedly to clean things up. You are not dragging us into this battle. None of us. You are on your own. The last thing we want, or need, is to give any intelligence to the Pope about our infrastructure, our size, our location, not to mention our very existence. Do you know how long it has been since the Vatican has rallied a team to hunt vampires? Any idea? Eighteen-seventy. That's right. Have they hunted witches? Yes. Satanists? Yes. Vampires? Not in over a hundred years. Until now. Until you brought them to New York. It's your mess. I suggest you clean it up. Quickly."

Victor lowered his eyes. This was not what he'd expected.

"And then I expect you to clean house. Your kids run amuck." Miguel stood by the door, hand on the knob ready to leave. "You can't be expected to run our finances if you can't run your own family. No one will respect you. Without respect, what have you got? You got nothing. Nothing."

Miguel pulled open the door. "And Victor, let me warn you. I want this to be clear. If your half-breed goes on a killing spree, if he draws police attention, makes headlines of any kind, I'll be back. You don't want me coming back."

Miguel turned and strolled out of the boardroom as if leaving a restaurant after a filling meal. Sauntering, hands back in his pockets, Miguel made his way toward the front door.

"It's what I told you," Sawyer said. "This is your business. Not mine." He stood.

"I'm sorry, Victor," Candace said, drained her glass and set it on the table.

Theron and Demitri finished their drinks, stood and silently followed the small procession out of the room.

Victor looked across the long table at his son. Marcus refused to lift his chin. "I'm sorry, Father."

At a loss for words, Victor merely shook his head and closed his eyes, wishing this could all be part of some nightmare. The rational side assured him it was not, and that closing his eyes was synonymous with burying his head in the sand. It was time to devise a plan and fight. Miguel might have washed his hands of everything, but that didn't mean he wanted out of the loop. He'd demand progress reports and expect resolution immediately.

"Call your brothers," Victor said, opening his eyes. "It's time to put an end to this disaster, and move forward."

Forty-one

David Bonsignore and his team stood around me. Once again, my wrists were secured around the pole. Father Daly stood across from me, arms folded in silent protest.

"Why didn't you run last night?" Bonsignore talked like he thought he was tough. Sure, he was big, strong, but tough? I wasn't so sure.

"I think I can help."

"Like we can trust him!"

"Cano!" Bonsignore silenced the priest. "Because you think you can help, you didn't run?"

I thought about Wayne, his words, God's plan for me. I shook my head, lowered my eyes. The jury was still out on whether I was crazy. "We don't have to kill the vampires."

Cano laughed. "See what I'm saying? He doesn't want to help us. He wants to help them, his kind."

"I'm not like them," I said. I twisted my head around, but still couldn't see Cano.

"We have an objective tied to our mission, Rossi," Bonsignore said. "We were sent here to execute vampires."

"But what if they can be saved?"

"Saved?" It was Bri. She leaned her butt against an old desk. For the first time I can recall, her weapon wasn't pointed at my head, and the way she held the gun was casual.

"We don't have time for this, Dave. You know we don't."

"Cano!" Bonsignore furrowed his brow, intensifying the stare that focused on the priest standing behind me.

"What if the vampires were offered a choice?" I said. I locked eyes with Father Daly. "Like I've been."

"You've been offered a choice?" Cano laughed. "Dave…"

"Can we just let him talk," Daly said. "Maybe you guys have spoken to tons of vampires, and I know you've been trained on how to handle them, but for me this is all new. Regardless, I'd think it improper to act without looking at all the points before jumping to any sort of action."

"Go ahead, Rossi. We're listening," Bonsignore said.

I explained to them why I was a half-breed because I hadn't made a kill and drunk human blood. "Wayne says…"

"Wayne? We back to him? Back to that?"

Cano got on my nerves.

God, help me find the right words to explain this, I prayed. *Help me not mess this up.*

"We all have free will. God made us that way. Whether we sin or not is up to us. But when we sin, and we all sin, if we ask forgiveness and turn from that sin, God forgives us. Am I right?" I asked.

"We're listening," Daly said.

"These vampires need to hear about Jesus and salvation. They need to be told they can still save themselves, still redeem their souls. Heaven is still a possibility for them, if they ask for forgiveness and turn from their sin," I said, hoping what I said made sense.

"Those soulless vampires murder people. You told us yourself that you witnessed two girls get butchered," Cano said.

"You're right," I said. "But when Jesus was up on the cross, two criminals were nailed to crosses on either side of him. They were close to death, bound for hell, I'd assume."

"So?" Cano said.

"One of them asked God's forgiveness, and what happened?" I said.

Silence filled the church basement. They knew the answer, of course. The point had been made.

"That's different," Cano said.

"How so? Did Jesus forgive the one who asked?"

"He promised a place for him in Heaven," Daly said.

"Are vampires any different than the murderer Jesus forgave?" I asked.

"I can't see a difference," Daly said.

"We can offer Carissa and her family a chance to find God, rather than just destroy them," I said.

"But they've had human blood. They can't go without it once they've had blood, can they?" Bri asked.

"No. Their bodies would require human blood." I kept my eyes on Daly while I spoke. He seemed to sense where I was going with this.

"So how would they…"

"They'd die. Starve to death," I said. "But their souls would be saved."

Cano stepped into view. "Are you kidding me? Are you for real? You want to make this a missionary mission? You want to, what, hand out pamphlets on God to vampires?"

"Yeah. I do."

"And what if they don't want salvation?" Bonsignore asked.

"Then we can't help them," I said.

"And where would you be in all of this?"

"By your side," I said to Bonsignore.

"If they refuse Christ, we'd have to kill them," he said.

"I could help."

"Help, how? You just told us you're a bleeding heart for the monsters," Cano said.

"Cano!"

"No, Dave, no. Why are we listening to him? This guy is one of them."

"He is not," Daly said. He stood up straight, arms at his sides. "He is clearly not a monster. You know it. I know it. And what he's just said—it makes sense. Something about his words resonates within me."

"What are you, a literary scholar? Resonates?"

"Cano—I don't want to hear another word!" Bonsignore suddenly looked tough. His words came out with bite. Muscles bulged and rippled in his arms and chest as he flexed. Cano stood down.

"We should offer them the chance at salvation," I said. "It doesn't seem right to go about it any other way."

Bonsignore sighed. "How do we do this? Invite them over for coffee and cake? We sure can't talk to them about God during a fight. It wouldn't be safe for us having our guard down."

"Let me talk to them."

This time Bonsignore laughed. "How are you going to talk to them?"

"Let me go," I said.

No one laughed. Bri tensed, changing her lackadaisical stance to full attention alert, her finger on the trigger.

"It's no ploy. I could have left any time. Still could," I said.

Cano snorted, tossed his head back. "Dave, tell Rossi here how it is."

"What would you do if we let you go?" Bonsignore said.

I'd given the plan some thought during the night. It wasn't flawless, and if anything promised danger—for me. "The Tantalos are hunting me. They want me. They're out there now—I sense them. I think I can smell them."

Bri shifted her weight again. Her eyes scanned the ceiling, as if her eyes could cut through the rafters and floorboards allowing her to see outside.

Cano looked all around as well, as he talked into a walkie. "Brandon, you see anything up there?"

Static-hiss. "Nothing."

"You looking out the windows?" Cano asked.

Bonsignore and Daly just looked at me.

"Going window to window. Nothing out of the ordinary," I heard Padilla's voice squawk from Cano's radio.

"They're out there," I said, assuring them.

"Okay. So the Tantalos want you. They're after you," Bonsignore said. "If we let you go, what happens? You going to run to them, or away from them?"

"To them," I said. "I'm done running away. They'd just keep hunting me, tracking me. My life has already been turned upside down, ruined. Running won't get me anywhere. What am I supposed to do? Go back to work? Pretend to live some kind of normal life?" My stomach gurgled. I looked to see if anyone heard. Hunger pains bit at my belly, gnawed on my nerves throughout my body. They didn't realize with all of them standing so close to me, all so worked up and excited, that their blood pumped furiously through their veins. It was like a fresh baked apple pie set on a window sill to cool, the aroma reaching out to tempt anyone within range. I was within range. To say I was tempted would be like saying an alcoholic is thirsty.

"Why not? Why can't you just fit back in with society? You're trying to convince us you're not like the vampires out there, that you're different," Bonsignore said.

"I'm not like them," I said. "But I'm certainly not normal. Not anymore. It wasn't something I asked for. I've mulled this over and over inside my head. I'm alone now. More alone than I'd been.

"When my wife was sick, I thought I could prepare for her death. There was no getting ready for it. The house was so empty without her, as were my days and nights. Months and months did nothing to ease that sense of seclusion that fell over me. But now, it felt worse. I wasn't even human anymore. I wasn't a vampire, either. I hated to say I was 'a man without a country,' but I was. I was a man without a race."

"I'm just not following you," Bonsignore said. It was a thoughtful response. He didn't understand where I was coming from. I couldn't blame him. I wasn't sure I understood anything much better.

"You let me go, I'll go to Carissa's brothers. In a sense, I'd be surrendering. Or they can claim they captured me. Whatever. Once they have me, as long as I'm not killed on the spot, I'll try talking to them," I said.

"Try to convert them to Christianity," Cano said. Again, he let out a crude snicker.

I couldn't scold him for snickering. I suppose I'd snicker, scoff, mock, too. It sounded ridiculous. An impossible task.

Impossible for me.

God worked weird miracles though, didn't He? "Think about Saul," I said. I closed my eyes. It had been some time since I'd read from the Bible, and equally as long since I'd been to a church service. Although I thought I'd forgotten much of what I'd learned over the years, so much seemed to be coming back, re-filling my memories.

They stared at me with blank expressions. I shook my head. "You know Saul," I said, perplexed.

"Of course," Bri said. "But you're not seriously comparing vampires to Saul?"

"Yeah, I am. If you think about it, Saul caught, tortured and killed Christians. It was his job. It's what he'd been taught to do from the time he was a child, from the time he witnessed the stoning of Stephen. And what happened to him? On his way to Damascus…"

"This isn't Bible study, Rossi," Cano said.

"It's important," I said, staring at Cano. "It's real. It's happening. Outside this church, people just like Saul are waiting to catch, torture and kill people. But God blinded Saul, spoke to him, and allowed him the chance to see the light and turn from his ways. Saul became Paul, who in turn became one of the strongest, most prolific disciples of Christ. Even the apostles, who knew the power God possessed, were afraid that Saul's conversion was a lie, that he was pretending to be a Christian in order to track them down and kill them. But it hadn't been a lie. God worked a miracle in that conversion. A miracle."

"And you think God wants to do more miracles, through you, by letting vampires accept Christ—starve themselves and die—in order to save their souls?" Bonsignore continued to ask sincere questions. I liked that. He was pondering everything said. Unlike Cano, he wasn't racing toward judgment.

"That's what I believe," I said. It's what Wayne told me. I saw no reason to share my burning-bush with them. This Pope-assembled team struggled with me enough without pressing the Wayne-issue. "I have the feeling, if we can save one, it will make a world of difference."

Silence filled the small, musty room.

I didn't break it. They were thinking. Even Cano.

"I think we need time to pray about this," Daly said. No one snickered. All of them nodded in agreement. "Joey, will you join us in prayer?"

Forty-two

Victor had Marcus call Antonio and Dean, then told his family to wait for him in his office.

The meeting with Miguel and the bordering heads hadn't gone well at all. He hadn't been sure what to expect once Miguel showed up uninvited, but a complete boycott had never crossed his mind. It wasn't that he blamed Miguel and the others for treating them like diseased undesirables; in fact, he understood where Miguel was coming from. The problem stemmed from something more internal, paternal. Despite living in separate cities, he always thought of the other covens as extended family.

Maybe that was the overall problem. No one else considered their ties blood-bound. *Paisani.* He might be the only one who looked at everyone else as if they were related. Family stuck together, not just during good times, but especially during the bad. If you didn't have family to count on for support, what did you have? You had nothing, was what you had.

Victor stood outside his closed office door. Everyone he loved was on the other side. He never felt so isolated and alone. He knew he could count on his wife and kids. They, at least, understood the commitment involved with being a family. Family was everything, all-important, and essential to surviving the span of time before them.

Rogue vampires existed. They kept to themselves. Hunted on protected territory, and continued to do so until detected and taken out. How many rogues had he put to death? How many times had he looked in their blackened eyes and seen nothing? No love. No anger. No sense of recognition. Rogues were more like animals than vampires, than humans. They existed in the wild where they hunted, fed, slept. Rogues kept instinctively on the move, never staying in one place too long, less they risk getting caught and dealt with by the likes of Victor and his sons.

It was hard to wonder at times if the carefree lifestyle of a rogue might not be the better way to live life as a vampire. No one to answer to. No one to worry about.

He heard the voices of his family through the office doors. Katrina laughed.

No. The rogues had it wrong. Backwards. They were the ones missing out. Their existence was lost and inconsequential. Once extinguished, they were gone and forgotten. No legacy left behind, no fond memories for family to recall and share and savor.

Victor sucked in a deep breath as he pushed open the office doors. Katrina offered up a warm smile. The situation was bad. They all knew it. Only the woman who loved him so unconditionally knew his nerves could be calmed with one of her smiles.

"I," Victor said. "I am upset. I am so upset."

He knew he didn't sound it. His voice was soft and casual. It took tremendous control not to yell and scream and throw things. He strode into the room, to his chair, and kicked it over.

No one moved.

"We are going to handle this situation on our own." Victor stood facing the window, his back to everyone. He didn't want to see their expressions. "I want Rossi. Now. And as far as the Pope's men, they're dead. They may not know it, but they are."

Victor knew it was Dean who hissed, the way any parent could identify the cries of their own child. "They'll be coming for us. We're not going to be on the defense, though. No. We're not waiting. We'll be on the offensive. We're going for them."

"They're holed up in a church," Dean said.

Victor spun around and hissed. Thick, dark ruts distorted his face, bulging over inset glowing red eyes and highlighted by elongated white fangs. "They can't stay in there forever," he said, his voice turned to gravel. He breathed heavily, saliva pooled behind his lower lip drooled over the side of his mouth and dripped in long strands off the end of his chin. "They're dead. All of 'em."

When he slammed his fist onto the end table, it made a loud thud. It took a moment for the split wood to wobble before the furniture fell in two halves, and the lamp in the center crashed to the floor. The light bulb flashed brilliant blue before the glass shattered with a pop.

~ * ~

After an hour of silent prayer, Bonsignore asked Daly and Joey Rossi to go to the basement. They'd all asked for God's guidance and wisdom, but now it was up to the team to decide what would be best for the mission. Unless there was a clear sign from above, they'd have to figure out a plan and stick with it.

"Dave, you aren't really considering letting Rossi go, are you?" Cano stood with his back to the sink, his hands propped on the countertop.

"I think Joey might be sincere. If he can get the monsters to surrender, if it is God working through him..." Bri did not finish her sentence.

Dave knew God answered prayers all the time. It was just that the cardinal wasn't always sure he recognized an answer when it was in front of him. Could Cano be the voice of reason, which meant not letting Joey go? Or was Bri the one he should listen to? He hated the shades of gray and longed for black and white. "What are your thoughts, Padilla?"

"Man, you ask me, we take care of Rossi and then we go after the others. The sooner we clean up this city, the sooner we go home." Padilla sat at the table and stared while his fingers intertwined with one another. Did that suggest internal conflict?

"We could put a tracking device on Rossi," Dave said. "We'd know where he was at all times. He'd lead us right to the Tantalo family."

No one looked surprised when Cano spoke. "How many did Rossi say there were? Five? Six if you count his vampire girlfriend? If we let Rossi go, even if we track him, if we're wrong about his intentions, then there will be seven of them. Worse. If Rossi tells them about us…"

"Like what?" Bri asked.

"That there's four of us. That we're heavily armed. That we have God and silver and blessed Holy Water and Bibles. That we're coming for them with the sole purpose of annihilation. We lose our edge a bit, don't you think? We lose any element of surprise." Cano's shoulders and chest heaved with each sentence. "Want my opinion? I don't like it. Daly's no help. He's almost more on their side than ours. What's up with that?"

"It's not Daly's fault. He's a simple congregation priest. He is trained to look for the good." Dave walked over to the basement door. He stood silently, listening. He didn't think the two down there were on the stairs listening, but wanted to be sure.

"He did call the Vatican," Padilla said. He pushed away from the table, tipping the chair onto its two back legs and balanced himself in this position for a brief moment before letting the chair come to rest on all four legs. "I like the guy. I trust him. He seems morally sound."

"I agree," Dave said.

"I was just saying," Cano said, spinning around to face the window.

"We need to move. We've been in the church too long. That's my fault," Dave said. "This is your first mission, and my first mission like this. I apologize. I didn't expect this to be as complicated as it's become."

"It's because of Rossi," Padilla said. "He was an unforeseen variable."

"Thank you, Padilla. I appreciate that, but no. This is all on me." Dave closed his eyes, adding extra personal prayers to the one they'd said as a group. *God, I need an answer. Please. What are we supposed to do?* "The only thing I know for certain is we're past waiting. It's time for action. It's time to get to work. And I think the best move will be to put a tracking device on Rossi…"

"Do we tell him?" Bri asked.

"No. Although some can read minds, not all vampires can. They may sense a trap, but might not realize it's a tracking device. Better still if Rossi doesn't know what's on him. We're out of options. This seems like a best bet." Dave laced his fingers together and let his hands fall in front of him. "Get the cross."

~ * ~

Father Daly and I sat on the old sofa in the basement. We were silent. Despite straining with my keen sense of hearing, I couldn't clearly make out anything being said upstairs.

"There's two options on the table," I said.

Daly nodded.

"They're either going to kill me…"

"I'm not going to let that happen."

I nodded, as if I believed the priest. His intentions might be good, but he'd never stop my murder. He was sworn to follow the laws of the church. If Bonsignore deemed my death necessary, Daly risked his vocation if he got in the way.

"They're either going to kill me or let me go," I said. "And I've got to be honest, Father, I'm not sure which way I'm hoping to see the tossed coin land."

"You're scared. I understand that," Daly said.

Scared was an understatement.

"I believe everything you've told me, Joey. Everything. I'm not a sucker or easily fooled. I don't send my parishioners to Mexico for healing when a statue bleeds, or cries, or to touch some wall that displays the features of Jesus on mold and chipped bricks. I know that miracles happen. I know that evil exists. What is happening now—it's a bizarre combination of both."

"You believe me about Wayne?"

"What you've told me can only be true," he said.

"How can you say that? You didn't see him, hear him, talk to him. You have my word. Right now, I'm the least likely trustworthy person I can imagine," I said.

"I disagree. What's going on is surreal," Daly said. "Vampires? I didn't think they were real. I felt so foolish calling the Vatican. I grew up watching Vincent Price movies, Dracula and all of that. I was almost certain the training I'd received on witches and vampires and cults was a trick."

"A trick?"

"Like a test. If a priest called, confessing vampires infested his parish, the Pope would know that particular priest was burnt out, in need of a sabbatical." Daly smiled and laughed. "I never expected some mercenary team to be dispatched by the Pope to come and kill legendary monsters."

I laughed, too. "Yeah, that's just crazy."

Daly laughed a little harder. When he composed himself, a solemn expression softened his features. He set a hand on my shoulder. "Joey, God wants you to do something for him. For whatever reason, He's picked you. Is it all right to be scared? Absolutely. Is it all right to refuse God? That's your call. That goes back to the whole free will thing you lectured us on. But if they decide upstairs to let you go, then you know you've been commissioned by God to carry out a mission of your own."

I bowed my head. "So what do I do? Got some fatherly advice?"

The door at the top of the stairs opened. "Father? Rossi? We're ready for you," Dave called down.

Daly stood up. I looked at him. He smiled.

"My advice is simple. Keep God close. Talk to Him nonstop. He has called on you. If you need Him, He'll be there, ready to guide your every step." Daly turned to leave.

I followed him up the stairs.

In the kitchen, I couldn't help but feel like I was walking into some kind of Star Chamber proceeding.

Bri stepped up to me. "We want you to wear this at all times," Bri said. She stood in front of me. I could hear her blood course through her throat. It smelled sweet. Wonderful. This realization sickened me. I wanted to vomit, but at the same time, I felt so hungry I feared I might begin drooling.

Everyone stood silent. Watching. They seemed to be waiting for something to happen, collectively.

I lowered my head so she could loop the cross over my head. For just the flash of a moment I envisioned the cross slamming into my chest and burrowing a searing hole through my flesh.

That didn't happen. I was wearing a shirt.

"We all have one. It's for protection," Dave said. "The fact that you can wear that cross without dying is a good sign."

I looked at the cardinal, who raised an eyebrow as if he'd been struck by an epiphany of some kind. "You thought this might kill me?"

"It was a possibility. If you were a vampire, it would have caused you a great deal of pain at the very least," Bonsignore said.

I exhaled, at a loss for words. They were letting me go. Either they believed I could save souls, or—more than likely—they wanted me to lead them to the Tantalos. Either way, I'd have a head start. I wasn't sure how much time I'd have to try and convince, or try and convert, vampires who had lived their lives a certain way for God only knew how long.

"Let's start with this… tell us as much as you know about each of the vampires," Bonsignore said. "I want to know what they look like, what they act like. Anything. Everything."

"I don't know them that well. Carissa. I knew her," I said.

"You at least know what they look like, right? That will help." Bonsignore crossed his arms.

"Yeah," I said. "I can describe them."

Forty-three

I left the church with two things: the Bible from Wayne tucked under one arm, and the cross from Bri around my neck. Although tempted to look back as I walked toward Carissa's vehicle, I didn't. I knew I'd see faces practically pressed to the glass watching my every step.

I turned the ignition, and while Carissa's car heated up, I brushed snow and scraped ice off the windows. The entire time I thought about what my next step might be. There was really only one way to go about this. Head on.

I climbed into the car, shut the door. The heat was turned up too high. I felt the blast coming out of the vents. It did nothing to warm me. The chill was internal, but was it eternal? I hoped not.

Was I getting worse, becoming more like them, like the Tantalos? How long could I survive without drinking blood? I worried I might be dying. The hunger was that intense. The idea of food didn't appeal to me. I couldn't recall the last time I ate. It had been days.

As I shifted into reverse I wondered about animal blood. Would that curb my desire? Was that a sin?

I needed nourishment if I was going to fight this battle. I had to believe the Tantalos were well fed, keeping them strong, focused.

Was it possible I was supposed to live what I preached and abstain from nourishment? Did God want me to die as well, to sacrifice my life as I worked to save the souls of those infected, or inflicted with whatever turned mortals into living dead beings?

I drove with both hands on the steering wheel. The car fishtailed as I pulled onto the main road. I turned into the skid, correcting the spin as I drove toward Webster.

"Here we go, God. If you have any ideas, I'm all ears," I said, and turned on the radio.

~ * ~

There was no flying during the day. That was a no-no.

Marcus followed his sister's car and tapped on his blue tooth. "Dad? I'm following Rossi. We're on One-o-four West."

Victor laughed. "It couldn't be… could it?"

"He's headed toward Webster." Marcus stayed several car lengths back. Rossi drove the speed limit. He stayed in one lane. If he was aware of the tail, he gave no indication, or didn't care.

"He's coming here," Victor said.

"Looks like it." Marcus licked his lips. His tongue ran over sharp teeth. He winced. Blood dripped from the wound. He sucked on his tongue, extracting the fluid and swallowing it.

"We'll be in position," Victor said.

The line went dead. Marcus shut off the blue tooth.

~ * ~

"Headed toward Webster," Father Daly said. He sat in the back seat, looking out the window. Bonsignore watched him through the rearview mirror, knowing the priest felt uncomfortable with using Rossi as bait.

"Bri, tell them what's up," Bonsignore said.

Bri used the two-way and called Padilla and Cano in the car behind him. "Daly says he's headed for Webster."

"I miss the old days of car-tag," Cano said. "Tracking devices take away all the fun. Since you got the monitor, can we at least take point and pretend we're playing some follow the leader?"

Bonsignore shook his head. "Tell him to keep his distance."

"Don't let them see you," Bri said.

Laughter came back over the two-way. Bonsignore checked his mirrors. Cano signaled and changed lanes. He and Padilla passed on the left.

"What's car-tag, and follow the leader?" Daly asked.

"It's almost impossible for one car to follow another without being detected," Bri said. "Especially if the person you're following is keeping an eye out for a tail. Using two cars is better, but three, even four is best."

"Why?"

"You let one car follow the mark for a bit." Bri twisted around, moving the seatbelt strap away from her head so she could face the priest. "Then, when you have some kind of sense of direction, a second car comes up behind the first, and the first can turn off at an exit, or drive past them. This lets the new car follow the mark even longer, without it looking suspicious."

Daly nodded. "So with three and four cars, you can, what, leap frog for longer periods?"

Bri smiled. "Exactly. With one car, as soon as the mark spots you—if they make lefts and rights, and see the same car still behind them, the gig is up."

"But with the tracking thing Rossi's wearing?" Daly asked.

Bri held up a palm-sized electronic device. A red light blinked on and off nearest the bull's eye on a screen of rings. "Right. He's not going anywhere we won't know about."

Static from the two-way filled the car. "Dave," Cano said.

Bonsignore nodded at Bri.

"Go ahead," Bri responded.

"We got vampires following Mr. Rossi," Cano said.

Bonsignore looked at Bri and then back at the road. He saw Cano's car about three cars ahead, and Rossi's maybe another six car lengths ahead of them. On the three lane highway, cars surrounded them.

"What have you got?" Bri asked. She sat facing front, set the radio aside, reached down between her feet and pulled her gun out of a duffle bag.

"I'm keeping back some, switching to the far right lane. No. No. It's merging to two lanes," Cano said.

"After the bridge it's two lanes," Daly said as they crossed over the Bay Bridge, the expanse of Lake Ontario to their left, the Irondequoit Bay, which looked partly frozen nearer the shore, on the right.

"Cano, stay a few cars behind the tail," Bri said, and looked up at Bonsignore.

"Must be. They had to have been watching the church." Bonsignore shifted his weight around, feeling restrained by the seatbelt and being as far behind the others as he was. "Ask Cano which car he thinks is the tail."

"Cano, which car you watching."

"Big black SUV. Tinted windows."

Bonsignore found it easily. It was two cars behind Rossi, and one in front of Cano and Padilla.

"Let me see the radio." Bonsignore held out his hand. Bri handed over the radio. "Cano, why do you think it's vampires? Can you see into the vehicle?"

"Negative. Can't see a thing."

Bonsignore looked over at Bri. "Why vampires? Cano?"

"They got vanity plates, sir. Rear plate reads Tantalo."

"Keep back, Cano. Stay the speed limit."

"Got it," Cano said.

Bonsignore handed the radio back to Bri. "Our boy's not going to have much time to preach. If the vampires are following him, they know what we know. Rossi's headed right for their house."

Bri looked over her shoulder, straining to see out the back window. "Think we're being followed?"

"I've been checking the mirror. Haven't spotted anything." Bonsignore sucked in a deep breath. It felt like pure adrenaline was coursing through his veins and arteries in place of blood. His heart hammered away. "Weapons check."

"Did it before we left," Bri said.

"Do it again. Call Padilla, tell him to do the same. This is going to come to a head soon. We need to be one hundred percent ready, one hundred percent!"

Bonsignore watched the SUV signal and switch into the exit lane.

The radio squawked. "Dave? Dave? You want us to follow the SUV?"

"Tell him, no. No. Stay with Rossi." There could be other Tantalos in the city. It wasn't that unique a name. "We are not dividing. We stick together, we stick to the plan. Tell him!"

Forty-four

I'd only been to the Tantalos' house once. Although Carissa and I had been talking, and I hadn't been paying complete attention to where I was headed, I felt confident I could find the place again. Couldn't be that hard. The huge house sat on a hill, a bluff, overlooking the lake.

I took the Maple Avenue exit, made a left on Maple and followed it down to Lake Road and made a right. I knew where I was now. It was either because I remembered how to get to Carissa's house, or because I remember Sodas Point, that everything looked familiar.

My brother-in-law brought me fishing at Sodas Point, at least a few times a year. Saturday mornings he'd pick me up. We'd stop at a bait shop for worms, and Dunkin' Donuts for coffee. I was never a fisher. I learned so the two of us would have something in common. Even though we spent most our time silently sitting beside each other, I can't recall better bonding moments between the two of us.

I saw the house as I got closer to Sodas Point. Just like I remembered. Big, like a mansion. It sat alone up on the hill. I found the driveway off Lake and started the ascent. Winding my way up, trees, like two forests, lined both sides of the driveway. Despite mostly bare branches, the density from the tall tree tops blotted from view most of the afternoon sunlight.

I concentrated on driving, getting closer and closer to the house. If I didn't, I knew my mind would wander, and I'd be stuck letting fearful thoughts fill my head. Carissa's family scared me. I'd sensed evil coming off them like cooked onions off grilled fajitas.

I was so hungry. Thirsty.

How long had it been since my last cigarette?

Too long.

I thought about old movies with firing squads. The idea of a blindfold and cigarette held alluring qualities I didn't care to dwell on. Not right now. If they time arose, if I was caught and sentenced to death, I might just ask for both.

I shook my head. I needed to jar loose the negative thinking. *God, clear my mind of junk. Please. Keep me focused.*

Even with the windows up, the heat and radio on, I could hear the car's tires crunch loose gravel as I reached the house. I stopped as I reached the last hundred yards of driveway, which, unlike the rest of it, was blacktopped and smooth. This was also where the "forest" ended. Snow covered the yard. Behind the house I saw white caps on rolling waves.

Nothing about this property, about the house, about the town, would lead anyone to suspect blood suckers were among us. The place, the view, was all so breathtaking. Bow windows, wrap-around porch, three car garage, off-white aluminum siding, solid wood double door entrance. There had to be fifteen to twenty rooms. The Tantalos' house could easily serve as a bed-n-breakfast, or Marriott.

I eased the car up the driveway and parked it up by the first garage door. I let the engine run, gave the heat a few extra moments to attempt warming me and then climbed out of the car. I held the Bible in my hands, up to my chest, and took in a deep breath.

They knew I was here. Had to. Although I didn't see any, I'd bet anything a number of surveillance cameras watched my every move.

Or maybe they didn't need that type of security. My enhanced sense of smell, hearing and sight were amazingly powerful as a half-breed. Hated that word. As full-fledged vampires, how much more intense were their powers of awareness?

The icy air burned as it entered my lungs. I sniffed to no avail at the wind as it howled and whipped around me. Although Father Daly had lent me his long, black trench coat, it did little to protect my body from the brutal assault Mother Nature unleashed.

As I walked toward the front door, I couldn't help but feel like I was being watched, my every step monitored. I tried to spot cameras, but saw none. I scanned windows as I walked past them, expecting to see Victor or Katrina or someone on the other side of the glass, but didn't.

At the bottom of the steps that led up to the front door, I paused. Time was limited. Bonsignore and his team weren't going to wait long before coming after this coven, if they actually planned to wait at all. They might have left the church soon after I did. More than likely I've led them directly to the Tantalos' house.

Turning to look back to where the driveway disappeared into the woods, I wasn't ready for the attack.

Caught off guard, Dean came at me from the sky like a bullet. He flew with his head up, and the rest of his body stiff and straight. At the last fraction of a second, his arms shot out from his sides. Talon-like fingernails cut through my shoulders, and dug into meat as I was lifted off the ground.

The Bible fell from my hands as I fought to ease the searing pain in my neck and muscle. I latched onto Dean's arms and tried pulling myself some, so that I supported my weight in my biceps, rather than by nails buried in my flesh.

Just as I got a good grip, Dean released me—his long nails slipped out of gaping, bleeding holes. I didn't look down. We had soared just above the housetop. That much I knew. He must have meant to drop me. I wouldn't let go of his arms.

"Set me down," I said. I wouldn't be able to hold on long. I was losing blood. Alive or living dead, I knew losing blood couldn't be good. At least six deep punctures ran along my back and chest, from where he had latched onto me.

"I'll set you down." Dean's eyes were completely black, while his cratered skin reminded me of white chunks of coal, shiny and ragged, sharp and ridged. When he laughed, his breath belted me in the face. Putrid, like forgotten Easter eggs hidden under a sofa only discovered accidentally when crushed and the rancid aroma escapes from the shattered shell in a mushroom cloud of bile stench.

He brought his forearms up, pulling me closer to him as if lifting a baby out of a stroller. When his forehead came racing at mine, I did not have time to avoid the smack. It wasn't like in the church basement when I could move five times as fast as the Pope's team. Here, in this element, in Dean's world, I was the slow one.

My nose crunched against his skull. Blood sprayed from my nose. My eyes watered and burned. Instinctively, I let go of his arms to cover my face.

I plummeted, fast. With no time to think, when my legs hit the ground, I let my knees bend to absorb the impact, and I fell to my side and rolled. If bones broke, I didn't have time to assess the damage. By all means, my legs and feet should have shattered my ankles.

I jumped up and ran toward the woods. Everything seemed to be working, at this point even though pain filled the upper half of my body. Ignoring a broken nose and pierced flesh, I concentrated on escaping.

I heard Dean laughing, closing the distance between us. My mind's eye imagined a hawk swooping down to scoop up petty prey, and just when I felt he was inches from impaling me with Krueger nails, I dropped to the ground. The snow did little to pad the frozen earth below. My chin slammed into a rock buried under a fresh layer of billowy snow. I grunted, and looked up. Dean had flown by.

I scrambled to stand. My feet slipped on ice. I planted bare hands in cold snow and pushed myself up, all the while watching Dean turn around just inside the thicket of trees. I decided to run for the car, but as I turned to look for it in the driveway, Antonio crashed into me.

Although I expected my back to smack against the ground, I never fell. Long spikes stabbed my back and under my arms.

Something howled, and shrieked in obvious anguish and pain. A full thirty seconds later I realized I was the one making all the noise.

"Let's get him in the house," Antonio said.

Wanting to fight, wanting to make another run for it, wanting to beg to be set free all sounded like great ideas. Instead, I gave no resistance as they hoisted me into their arms and carried me toward their house, and, oddly, it made sense to close my eyes and try to sleep. Just before letting my eyes close, and darkness to surround me, I caught sight of the Bible on the ground, kicked up snow, and droplets of blood sat on the leather cover.

Forty-five

"C'mon, wake up."

I heard the words, vaguely, as if spoken in a whisper from across a crowded room. It was the ice cold water that splashed against my body that caused my eyes to open wide.

My head lolled from side to side, but it took strength to lift it, to see who was treating me like a campfire. Everything looked hazy. One thing registered. I was naked, naked and suspended off the ground. Chained at the wrists and ankles, my limbs were pulled taut and spread in an X. The weight of my body was supported by my arms. Blood covered my chest and thighs. It must be dripping from at least a dozen deep wounds. I didn't know enough about my new condition to know if I could die from hanging like this. Sure felt like I could.

"Look at this." Dean stood, cuddling an empty bucket in his arms. "He's awake."

I had no problem closing my eyes and going back to sleep, if sleep, in fact is where I had been. Might have been a blackout caused by a concussion. Either way, I did not wish to be here, alert, at their disposal.

I thought about Carissa.

"I want you to let me down now."

"Ok. Let's let him down now," Dean said. He walked slowly forward, as if in a trance. He stopped when he was inches from my face, then reached up for one of my wrists.

"Dean!" Antonio stood at attention, ready to coil and spring.

"Antonio, you will help Dean set me free?" I said. I willed them to do my bidding.

Antonio's expression lost focus and became more lackluster. He walked up to me and reached for my other arm.

I couldn't believe this was working. It was so simple.

And then the wind was forced out of my gut. I gasped, trying to figure out how my rib cage could have collapsed into my lungs.

"Are you kidding me?" Dean took a step back. "Is he kidding me?"

Antonio let knuckles berate against my chin. My head snapped to the left. I let it stay there, me ear using my shoulder as a pillow.

"You can't use that on us. It only works on dumb humans and weak-minded people, Rossi."

"It's why I tried it on the two of you," I said, immediately regretting having spoken.

Antonio used my body like a punching bag, and I figured if he ever got tired of sucking people blood-dry, he had a real chance as a heavyweight contender. Eventually he paused, perhaps to assess the, what felt like, irreparable damage inflicted.

A cell phone rang. Dean looked at the display on it.

"Where's Carissa?" I said. I wasn't sure they could hear me. Maybe I'd only thought the question. Either way, they didn't respond and acted like I wasn't in the room.

"We got him, Marcus," Dean said. "In the basement. Antonio just went up to get Dad." Dean nodded at Antonio and the shooed him away with his hands.

Antonio looked at me, smiled and winked, before heading toward stairs.

"Don't be too long," I said. "I'll get lonely."

Wisecracks helped me keep sane. Otherwise I'd be crying. Somehow I don't think crying would do me any good.

Dean snapped his phone shut. "You know, I'm kind of sorry it's come to this," he said. He walked toward me, hands stuffed into pockets. "You're not so bad. Carissa's got a good eye. You'd a made a nice addition to the family."

"You know," I said, careful to save wit for if things turned—worse. "I came here for a reason."

Dean nodded, slowly. "And I'd love to hear why. Because to be honest, what you did, coming here, is about the dumbest move, but one I'd never have seen coming."

"I'm not here to fight you, or your family," I said.

He laughed. "No kidding? Of course you're not. It's not what I meant. It's not what I thought."

"What'd you think?"

"You came to get my sister."

Good point. "In a way, yes. But I'm here for another reason." I was thankful for the time alone. I felt one-on-one I'd be able to make a stronger case for salvation. If the coven was together, they'd reject the message as one. Peer pressure and all that.

A door squeaked. I tried to move my head toward the sound. Steps creaked. Shadows came toward me. Antonio was back and behind him stood a solemn Victor.

I closed my eyes. My head dropped, my sore chin banged against my chest. Although I didn't know what to expect, the position I now found myself was farthest from my imagination. In short, this was not good.

God, if you're hanging around, I'd love a hand, I thought.

"Rossi was just telling me, that aside from plans to kidnap Carissa, he was coming here to kill the rest of us," Dean said.

I winced as my eyeballs rolled behind closed lids. "It's not true," I said. Welcome thoughts of that blindfold and last cigarette filled my head. "I came to talk."

"The time for talking passed long ago. The time for begging, gone," Victor said. His voice boomed. If my hands were free, I'd have covered my ears. The words he spoke reverberated inside my skull, bouncing off my brain like a ricocheting bullet.

"Do you want this life?" I said. "To stay this way?"

Someone snickered. Had to be Dean. No one answered. I swallowed, tasted my own blood as it slid across the back of my tongue, igniting not just a hunger but a perverse desire to feed.

"There is a way to put an end to who you are," I continued.

"Who *we* are." Victor insisted on talking in a loud, deep voice, reminding me of *Mufasta*, the great James Earl Jones.

"I'm not like you," I said.

Dean laughed. I opened my eyes, forced my head up, my chin off my chest. I didn't think as a vampire I needed to breathe. Maybe as a half-breed, the laws—the requirements to exist—were different.

"But there is a way," I said.

Sweat, or blood coated my eyes. I saw the three of them like looming dark shadows. Victor stood between his sons.

"Tell us about the team of assassins," Victor said. He stood with his hands folded in front of him. He wasn't the muscle. I had no doubt if he wanted, he could inflict additional hurt on my already aching body. Why would he dirty his hands when his sons weren't just capable, but more than willing?

"God has not given up on you," I said.

All three hissed at me.

Antonio's fist seemed to manifest out of thin air. I saw it, only as it was clobbered against the side of my skull. Inside I screamed, lacking the energy and strength to vocalize the agony.

"What do the Pope's men plan to do? Where are they? When can we expect an attack? How many are there? What weapons have they come with? Do they know you're here? Did you escape from them? Did they send you?" Victor shot the slew of questions at me, as if his jaw were part Tommy-gun.

If I answered one or all of Victor's questions, they'd kill me sooner. I wasn't here to stall, but neither was I in any hurry to die. There was work to do.

I coughed, choking on blood. I suspected I was in fact dying. Slowly. My shoulder blades and back muscles felt stiff and sore. I kicked my legs as much as I could in the tight restraints, hoping to get a footing in order to eliminate the strain on my upper body.

"Hose him down. The site of his filth is making me sick," Victor said.

Dean disappeared from my view, stepping back into it a few seconds later. He squeezed the spray gun on the end of a garden hose, and icy water rained on me.

"Clean him off good," Victor said.

The raining became more centered and hard, as blood and sweat and dirt was hosed off my body. I shook, shivering. My teeth chattered.

"Get used to it. Warmth, as you knew it, is nonexistent," Antonio warned.

"Doesn't have to be that way," I said, before the water shot into my face, filling my nostrils and mouth. I spat, and turned my head. The firing of water followed me. Dean, no doubt, enjoyed the assigned task.

"Why would we want to be mortal again? Why would we want to surrender this wonderful existence? And even if we did, Mr. Rossi, even if we longed to be mortal again, you want us to believe that you have the ability to complete such a transition?"

It was the first question asked by Victor that I wanted to answer, but couldn't. Fireman Dean did not relent. I couldn't catch my breath. I might be drowning. Why was this any different than when Carissa and I swam along the bottom of the river? Maybe I wasn't dying, and it only felt that way. Was it possible that I could be tortured forever, without receiving the satisfaction of death?

No. I hadn't eaten. No blood had passed my lips and filled my gut. I would die without blood. This much I knew. It was why I was here, to ask them to consider the same, voluntarily.

"Enough!"

The water stopped.

"There is a way to save your soul," I said.

"But we'd still be vampires, wouldn't we?" Victor asked.

"You would," I said. Cold water rolled in beads down my raked over flesh. "But when you die, there'd be a place for you in Heaven."

This got a laugh out of them. Winning them, even one of them, over seemed out of reach. I was failing at my mission. God had to be disappointed in choosing me, an inadequate spokesman.

"Heaven?" I didn't expect Victor to taunt, seemed beneath him. "God has damned us from the beginning. There is no way, now, He'd invite us home."

Home. It was not the word I expected to be spoken. Even though Victor had never been to Heaven, it was like instinct, something passed down from vampire to vampire all the way back to Lucifer and his fallen angels, that he said the word with certain warmth and longing.

"You're wrong," I said.

Antonio ought to change his name to lightning. His backhand slammed into my already bruised and broken nose, flattening cartilage and shattering more bone. "Watch your mouth!"

With swollen flesh, and puffed and closing eyes, I wasn't sure I'd ever see anything, much less be able to watch my mouth.

"I'm sorry, Mr. Rossi, but we have no time for *what ifs* and fairy tales." Victor backed away from me. "Your friends will be here shortly. And I want to be ready. Store-bought blood is a wonderful delicacy, but it has been some time since I've hunted for my own food, and I must admit, I'm rather looking forward to it." He turned around. At the stairs he stopped. "Think your God would still be willing to work with the likes of me?"

"I do," I said. As my head dropped to my chest, I caught Victor look at me before climbing the stairs out of my torture chamber that was their basement.

Forty-six

"They've got surveillance." Cano consulted a hand-held device. "Cameras everywhere." He looked up at treetops, and through the woods.

"The house must be at the top of this road," Bri said.

"Think it's a driveway," Padilla said. "No street sign. Mailbox at the end."

They stood outside their cars at the bottom of the Tantalo driveway. "Let's find a place to park. Come back on foot. Plenty of trees to use for coverage. Cano, can we jam the cameras?"

"Absolutely," he said.

"Good. Let's go."

They got back into their cars and pulled away, looking for a place to ditch the vehicles.

~ * ~

Marcus drove around the bend and turned up the driveway. He sped to the top as his cell rang. It was father. "Yes?" he said, answering the phone.

"Where are you?"

"In the driveway. I took a side road, hoping the mercenaries would follow me."

"They didn't?"

"No. They stuck to Rossi."

"Then they're close," Victor said.

"If they're not already here." Marcus saw Rossi's car and parked next to it. "I'll do a perimeter sweep before I come in."

"We've got nothing on the cameras. If they were on the property, we'd know."

Marcus shut the engine. "My guess, they're regrouping now that they know where we are. Probably devising a plan of attack."

"Come on in. We're in my study."

"Yes, Father." Marcus snapped his phone shut and climbed out of the SUV. He stood, scanning through the trees for any sign of movement. The snow would be a wonderful ally—footprints would be impossible to hide.

~ * ~

"Joey? Joey?"

Kelly? Is that you?

"Can you hear me?" Cold breath filled my ear. The voice was just above a whisper.

I opened my eyes. Not Kelly. She was dead.

"Carissa," I said. I tried to swallow. My throat felt dry, raw. I closed my eyes again. Keeping them open hurt too much.

"I'm going to get you out of here," she said. Her hands grabbed the chains and bracelet secured around my wrist.

I groaned. My arms had been in the same position so long that her jarring sent pain shooting through my body. "Stop, stop. That hurts," I said.

"I'm sorry," she said. "But I need to get you out of here. They're planning to kill you."

I started to nod my head, but stopped, fearing it might fall off my neck. Lightning Antonio must have jarred my brain loose, too. Something felt like it sloshed around inside my skull. "I'm not going anywhere," I said.

"I can get you down. I know a way out," she said.

"I didn't come here to escape," I said.

She paused. "You came for me?"

"I did. I wanted to talk to you—you and your family," I said. This wasn't going to be easy. Her family hadn't given me a chance. Carissa might. But what would happen after I said all I needed to say? She'd leave me, that's what. I didn't want to be alone anymore.

"Talk?" she said. "Talk? Joey, they are preparing for war upstairs. And once they finish killing the Pope's small army, they plan to come down here and finish you."

I slowly shook my head. "That doesn't make sense. They could have killed me already. Your father could have had one of your brothers end this. What's the point of tying me up? Leaving me till last? They aren't planning on killing me. They're going to offer me another chance."

Carissa stared into my eyes. She smiled a thin smile. "That's not what's going on," she said.

"It's not?"

"You're down here because they want to break you, they want you to suffer. They are going play with you, tempt you with blood and watch you squirm. You've brought the family more trouble and exposure in the short time they've known you, than anyone else ever dared. No, Joey, they're not giving you another chance. They're going to just enjoy killing you slowly." She looked away, pulled away, stepped away.

"I still didn't come here to run," I said. I thought about what she'd said. I didn't wish to be tortured. So far, it had been terrible, but bearable, if that made any sense. But how much more could I take? "Right now, though, I could use help."

"You need blood," she said. "It will heal all these wounds. You'll get your strength back."

"I can't."

"Not human blood. Animal blood. I can get it, bring you some," she said.

I thought about it. Although I loved Carissa, I worried about being tricked. If she fed me human blood, would that be different than me killing and drinking the blood on my own? "Animal blood?"

"There are rabbits all over the place. I'll be back in a few minutes," she said.

"Carissa, will animal blood change me?" I asked. "Will it complete my transformation?"

"It won't. And it won't help you as much as human blood, but it will help. It will heal."

"Hurry then," I said. I licked dry, split lips. "I want us to talk, so please, hurry."

Forty-seven

I felt confident I'd get sick. Vomit. Drinking blood did not appeal to me. It revolted me. Yet, as Carissa brought a glass to my lips, despite peeking at the thick fluid sloshing around, the smell caused me to salivate.

"Drink slowly," she said, cupping her hand behind my head. "Not too much, okay?"

I closed my eyes. Warm blood touched my lips, thick like syrup. The aroma shot straight into my nose. The smell alone seemed to do wonders for my energy, releasing hormones inside my brain. I imagined it wasn't much different for a starving homeless person who is next in a soup line.

My lips parted. Carissa tipped the glass. Blood poured into my mouth. Copper and sweetness tickled the buds on my tongue. I savored the flavor for just a moment before swallowing.

Once the first gulp made its way down my throat, raw hunger took over. My lips, my darting tongue, fought for more. Carissa continued to tip the glass, all the while cautioning me to slow it down.

There was no way to drink slowly. The thirst seemed insatiable. When there was nothing left to swallow, I licked all around the inside of the glass, the way a child would clean the bowl after making a cake with his mother.

"How do you feel?" Her words sounded muffled.

All I could hear was my beating heart, and other noises coming from inside my body. *God, what's happening?*

For a moment I actually think I felt myself get stronger. Was it possible to feel muscles grow?

My vision cleared.

"You're healing." Carissa said, setting the glass down at her feet. "Please, let me get you down."

"We don't have long," I said. The blood quenched my physical thirst. I wanted more. So much more. For now, though, the rabbit blood offered enough sustenance to help me focus once again. "We need to talk."

"First, we're going to get you down," she said. She grabbed the chains and cuffs. I expected pain to wrack my body. I even closed my eyes in anticipation. But nothing happened. In fact, I was able to pull with her. Together we snapped the chain. One down. Three to go.

Once freed from the wall mount, I sat on the ground, shivering. The vampires promised I'd never feel actual warmth again. A disturbing thought, disheartening.

Carissa laid a blanket over me. "I'll find your clothes."

"Please, later. Later," I said.

She kneeled in front of me. "What is it you want to talk about? Why did you come here? You had the chance to escape. You could have been free."

"I wouldn't have left you," I said.

She reached for my hand. "I'm not worth this."

I smiled. "To me, you are. That's why I wanted us to talk. Our time on earth, it's limited. Even if you live for centuries as a vampire—it's limited. It will come to an end."

She shook her head. "What are you talking about?"

"I'm talking about forever, Carissa. Eternal life."

"I have that. I tried to give it to you," she said, sounding apologetic.

"What you are, your parents, your brothers, that's not eternal life. You do age, and you will die. And when that happens, you will have to stand before God. And He will pass judgment on your life," I said. "If you turn away from this life you live, you vow never to drink human blood, if you ask God's forgiveness—your life can be saved."

When she let go of my hand, I knew we'd reached a pivotal point. As she got to her feet, I worried I'd lost her. "Joey, if I stop drinking blood, I'll die in a matter of months. I've heard of vampires starving themselves before. It's not pretty. It's not like you just become weak and complacent and pass in the night. That's how humans go. We don't die that way. It's ugly. We age. Our flesh rots. The final days are filled with constant pain."

"But you will have something to look forward to, an eternal life in Heaven," I said.

She took two steps back. "And what about you? Are you going to starve yourself? You just let me feed you blood."

"Animal blood," I said. It felt cheap. Like I'd latched onto a loophole. "Can you live on that?"

"I don't know. I don't think so," she said, as if it would be like going from prime rib to Spam meals.

"Would you consider giving it a shot?" I asked. I didn't know the ins and outs. I didn't know if God had rules against animal blood for nourishment. Was it all blood he wanted them to abstain from ingesting, or human blood specifically?

"I need to get you out of here," she said. "You said what you wanted to say."

"I need to talk to your family about this," I said.

She laughed. "Joey, they are not going to listen to you. What you just told me, if you told that to them, they'd impale you on the spot."

"That might not be so bad," I said.

"Please, let me get you out of here," she said.

I shook my head. "Are you going to come with me?"

"I have to think about things." She looked at the basement stairs for a moment before lowering her eyes. "I could do that, drink animal blood. I could give up human blood. I'm not sure it would be for God. It would be so I could stay with you."

I nodded. I wasn't positive if God would accept that type of conversion. It had to do with following me, not Him. If I had to guess, it wouldn't cut it, but was still better than nothing at this point. "Find my clothes," I said.

"We'll leave?"

"Not yet. Soon," I said. First, I wanted to find Victor and the rest of his family. I needed to persuade them to listen to all I had to say. The decision then would be theirs.

Forty-eight

Bonsignore led his team back toward Tantalo property, leaving Daly with the cars. They walked along the side of the road, hoping not to attract attention. Each of them carried a duffle bag filled with enough weapons that, if the police stopped them, they could bet they'd be detained for a while. As soon as they could, they stepped into the trees, counting on the woods to conceal the approach from people in cars driving by.

They wore light, voice-activated headsets. Thin-wire microphones sat positioned in front of their mouths. "Radio check," Bonsignore said.

"Check," Bri said.

"Check," Padilla said.

"Check," Cano said.

"Cano, the cameras," Bonsignore said. He wore gloves without fingertips and blew into cupped hands.

"Working to jam them now," Cano said. "There. It's done. Their monitors should be showing nothing but static."

Bonsignore stopped in front of a cluster of trees and set down his bag. The others did the same. "Let's get ready. We have no time. Once they see static, they'll know we're here, just not where we are."

Cano knelt by his bag, unzipped it and removed a basket of arrows. He strapped it on his back, and quickly practiced reaching over his shoulders into the supply of carbon arrows. When he removed the crossbow, he held it with delicate hands, and stared with eyes wide. "I love this thing," he said. He removed an arrow from the basket and loaded it onto the crossbow. "Look at that tip. It's solid silver. Four blades. There's no pulling this out of an entry without bringing chunks of innards with it."

Bri groaned as she removed hand guns from her bag and placed them into holsters on her hips, and one down around her calf muscle. She strapped a belt across her chest and shoulders, replacement clips for her guns in place for easy access and quick reload.

Padilla squatted next to his bag and removed three items: a sword, Chinese throwing stars, and a semi-automatic machine gun.

Bonsignore, like Bri, holstered three handguns and secured extra clips to a shoulder harness. "We have a read on Rossi?"

"He's in there," Bri said. "It's a strong reading."

"Yeah, but is he trying to show them the light? Or is he plotting with them on the best way to kill us?" Cano said.

Bonsignore ignored Cano. "We ready? Leave the rest, but get it out of sight."

~ * ~

"They're here," Katrina used the walkie-talkie feature on her cell. She stood in the security room on the first floor. She'd spent most of the day watching monitors. She'd seen Rossi and Marcus come up the drive. When nothing but snow filled the five screens, she knew the time had come. For a moment she closed her eyes. This would have been so much easier if Miguel hadn't of cut them off from the others. United, they'd have cleaned up the mess in a heartbeat. Divided, the battle might be more vicious. She could not bear the thought of harm coming to any member of her family.

She let out a long, agonizing hiss as she transformed from mistakenly human, to unmistakably dead. Fingernails dug through plaster as she ran from the room, down the hall and toward the front door.

~ * ~

"Victor!" I stood in the kitchen. The house was far too big to search. "Victor!"

"What are you doing?" Carissa, behind me, placed a hand on my shoulder. "We need to leave. Now."

"I can't," I said. "Victor!"

Marcus appeared in the kitchen, arms folded and a sinister half-smile on his lips. "Dear sister, why do you insist on bring this family down? You're playing with our food."

"We're leaving," Carissa said. "You can't stop us."

"Not only will I stop you, I'll kill him while you watch," Marcus said.

"I'm your sister," she said.

"You're an embarrassment. You think only of yourself, your own loneliness. We have survived for centuries and centuries because we've been able to set emotions aside. You're more like the rogues out there, lost and wandering. And I can't understand why, You've had nothing but the best. A supportive, educated and wealthy family isn't enough for you?" Marcus walked toward us.

"I want to help," I said.

"Oh yes. Father told me. You can save our souls. Offer us a place in Heaven, is it? Thanks, but no thanks. I like who I am," Marcus said. He hissed, mouth wide, fangs dripping wet.

"But when you die…"

"I won't," he said.

"You will," I said.

Marcus swept his arm over the island between us. Everything on it fell to the ground. It sounded like thunder when pots and pans struck the marble tiles. "Come here," Marcus said.

"They're here!" It was Katrina yelling.

It was the best distraction I could hope for, but I had no plan. I wasn't here to fight and definitely not to kill. Running was not even an option. "Our Father," I said, eyes closed, concentrating on the words I spoke. "Who is in Heaven, Holy is His name…"

Marcus hissed, but so did Carissa. They fled the kitchen, together.

"Carissa," I yelled.

~ * ~

"Katrina, no!" Victor was at the top of the stairs, Dean and Antonio beside him.

Katrina threw open the front doors and ran outside.

"Get her," Victor shouted.

Dean leapt over the rail, and flew toward the front door.

Marcus and Carissa ran into the alcove and looked up.

"Father?" Marcus said.

"Your mother ran outside!" She wasn't supposed to do that. The house was a fortress. The Pope's team would never have gotten in. The plan was simple, to pick the others off, one at a time, and would have worked.

"Help your brothers," Victor ordered.

Antonio jumped the rail and flew after Dean and Marcus.

"Carissa," Victor said, but it was all he could say. He knew she'd not be able to help. Maybe Miguel had been right about her. Uselessness had no place in the family, and as much as he hated admitting it, Carissa was useless.

Victor watched her turn from him and run deeper into the house.

Rossi, he thought. She'd come from the kitchen. Rossi was in the basement. He descended the stairs running.

He rounded the corner and found himself staring at a dressed and completely healed Joey Rossi.

~ * ~

"Padilla!" Bonsignore said into his radio.

They came through the trees and stationed themselves around the perimeter, one at each corner of the property.

"I see her," Padilla responded. "Target's mine."

Padilla held a star like a Frisbee as he centered his attention on the woman. He flung the star with all his might. It flew silently through the air.

A flying man exited through the front door, knocking the woman to the snow. The star embedded itself in the house with *slithump!*

The two looked up, and back at the star, then right at Padilla.

"Sir?" Padilla said. "I missed."

"Saw that," Bonsignore said. "Hold your position. Bri, circle around. Do you have Padilla in sight?"

"I do."

"Be ready," Bonsignore said. "Cano. Don't move from your position; watch the back of the house."

Bonsignore held a gun in each hand. Training was officially over. Fighting automated, mechanical monsters in the Vatican was long gone, but hopefully the skills acquired were not forgotten.

The vampires stood up and rocketed into the sky.

"Padilla?" Bonsignore called into the radio.

"I lost them," he said.

They could be anywhere. Despite a gray, sunless sky, he couldn't spot the creatures anywhere. "Be ready. Bri—eyes open."

Padilla unsheathed his sword and held it with both hands. He spun left and right, head moving, ready for the attack.

Bonsignore kept an eye on the front door. He moved slowly to his left, trying to get closer to Padilla without giving up his own location.

Another vampire flew out the front door. He landed in the snow, a few feet from the door. He stood with hands on his hips, looking from left to right.

When he pointed at Bonsignore, a chill ran up and down the cardinal's spine.

The vampire did not fly off, but instead ran right at him.

~ * ~

Padilla saw them before he heard them. He took two giant leaps backwards. They came at him from opposite directions. The woman would reach him first. The man looked like more of a challenge.

Taking the offense, he ran at the woman. Since he'd seen Carissa, he figured this had to be Katrina, the mother.

She didn't slow up like he'd suspected. She might even have been smiling. It was hard to tell. Her face was contorted, and her eyes looked like they might be on fire.

As Katrina came at him, he dropped to the ground onto his back and slashed outward with the sword. He heard a gunshot ring out as well. Bri must have fired from her position. The blade tore open Katrina's gut as she flew by, dripping guts to the ground before she crumbled and rolled into a tree.

"No!" The other thing screamed. Had to be Dean, the youngest. It was the black eyes that gave up his identity. He stopped by Katrina.

When Dean looked over at Padilla, he wiped his mouth on his sleeve and then stomped toward him.

Padilla slipped getting to his feet. He steadied himself, held the sword out in front of him and then pulled it back, ready to swing.

"That," Dean said, "was my mother."

Padilla swallowed.

~ * ~

Bonsignore raised his weapon. Before he could fire, the vampire changed direction and ran toward Padilla.

He covered his ears when something shrieked. The vampire that had come at him was now crouched on the ground, lifting the dead woman in his arms.

One down.

Padilla screamed. The noise nearly blew out Bonsignore's eardrums. He pulled the earpiece from the radio away from his head. "Bri!" he shouted.

"It's got him—I don't have a shot," Bri shouted. "I don't have a shot."

Bonsignore ran toward the monsters. He saw the one had the woman in his arms still, but his attention was turned.

The other male vampire had lifted Padilla in the air. It took Bonsignore a moment to realize what he was seeing. The thing had impaled Padilla with his hand. The vampire had buried his arm up to his elbow into Padilla's gut. Padilla's body jerked, twitched.

Bonsignore had the shot. He crouched. Aimed.

He fired.

The vampire spun, lowered Padilla and used the priest as a shield. The silver bullet slammed into Padilla's back.

The vampire shook Padilla off his arm, like sliding a bad piece of meat off a fork.

At the same time Bonsignore heard a shot, the vampire flew up and was lost in the tree branches.

Bonsignore spun around. The dead woman and the other vampire were gone. The cardinal looked up. He saw nothing.

"Bri?" Bonsignore said.

"I got off a shot. Missed."

"Same here," he said. "Cano?"

"What's going on guys?" He spoke fast.

"Padilla's down," Bonsignore said. He knew the priest was dead. Now was not the time.

"Is he all right? He going to be okay?" Cano said.

"We'll see," Bonsignore said. He knew Bri was listening to the exchange, and knew she'd seen enough to know he wasn't being completely upfront with Cano. "Anything on your side, Cano?"

"Nothing."

"Watch the sky, too," Bonsignore said. "I'm going to center myself to the front of the house. We need to figure out where everyone is. One's down. The woman."

"Carissa?" Cano asked.

"No. It wasn't her."

"The mother," Cano said.

"Yes," Bonsignore said. "Padilla took her out."

"That a boy, Padilla," Cano said. "Buddy?"

"He's not wearing his radio," Bonsignore said. That would tell Cano things were worse than he'd initially made them sound. The lingering silence confirmed this.

"Action?" Bri said.

"Three brothers. The father. Carissa," Bonsignore said.

Forty-nine

"Mr. Rossi." Victor stood stiffly. "You look well."

"Let's talk this through," I said. "There doesn't need to be a fight. Not between us, you and me. And not with the Pope's little army."

He laughed. "You have the authority to call off the Pope's mercenaries?"

"Authority? Let's say there's an agreement in place. If I can convince you and your family to change, then they will not... do what they were sent here to do," I explained.

"Like Abraham?" Victor said.

"Abraham?" I asked.

Victor cocked his head to one side, clearly amused. "Sodom and Gomorrah. God told Abraham he was going to destroy the cities. Abraham worried for the innocent. He pleaded with God to be allowed to first go and warn everyone so God's followers could flee and be saved."

I knew the story. Abraham said if he could find 50 worthy people would God spare the city. God said He would. Abraham, perhaps, knew that despite the size of the city, he'd never be able to find 50 good people. He then asked God if he found 40, would God spare the city, and then 30, then 20 and then 10... in all instances,

God agreed to spare the city if good people were found. In the end, Sodom and Gomorrah were destroyed. "I just want to help," I said. "Is it so wrong to ask you not to kill and drink human blood?"

Victor laughed. "Do you know how long I've been like this? So long, I don't know any other way. And blood—I love it. It nourishes and heals me. It keeps me young and full of life."

"But it's not real. It won't last," I said.

Victor took two aggressive steps toward me. The island between us was an ideal barrier. "Victor, if not for you, then your family. As a father, don't you want what's best for them?"

Victor lowered his eyes.

Was it possible? Was he listening to me? Was he considering the alternative? "What if you consumed a diet of animal blood until we could find a way…"

"Father! Father!"

Victor spun around and ran from the kitchen. I followed.

Marcus was in the foyer. Katrina lay on the hardwoods.

"No," Victor said. "What happened? Who did this?"

"Dean got the man responsible," Marcus said. He looked at me over his father's shoulders, as Victor fell to his knees and cradled his dead wife in his arms. "You're responsible."

"I did not harm Katrina," I said. "I came here to talk. Not to fight."

"Talk?" Marcus got to his feet. "All of this, all this trouble is your fault. Yours!" He pointed at me. Hissed.

"Marcus, I…"

"You brought them here."

"I came alone."

"They followed you. I followed you. We might have well been driving in parade procession," he said.

"I did not bring them here."

"You told them about us," he said.

He was right. I did. "Marcus…"

"Where's Dean, and Antonio?" Victor asked.

"Dean flew away. I, I don't know where he went. I haven't seen Antonio."

Victor lowered his face to kiss the top of Katrina's head. He rested his cheek on her hair. "Kill these monsters," Victor said. "Kill them!"

~ * ~

Cano looked up. He had to watch the sky? Would they really come from up there? Being told the vampires flew was one thing. Seeing a flying person—vampire—was quite another.

Spinning in slow circles, Cano watched the sky and the house and the woods around him. The air felt colder than just moments ago. The temperature seemed to be dropping rapidly.

Cano shivered. As he came back around to the house, he jumped back. A large man with blue, gunmetal gray, eyes stood in front of him.

Antonio.

And then the man changed. His eyes went from blue to yellow, to orange, to crimson.

Bile slid up Cano's throat.

The pupils danced around inside the eyeballs, like a burning flame. Cano watched wrinkles first appear on Antonio's face, then deepen, and then darken.

Antonio moved the same way Rossi had in the church basement, like lightning. The vampire was gone. Cano didn't know if the thing went left, right, or up. Cano spun around and around, looking.

There was no sign.

But there was sound.

Cano should have fired an arrow through the creature instead of watching it become a monster. That opportunity was gone. This one wasn't.

Throwing himself forward, Cano hit the snow and rolled.

Antonio hovered just over where he'd stood.

Cano knew he hadn't jumped far, or fast, but the small element of surprise was his, regardless.

As Antonio dropped back to earth, and lunged forward, Cano fired an arrow. It traveled less than four feet before piercing Antonio's chest. The beast dropped onto Cano. Talons slashed and hacked at the air in an attempt to either rip off Cano's head, or to grasp onto and remove the arrow from its writhing body.

Cano kicked and wiggled and managed to get out from under the thrashing vampire.

He loaded a second arrow into his crossbow. He aimed it at Antonio's back, behind the heart, and, without hesitating, he fired. The vampire fell flat on the snow. It stopped moving for a moment and then the body imploded; flames jutted out from the wound the second arrow caused.

"Dave," Cano said as he loaded a third arrow into his crossbow. "I got one. Antonio. Looks like Antonio, I'd say."

~ * ~

Marcus screamed. He knew human ears would hear it as a high pitched wail, and that he'd expose his location, but he couldn't help it. The vampire hunters had killed his mother, and now he'd watched them slay his brother.

The priest with the crossbow spun around faster than Marcus would have anticipated.

He saw the arrow and moved, but was not fast enough. The silver tip chunked away flesh from his thigh. On suddenly unstable legs, Marcus fell. His blood stained the snow.

"Marcus!" He looked up. Dean.

Marcus looked at the hunter, saw the man running at him, loading another arrow into his weapon. Wincing, Marcus raised his arms. It took a moment before his body responded, but then he was up, in the air and over the trees following Dean out over the lake.

~ * ~

"Dave? Bonsignore?"

"Cano…"

"I hit another one. He's not dead. But hurt. He's definitely hurt. I couldn't tell. Might have been Marcus, the oldest. But I don't know," he said.

"Where are you?" Bonsignore said.

"Still in position."

"We believe Victor is in the house, maybe the daughter."

Cano kept his eyes roaming over everything. His skin crawled as if bugs were scurrying over his flesh under the layers of clothing. "Okay. The two brothers flew away," he said, shaking his head. It sounded unbelievable, and beyond surreal—flew away. "Sounds crazy, but they looked like they might be headed for Canada."

Fifty

"Victor," I said.

"Get. Out. Of. My. House."

I moved away. If I thought he would let go of Katrina and come for me, I'd have run. "Victor, please," I said. "We can end this now. We…"

"It's over," he said. "Over!"

"You'll consider…"

He looked at me. The expression, if looks could kill, didn't come close to capturing the furious anger boiling behind fiery retina.

I stepped away and out the front door.

"Down, down now!"

It was Bonsignore. I didn't feel a need to explain who I was. I dropped to my knees, raised my hands. Out of the corner of my eye I saw my Bible.

"Turn around," I was told.

I moved snow, with my slide. If I were warm-blooded, the snow would have melted and water would have soaked my jeans. "Cardinal, it's me."

Silence.

"Bonsignore," I yelled.

306

"On your feet. Head to the driveway. Follow it to the trees," he said.

I moved slowly. Picked up the Bible, held it so Bonsignore could see it wasn't a weapon, one that could be used against him. I put my hands in the air. I wanted to run. I didn't want to give them a reason to shoot. So far I'd failed, done nothing to further God's plan.

"Victor's in the house," I said. I didn't know where anyone else was.

"The trees," Bonsignore yelled.

I kept walking.

~ * ~

Marcus followed Dean out over the lake. They flew low, close to the water. His body split the winter wind. Dean flew upward. Hovered. Marcus followed.

"Your leg?"

"It grazed me," Marcus said. "Pint of blood will heal it in no time."

"That's good, brother."

"Antonio's gone," Marcus said.

"And Mom." Dean looked distracted. He looked toward Canada.

"You're not thinking about leaving. Dad, Carissa, they're still back there," Marcus huffed. His leg felt heavy, as if it weighed a thousand pounds. He wasn't sure he'd be able to walk. Blood spilled from the wound.

"Father may have led us into a no-win battle," Dean said. "If we go back, we're dead. It would just be the two of us."

Marcus grabbed his brother by the shoulders. "We could take them."

"Maybe. But at what cost? Look at you. You aren't going to be worth anything in a fight."

Marcus sighed. "We've got to go back."

"I absolutely agree," Dean said. "The house. It's on fire."

Marcus turned. Saw smoke rising from their home. "They burned our house?"

Marcus heard the snap. It took a moment before he realized it was his neck.

"I told you, don't ever touch me," Dean said.

Marcus felt weightless as he plummeted down to the water. He couldn't control his arms, or legs. Couldn't fly. Couldn't move. As he fell, he looked up at his kid brother. Dean waved at him.

~ * ~

I made it to the woods, turned and saw the flames licking out of the front door. The house was quickly engulfed. Black smoke billowed toward the sky. Soon fire trucks, police and ambulances would arrive.

An upstairs window shattered. Glass sprinkled in shards onto the snow-covered ground. Carissa flew out the window, howling as embedded glass raked her skin.

"Carissa!" I shouted.

She flew at me, spun me around, knocked me onto my back. Kneeling beside me, she panted. "I can do this," she said.

"Do what?"

"Follow God. I want to. I can. But I'm not sure what I need to do," she said.

On my back, I sensed the flames, the heat, increasing behind us. I could see the flames dance on her rutted skin. Her physical beauty was masked by what she was, but her inner beauty seemed to shine. "Are you sure?"

"I don't want this. Not anymore," she said.

I wondered if the demise of her family helped her find religion. I didn't care. She wanted a shot at redemption. I hadn't failed.

"I brought you this," she said. She held up a leather-bound book. "My father called it the Book of Names. It's loaded with information. He handled the money for the New York families. I want you to have it."

I reached up for the book.

"I love you," she said.

The hair on my arms and behind my neck stood. We weren't alone. "No!" I screamed.

Carissa looked at me, her head tilted to one side.

I saw the arrow exit her chest before she reacted. Then she bowed her back. The shriek that erupted threatened to explode my ear drums. Blood sprayed all over me. "No!" I screamed, again. I tried to get up. She fell over me.

"Joey," she said.

I pushed her off me. Got to my knees, rolled her onto her side.

"Are you all right?"

Cano stopped a few feet away. He'd already loaded another arrow into his crossbow. "Stop," I said. "She was helping. She brought us this!" I held up the book. "She wasn't attacking me. She wanted to change. She was giving her life to God," I said.

Cano dropped to his knees.

Bri and Bonsignore ran over. "We have to get out of here. Victor must have started a fire. We don't have much time. Our car's parked just past the trees in a vacant lot. That way!"

"I can't leave her!" I grabbed onto the end of the arrow by her chest. If I could break off the jagged silver tip, I could pull the wood out her back. Maybe she'd be all right. "Help me!"

Bonsignore pulled a knife out of a sheath strapped to his leg. "We don't have time for this," he said. But he worked, regardless. "Hold the arrow."

I held it with two hands. Blood coated the wood, gushed in my palms and out between my fingers.

Bonsignore chopped the tip off the arrow. "This is going to hurt," he said. "Bri, help."

Bri took the arrow at Carissa's back and pulled it out in one swift motion.

"Cano, carry the girl. But first, I want the rest of the bodies tossed into the house. We need to get Padilla," the cardinal said, and looked at the ground. "We're not leaving him here. Then let's go. Now. Move!"

Cano didn't argue. The team scrambled.

I stayed by Carissa, whispering into her ear that everything would be all right.

When Cano returned, he squatted to lift Carissa.

"I'll take her," I said. I tucked the Bible in the back waistband of my pants and handed Cano the Book of Names. "Put this in your bag."

Cano didn't argue. He stood up, looked relieved.

I draped Carissa over my shoulders. She wasn't as heavy as I suspected. I felt like I could carry her in one hand, if I needed to. "I'll meet you at the car," I said.

When I ran past the Pope's team, I wasn't sure they saw me, that's how fast I was running. As I reached the end of the trees, and the main road was in sight, I fell. Carissa rolled out of my arms. She grunted and moaned. A great sign. She wasn't dead.

Knowing I must have slipped, I stood up, brushed away the snow and stepped toward Carissa.

When Dean landed between us, I gasped, but tried to remain calm. "It's over, Dean."

"Not even close," he said. "My sister gave you something. I want it back. Now."

"She didn't give me a thing," I said. "It's not too late. You can come with us."

He laughed. "The book. I want it. I will not ask again."

I shook my head. "Is a book worth your soul?"

"Yes. It is."

I reached behind me.

"Slow." He was ready to attack if I made a fast move.

I raised my hands. Turned around. Lifted my shirt, showing him the book.

He reached for it, grabbed it, pulled it out of my pants and screamed.

When he dropped the Bible, I scooped it up and tackled him. I thrust the Bible onto his head. I smelled burning flesh before I saw smoke rising off his skin. The Bible bore a hole into his skull and cooked his brains.

"Rossi!" Bonsignore stood beside me, weapon drawn, ready to fire.

"You don't need that," I said, stood up, bringing the Bible with me. "Carissa's the last of the Tantalos."

I looked behind me. Cano and Bri stood side by side. Behind them the house was engulfed in flames. Sirens screamed in the near distance. "We have to go."

Cano lifted Carissa into his arms. "I'll carry her."

Fifty-one

We were packed tight into the car. Bonsignore and Bri sat in front. I sat in back with Carissa in my lap, draped over Daly and Cano. Padilla rode in the trunk.

"She's lost a lot of blood," I said. There was no pulse in her wrist. Had there been one before?

"Will she be all right?" Bri asked.

"She's going to need blood," I said.

"This isn't how things work," Cano said.

"She'll die," I said. I brushed her hair with my fingers.

"We can't let her feed," Bonsignore said. "It's not going to happen."

"Not human blood. Animal blood," I said. "That should work."

"You don't get it. We weren't sent here to save vampires," Cano said.

"She gave her life to Christ," I shouted. "She's not the same person. Not anymore."

"If she needs blood to survive…"

"Animal blood, Cano. God created the animals for us to consume," I said.

"That means eat. Not drink," Cano said. "The Bible talks at great lengths about the sin of consuming blood!"

"Old Testament," I said. "Not the same thing."

"But it is."

"Then let us out." I reached for the door knob.

"We're not letting you go anywhere," Bonsignore said.

I wasn't asking permission. I pulled open the door and felt Daly's arm on mine. "Father, you have to let us go," I said.

"But you can help the mission. You know that."

"Not if they won't work to help me save Carissa. And myself. Without at least animal blood, we're dead. Dead. I'm not sure if it's right or wrong," I said. "But I'm not ready to just starve to death. I can help, I know I can, but not if I'm starving to death. I'd be useless."

Carissa convulsed. Her head snapped back, her body shook. I gripped her shoulders with one hand and closed the car door with the other. "We can't let her die," I said.

Daly pulled the hair from her face. Her eyes wide open. She didn't blink. "She's gone," he said. "I'm sorry, Joey."

I thought of my wife. She quit on me, too. Quit. I touched her face, closed her eyelids. She'd tried. She wasn't like my wife. Not at all. The fight was in her. She'd held on as long as she could.

"You got that book I gave you, Cano?" I asked.

"It's in my bag."

"I want to see it. Where's your bag?"

"Bri has it," he said.

"This?" Bri said. She held up the Book of Names.

I snatched it out of her hand, threw open the car door again and jumped out of the car. I hit the pavement hard. My body rolled off the street, over the curb and into the grass.

"That wasn't smart."

I looked up. Wayne stood off to the side. "Oh? Why not?" I said.

"God still has plans for you," he said.

"I figured. I just thought I could do better at this on my own," I said. Not sure that was the truth. It was all I had to offer at the moment.

I stood up, brushed wet salt-mixed snow off my clothes and held both the Bible and the Book of Names in my hands. I watched the rear brake lights of the car I'd jumped from come on, and go off as the car kept driving farther and farther away. "Besides," I said. "I'm not alone."

"Oh?"

"I got you." I started walking in the opposite direction the car headed in. Wayne fell in step beside me.

"I guess that's true," he said.

"And, by looking at the size of this book, I'd say we got our work cut out for us."

Wayne laughed. "Joey, the Lord's work is never done. Never done."

The End

Meet

Phillip Tomasso

Phillip Tomasso is the award winning writer of 8 previous novels, including Johnny Blade and Adverse Impact. He lives in Rochester, NY with his three children, and is hard at work on his next thrilling suspense novel

www.ingramcontent.com/pod-product-compliance
Lightning Source LLC
Chambersburg PA
CBHW061011120726
47910CB00006B/1878